Also by Brent Ghelfi

Volk's Game
Volk's Shadow

Check Out Receipt

Baldwinsville Public Library (BV)
315-635-5631
www.bville.lib.ny.us
Wednesday, September 15, 2010 7:36:40 PM

28746

Item: 39850030842317
Title: The Venona cable
Material: Book
Due: 10/6/2010

Total Items: 1

NEW HOURS!
the library now opens at 9AM
Monday through Friday

The Venona Cable

The Venona Cable

a thriller

Brent Ghelfi

HENRY HOLT AND COMPANY

New York

Henry Holt and Company, LLC
Publishers since 1866
175 Fifth Avenue
New York, New York 10010
www.henryholt.com

Henry Holt® and ▮® are registered trademarks of Henry Holt and Company, LLC.

Distributed in Canada by H. B. Fenn and Company Ltd.

Library of Congress Cataloging-in-Publication Data

Ghelfi, Brent.
    The Venona cable / Brent Ghelfi. —1st ed.
        p. cm.
    ISBN-13: 978-0-8050-8894-6
    ISBN-10: 0-8050-8894-6
    1. Code and cipher stories.   I. Title.
    PS3607.H46V46 2009
    813'.6—dc22   2009002369

Henry Holt books are available for special promotions and premiums.
For details contact: Director, Special Markets.

First Edition 2009

Designed by Meryl Sussman Levavi

Printed in the United States of America

1   2   3   4   5   6   7   8   9   10

For Lisa

The Venona Cable

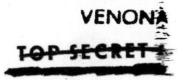

USSR   Ref. No: (of 8/7/1953)

                         Issued: 10/9/74

                         Copy No.: 301

3RD REISSUE

"19" REPORTS ON DISCUSSIONS WITH "KAPITAN", "KABAN" AND
ZAMESTITEL' ON THE SECOND FRONT

(1943)

From: NEW YORK

To: MOSCOW

No: 812   29 May 1942

To VIKTOR[i].

    "19"[ii] reports that "KAPITAN"[iii] and "KABAN"[iv], during conversations
in the "COUNTRY [STRANA][v]", invited "19" to join them and ZAMESTITEL'[vi]
openly told "KABAN"

                    [10 groups unrecovered]

second front against GERMANY this year. KABAN considers that, if a second
front should prove to be unsuccessful, then this [3 groups unrecovered]
harm to Russian interests and [6 groups unrecovered]. He considers it
more advantageous and effective to weaken GERMANY by bombing and to use this
time for "[4 groups unrecovered] political crisis so that there may be no
doubt that a second front next year will prove successful."

    ZAMESTITEL' and

                    [14 groups unrecovered]

". 19 thinks that "KAPITAN" is not informing ZAMESTITEL' of important military
decisions and that therefore ZAMESTITEL' may not have exact knowledge of
[1 group unrecovered] with the opening of a second front against GERMANY and its
postponement from this year to next year. 19 says that ZAMESTITEL'
personally is an ardent supporter of a second front at this time and considers
postponement

───

                                    [Continued overleaf]

[15 groups unrecovered]

can shed blood

[15 groups unrecoverable]

recently shipping between the USA and

[40 groups unrecovered]

The "COUNTRY" hardly [9 groups unrecovered] "insufficient reason for delaying a second front."

No. 443   MER[vii]

Benes Czech delegation?

Footnotes:	[i]	VIKTOR	:	Lt. Gen. P.M. FITIN.
	[ii]	19	:	Unidentified cover designation.
	[iii]	KAPITAN	:	i.e. "CAPTAIN"; Franklin D. ROOSEVELT.
	[iv]	KABAN	:	i.e. "BOAR"; Winston CHURCHILL.
	[v]	COUNTRY	:	U.S.A.
	[vi]	ZAMESTITEL'	:	i.e. Deputy – therefore possibly Henry Agard WALLACE, who was ROOSEVELT's Deputy (Vice-President) at this time: later he is referred to by the covername "LOTSMAN".
	[vii]	MER	:	Probably Iskhak Abdulovich AKhMEROV.

more likely to be Hopkins ?

VENONA

PART I

Source No. 19: unidentified highly placed asset who at the time of the Trident conference in 1943 reported to the KGB on a conversation with Roosevelt and Churchill.

—John Earl Haynes and Harvey Klehr,
Venona: Decoding Soviet Espionage in America

I'm trapped, nearly out of time.

I have to *think*.

But I can't trust my judgment. Perceptions blurred, memories distorted and incomplete. No sleep for thirty-six hours, a punch behind the ear with the butt of a Glock, and a sickening tumble down the embankment of one of L.A.'s ubiquitous freeways have taken their toll. I landed in a drainage basin beneath an overpass, where a crawl of sixty meters through a nearby culvert saved my life. The tunnel led to the other side of the expressway. From there I hot-wired an ancient Datsun pickup, abandoned it ten miles later in a mall parking lot, then walked here, to a run-down motel near the airport.

I figure I bought an hour. Two if I'm lucky.

My cell phone is gone, but that doesn't matter, not anymore. The only person I trust is Valya, and she is half a world away. I'm on my own, hunted by the police and by American intelligence agencies. My adversaries could be from any of half a dozen organizations. What I don't know is who is pulling the strings. If I can't figure that out soon, I'll be dead.

Somehow I need to wrest answers from the document on the stained bedspread in front of me. Two pages, winged open at the folds, crumpled and smudged from much handling. Labeled VENONA, ~~TOP SECRET~~, it is a decrypted Soviet cable, originally sent from New York to Moscow on 29 May 1943.

No matter how many times I look at it, revelation fails to come.

I lean forward, elbows on my knees. My suit is mud-streaked, torn at the knees. A subcompact Beretta rests in my lap, only four rounds left in the magazine. It smells of burnt powder and gun oil. Opposite the bed, the door is locked and chained. A creaky wooden chair, the twin of the one I'm sitting on, is wedged beneath the knob. Next to the door is a window, the blinds closed as tight as they'll go but still admitting slits of electric yellow light that stripe the carpet and one corner of the bed where the glow cast by the feeble overhead bulb fails to reach.

I don't know how the Americans will handle a situation like this. Their methods in this country are restricted "by law and convention," as a British double agent once famously put it, but the usual rules won't apply in this case. In their position I would clear the area and launch a grenade or pump several hundred rounds through the window rather than risk any people in an assault.

My trembling hands are all that remains of the adrenaline rush brought on by the near miss on the freeway ramp. I clamp them together to steady myself. I need to concentrate in the little time I have left.

The decrypted cable in front of me is marked "3rd Reissue." Each reissue meant that more parts of the cable had been deciphered by the code-breakers at Arlington Hall's Venona Project or their successors in the NSA. This one was dated "10/9/74." More than thirty years after the original cable was sent. But less than two months before my father defected in a Soviet spy plane carrying reconnaissance equipment so advanced for its time that the Americans were desperate to have it.

Through the motel's paper-thin wall I hear a family moving their luggage into the room next door. A baby cries. A boy complains that he's hungry, and his father gruffly tells him to shut up. Jet engines scream overhead as another plane approaches the runway. Hoping the family will leave soon—dinner, a movie, anything—I reposition myself on the hard edge of the chair and bow over the papers again.

The decrypted cable is titled *"19" REPORTS ON DISCUSSIONS WITH "KAPITAN," "KABAN" AND "ZAMESTITEL" ON THE SECOND FRONT.* According to footnotes prepared by the Venona analysts, "19" was an "unidentified cover designation." "Kapitan" was Franklin D. Roosevelt. "Kaban," Russian for "boar," was Winston Churchill. "Zamestitel," the Russian word for "deputy," is believed to have been either Roosevelt aide Harry Hopkins or Vice President Wallace.

Before leaving Moscow—how long ago was that, four days, five?—I was briefed by a former KGB field operative, an aged Cold War veteran named Isadora, who described the Soviet encryption process to me. There in the glade near her dacha, her gaze flitting from one spot to another but rarely meeting mine, she told me how the Soviets' wall of secrecy was breached. Wartime madness, Soviet mistakes. "Point to whatever reason you like," she said. "Venona was still a singular counterintelligence achievement."

The phone in my room rings. One, two, three jangling peals before it goes silent. Nobody knows I am here. Nobody. I draw a deep breath, then another, casting through my memories of the past two weeks for answers. Starting with Everett Walker, a renowned Hollywood filmmaker and cinematographer found dead in my Moscow warehouse with the Venona cable hidden in his possessions, photographically shrunken to a microdot. He had come to Moscow looking for me, the son of Soviet defector Stepan Volkovoy.

Why?

I rub my eyes, picturing my father shivering in the cold cockpit as American interceptors escorted him toward a secret base above the Arctic Circle. What was he thinking at that moment, thousands of meters above the ice, guiding the enormous plane lower, ever lower, approaching—what? Foreign riches? Duty? Fate, I suppose. Either way, traitor or patriot, he was descending toward his new life.

My hand comes away from my eyes smeared with blood. A red trail stains the crinkled whiteness of the cable as I pull it closer, determined to see it anew, to find the clue I believe must be hiding among the words.

The Venona decrypts helped the Americans and British identify hundreds of Soviet spies—among them Julius Rosenberg, Kim Philby, and Alger Hiss—many of them placed at the highest levels of their governments. But despite the American and British successes, they never discovered the identity of 19. They never learned the name of this Soviet source.

A lesson I learned during a training course on counterespionage at Balashikha-2 springs to mind—the paradoxical truth that the more valuable an agent, the more reason to fear deception. If Source 19 was able to get this close to Roosevelt and Churchill at this most critical stage of World War II, he was as valuable as any agent the Soviets had, and therefore the most dangerous one to both the Soviets and the Americans. All of which should be simply a historical footnote, but it's not, because somebody protecting 19's identity wants me dead.

Think!

The KGB assigned cover names to its agents. Julius Rosenberg was "Antennae," then later was known as "Liberal." Alger Hiss was "Ales." The GRU—the Soviet military intelligence agency—often used numeric cover names. Everyone knows this, including all the people who have speculated about the identity of Source 19 for decades. But I know more. I know that GRU Captain Oleg Bassoff has been sniffing around Moscow, rooting through old files, pressuring former agents, and pushing me and others for answers. Does that mean 19 was a GRU source? Why would it matter anymore?

The certainty that nothing can be known or trusted entirely has been drilled into me by training and experience. Truth is elusive, and never more so than in the world of espionage, where patterns are concealed within webs of disinformation and misdirection. Somehow I need to see past the distorted mirrors of deception and time. I need to start at the beginning, make the connections between what I know and what I can infer, find the relationships. My life depends on whether I can solve the puzzle.

What started me along the path to this squalid room? *Your father was a traitor.* A man named Filip Lachek said that four months ago, when he held me in a torture chamber in the bowels of the Lubyanka. He said it again ten days ago, just before I killed him on a foggy night in

Macao. That was the moment, I decide, when the past erupted into the present. That was when I changed from predator to prey.

I settle back into the creaking hardness of the motel chair, cup my face in my hands, and drag them downward, stretching sandpapery skin, pulling my eyes wide open. Another jet passes overhead, followed by a roll of thunder and hissing sheets of rain. The color of the thin blades of light between the blinds has changed with the weather. The parallel slashes are bone-white now, strobing as fitful gusts blow from the floor-mounted air vent.

A figure darkens the window.

My hand drops to the butt of the Beretta.

PART II

There is a man, there is a problem. No man, no problem.

—Joseph Stalin

I pursued Lachek for more than four months. Or maybe it is better to say I followed a trail of whispers and innuendo. He was rumored to be in Jakarta, Phuket, and as far north as Beijing, but I could never find any sign of him when I went to look. "Wasted days," Valya said of those trips, worried that my obsession with revenge was causing me to lose touch with what was truly important. "The General has work for you in Moscow, Tbilisi, London. How much longer is everyone supposed to wait while you chase a ghost?"

True enough, although I think her comment about the General reflected her impatience, not his, because he never questioned me during that time. But I didn't listen to her.

My life-and-death game with Lachek began when I killed his son during what I thought was a terrorist attack. I didn't intend to kill him, just to get him out of the way while I subdued two terrorists holed up in a burning building. But a blow to the head with the flat of a gun barrel speaks for itself.

Later I discovered that Lachek and others had staged the explosion of the offices of an American oil company to simulate a terrorist bombing, trying to frighten American investors and inflame passions against Chechen separatists in a bid to take over oil routes. He lost his bid and fled to Southeast Asia, but only after he raped and murdered my friend and business partner, Alla.

Then word leaked to one of my sources that China's Ministry of State Security's counterintelligence section, known as Sixth Bureau, had located him in Macao. I jumped on a commercial flight to Hong Kong, rode the jetfoil ferry to Macao's Outer Harbor, and spent two fruitless days patrolling cobbled streets with their names etched in blue enamel tiles—exotic leftovers from the days of Portuguese colonialism.

Lachek should have been hard to miss. Tall, cadaverous, thinning white hair combed back in oily strands. He would stand out even among all the tourists. But I trawled hotels, theaters, nightclubs, restaurants, bars, Internet cafés, food markets, and a giant shopping mall without a hit.

I showed his picture to chambermaids, waiters, street vendors, beggars. Cabbies smoking dark cigarillos as they leaned against dented fenders, waiting for the next fare. A lounging shopgirl, who jutted her hip, ticked a shiny red nail on the photo, and batted lashes long as butterfly wings as she slowly shook her head no. I trolled the Jockey Club while the thoroughbreds barreled around the turns at Taipa racetrack. Cruised among the flashing lights and burbling machines in the casinos, bumping shoulders with gamblers, junkies, painted hookers.

No sign of him.

Valya phoned me on my last night in Macao. I was done in, ready to call it another useless trip, trudging through a back alley so narrow a driver had to fold back the side mirrors of his delivery truck to squeeze through. Past the kitchen of a noodle shop, its recessed rear door propped partway open, leaking steam and the clamor of pots and shouted Cantonese. On the other side of the alley stood three rows of boxlike housing units that looked like metal shipping containers stacked beside and on top of one another. Wet clumps of fog absorbed the orange light cast by a bulb caged in metal over the delivery door of the restaurant.

"No luck?" Valya said.

"Nothing. The man is everywhere and nowhere."

"I went by the warehouse today. You don't have anyone watching the place, do you?"

"Not since Alla . . ."

I leaned my back against a wall made of sooty brick and propped my left heel behind me to relieve the pressure on my prosthesis. Alla ran my operations with dictatorial efficiency. She was so omnipresent that closing everything down had seemed inevitable after she died.

"Why?" I said.

"I went there to look for Vadim. One of the cooks told me he'd gone to get something at the warehouse."

Two people turned into the alley and strolled my way, shoulder to shoulder, holding hands. Another figure rounded the corner behind them, weaving, probably drunk.

"Three men were there," Valya said. "One out front talked on a cell phone while two others searched for something on the side nearest the river."

The couple turned into a gap between two buildings. Just before they disappeared, his hand dropped to her bottom and she slapped it away, giggling. The third figure resolved itself into an old man, jerking and swaying with an uneven gait. He appeared to be having difficulty finding purchase on the slick cobblestones.

"Police?"

"Probably."

"Did they see you?"

"You're joking, right?"

The old man drew even with me. Tall and thin, head down, one hand buried in his pocket, the other brushing the wall on the far side of the alley for balance. The upturned collar of his coat hid his face but left the top of his head exposed, revealing white strands of hair. He moved spasmodically, stooped, loosely placing one foot in front of the other before he stiffened his spine for the next step. That was what did it. His spastic movements triggered recognition.

"Got him," I said into the cell phone, then dropped it into my pocket, gathered a head of steam in five long steps, and smashed into Lachek like a battering ram.

chapter 3

Lachek slammed ass first onto the broken asphalt of the alley with me on top of him. Before he had a chance to take a breath, I elbowed him to the side of his head. Pistoned my knee into his groin. Hoisted him off the ground and drove him backward into the brick wall, all of my weight behind my shoulder. Ribs cracked as he hit with an explosive grunt. I held him there for long enough to see that he was done, then let him drop to the gutter, where he lay curled, clutching his midsection and groaning.

The delivery door of the noodle shop swung all the way open, casting a shaft of light into the alleyway. A Chinese cook stared without expression at us. He tucked his unlit cigarette behind his ear and looked off into the orange glow above the roofline of the building. Then he deliberately wiped his hands on his apron, turned away, and eased the door closed behind him.

I jammed the barrel of my Sig under Lachek's nose while I frisked him. Bony shoulders and hips, ribs that felt like broom handles. He cried out when I jostled one of the broken ones to find a chrome-plated Makarov in a shoulder holster and a nasty switchblade in a belt sheath.

I transferred them to the pocket of my leather jacket. Found two keys on a ring in his pants pocket.

The twin headlights of a car swept into the alley, lit the scene, threw long shadows.

"Volk," Lachek said matter-of-factly while I watched the car reverse out of the alley. I had to assume the driver was dialing the police on his cell phone. Meaning I didn't have much time.

Without bothering to look directly at Lachek, I slashed the barrel of the Sig across his face. Skin split as his head snapped back. Blood welled between his fingers, and he pedaled his feet against the asphalt trying to escape another blow.

"Where are you staying?" I said.

Still holding his face, he aimed his chin toward a flight of metal stairs crawling up the side of the stacked housing units. "Second floor."

I pulled him to his feet and frog-marched him ahead and up the stairs, grinding the barrel of the Sig into his lower back. He stumbled when we reached the landing, so I lifted him by the neck in a stranglehold and drove him up the last flight and along a breezeway.

"Here," he wheezed outside a door numbered 243B. I twisted the key in the lock, then shoved him through the doorway as it swung open, holding his body in front of mine, aiming the Sig around the room under his arm.

Nobody in sight. I kicked the door closed with my heel, clouted Lachek in the back of the head to make sure he wouldn't get ideas about hideaway guns and knives, and rushed to recon the flat as he lay dazed on the floor.

In the back was a bedroom. Unmade bed, scattered clothes, two dirty syringes, the whole mess bathed in green neon from a sign outside the window advertising some energy drink. The window looked onto a steel-and-glass commercial mid-rise surrounded by a ramshackle collection of older buildings.

The combination dining room and kitchenette held a folding table, a built-in stovetop and oven combo, and a rust-stained sink. The door to the right opened onto a bathroom barely big enough to turn around in.

No bodyguard, no nurse, no maid.

Lachek had money. Not as much as he once had. Much of his wealth had been stripped away, along with all of his power and prestige, when the General and his group chased him out of Russia. But still, more money than most people could accumulate in several lifetimes. He didn't have to live this way. This was a choice.

I went back to where he lay sprawled in the front room. Half-eaten cartons of food, periodicals, and discarded clothes littered the floor, everything coated with the sour stink of neglect and decay. No pictures or plants or personal touches anywhere.

As I waited for Lachek to regain his senses I flipped through the newspapers and magazines. The *South China Morning Post*, the *International Herald Tribune*, the *Vladivostok News*, *Time* magazine's international edition, *The Economist*—some of them dated as far back as February. Lachek hadn't been traveling every corner of Southeast Asia during the last four months. He had been here the entire time, holed up amid the squalor and the putrid smell of spoiled food and dirty socks. Waiting to die, judging by the look of him.

He stirred. Fluttered his eyelids. Drew his knees to his chest and held his bloody cheek in his hands, making a whimpering sound. Looking at him, I finally understood how he had been able to evade me for so many months. I'd been searching for the wrong man. The towering operative with a face like the blade of an ax and rabidly bright eyes was gone, replaced by this empty husk.

After another minute or so his hands dropped from his face. He stared around the room, looking lost for a few seconds before he saw me. I watched the memory come back to him. He started to say something, stopped, and looked around again. Then his expression changed as a different kind of understanding dawned. He was seeing himself through my eyes.

"Cancer," he said. "You can't do anything worse to me."

I started to correct him, then didn't. I had come here intending to destroy him. Make it last for days, I'd told myself. But now that the moment was upon me, I no longer had the taste for it. Nothing could bring Alla back to life. Killing Lachek would give me no more satisfaction than stomping a cockroach.

"Do it," he wheezed. He tried to sit up, then cried out and fell back, clutching his rib cage. "Do what you came here to do, just get it over with."

I stood and exchanged my Sig for his Makarov. Racked the slide. "You're vermin, Lachek. I'm not going to waste time pulling the wings off a fly."

"Fuck you."

His gaze followed the barrel as I raised my arm. But no fear showed on his face. Instead, his lips curled in the shape of a smile.

"Major Stepan Volkovoy," he said, dragging out each syllable.

"What?"

The Lachek I remembered blossomed back to life. Vicious, all curdled malevolence, a wild, gleeful light in his eyes. "Your father was a traitor. A pig."

My finger tightened on the trigger.

"He defected. Stole our most valuable spy plane and gave it to the Americans."

I never knew my father. As far as I had been able to learn, he disappeared not long after my mother died as I clawed out of the womb. As an air force officer, he could have been killed in any one of dozens of Cold War theaters or exiled to one of many Soviet detention camps.

I firmed my grip on the Makarov, ignoring Lachek's demented eyes, my thoughts turned inward. I had gone through a period of several years during which I'd search the archives for news of my father whenever I was on leave or had spare time. Even during rehab while I was learning how to walk again I made calls and requested records, swimming upstream against a torrent of Soviet and post-Soviet falsifications. The name S. Volkovoy appeared among the records of the political prisoners of a camp in Kolyma during the winter of 1979, but Volkovoy is a common name, and the reference led nowhere. The idea that my father might have betrayed his country and left his son to live an orphan's hellish existence . . .

"A defector, Volk."

Where not covered in blood Lachek's skin was parchment-dry, his hair oiled and ropey across this skull. Snot seeped from his nose, but he didn't seem to notice. He twisted his glistening red lips, visibly glad to have one last chance to injure somebody.

"He goes down in history as one of the vilest pigs our military ever produced. And it's not over. I've made sure of that. All of you are going to pay. Tell your precious General I said that. All of your worst secrets will come back from the dead when you least expect."

I knew the right thing to do if I wanted to learn more. Burn him, cut him, pistol-whip him. Tear every scrap of information from his ruptured flesh—whispered words from a former colleague in the KGB or one of his long-ago informants, or perhaps a connection he had made between the lines of one of his magazines. Who knows? But at that moment I didn't have the stomach to be in the same room with him any longer. I thought that anything else he said would be either a hateful lie or a truth I couldn't stand to hear.

Something in my bearing or expression forewarned him, gave him the chance to sink his fangs one last time. "Wait until you see what's coming. You, the General, Bassoff, all of you will pay. Wait and see," he said again, just before I crammed the barrel between his teeth and squeezed the trigger.

chapter 4

Two Moscow police officers arrested me at Sheremetyevo-2 terminal as soon as I got off the plane from Hong Kong. I was tired from the long trip—seventeen hours, including the ferry from Macao and a layover in Bangkok—emotionally spent and preoccupied by Lachek's final words. So I failed to notice the green uniforms until just before they yanked me out of the passport control line.

The bigger of the two cops led me away. He had a shaved skull the shape of a dented bullet and shoulders as wide as a crossbeam. The smaller of the two held my elbow, looking up at me each time we rounded a corner, his face so cramped and chin so shrunken that he looked like a parakeet. When we came to a deserted hallway away from the arrivals concourse, Bullethead pushed my face against a cold pane of glass overlooking the airfield and kicked my feet apart while his partner crunched metal cuffs around my wrists.

A third man appeared from the other end of the hall, heels clacking the tile as he approached. Middle fifties; average height and build; wispy blond hair combed forward and then to the side, the roots beginning high on the sloping dome of his skull; sharp, pale features marred by a rosette birthmark on his left temple. Dressed in a wrinkled blue suit and wearing a sour expression, he stood to one side and tapped his index finger against the side of his long nose while his men searched me.

"What was your business in Hong Kong?"

I stared through the glass at the night outside. Light from inside the terminal fell to the tarmac below in geometric patterns. Baggage handlers unloaded luggage from the belly of the plane I had just debarked. In the distance a Lufthansa Airbus lifted away, casting a rippling glow over the pine and birch trees beneath its lit wings. The rest of the outside world was inky blackness except for two parallel strings of lights, one white, the other red. The M10, pointing the way to central Moscow.

"Tell me what you were doing in Hong Kong."

I still didn't answer, just stood still while the cop with the parakeet face plucked at my pockets. Something had gone very wrong. I didn't know what it was, but talking to this man wouldn't help me. When I looked at his reflection in the window, his gaze caught mine. Washed-out blue eyes, weighing, assessing, calculating. The look of a man who distrusts the world.

The cop handed him my wallet, cell phone, a banded roll of large-denomination rubles and Hong Kong dollars, and a civilian passport. He put each item into his pocket in turn, but held on to the passport, absently riffling its pages with his thumb before opening it to stare at my picture and the information next to it.

"Vasily Pravdin? How many names do you have, Colonel Volkovoy?"

A family of tourists passed, obviously lost. Their steps faltered as a group, then they averted their eyes and kept walking. The youngest, a girl, turned back to look at the handcuffs on my wrists, her eyes cartoonishly round. Her mother whispered in her ear and quickly herded her away.

The name "Pravdin" had served for seven years as a cover on various missions for the General, taking me from the Far East to western Europe to America. Right then I didn't care that it was going to have to be retired. I was too busy recalling my last conversation with Valya about the three men she had seen stationed outside my warehouse.

"Aeroflot's records show you flew Moscow to Hong Kong three days ago. That is correct, yes? Can you account for your whereabouts during the twenty-four hours before you left so suddenly?"

The day before I left Moscow I had three meetings in my spartan office in the basement of Vadim's Café. Two involved a lost shipment of heroin from Yekaterinburg to St. Petersburg. Somebody was going to have to pay, one way or another, and it wouldn't be me or the General, I explained to one of the leaders of a drug cartel and, later, to his frightened partner.

My third visitor was Brock Matthews, an American NSA agent who had accompanied me on a journey to Chechnya four months ago to meet a rebel warlord. Matthews made vague references to "future co-operation" and more "joint projects"—his usual ambiguities that got nothing but equally meaningless responses from me—and asked whether my business was back in operation. "Not since Alla died," I told him and he nodded thoughtfully. He was fishing for something, but I didn't know what.

After Matthews left I made a quick trip to my warehouse to scavenge a computer for Valya. A few hours later came the call from my Kremlin source saying that Sixth Bureau had located Lachek, and I was off to Macao on the next available flight.

Bullethead rapped his knuckles on the back of my head. "Answer Mr. Rykov."

I considered a kick or a head butt, but decided I would have to settle with him later.

Rykov smiled thinly, reading the direction of my thoughts. "You'll just make things worse for yourself. Tonight you'll be in Lefortovo prison at his mercy. How do you think *that* will be for you?"

The list of reasons why someone might want to put me in prison was a long one. Most of them would never stick. If I didn't have the resources to buy or negotiate my way out of the problem, the General would. But this—this struck me as different. *Rykov* struck me as different.

My interrogator tapped his nose, studying me for a reaction. When he didn't get one, he offered another thin-lipped smile. "This isn't something you can walk away from, Volkovoy. You can't murder an American tourist in cold blood without consequences. Especially not one who has buckets of money."

An American? I almost said the words out loud, I was that surprised. Matthews sprang to mind, but nobody would mistake the intense NSA operative for a tourist. No matter who it was, though, a murdered American meant problems. Political, diplomatic, economic—the kind of trouble that requires a story. Facts gathered, contained, altered as need be, and then, and only then, selectively released.

Rykov started back down the hall, motioning for his men to bring me along.

"You'll leave Lefortovo in only one of two ways," he said, not looking back. "Transferred to another prison. Or dead."

chapter 5

Even though I was already handcuffed, the two cops attached leg restraints before they loaded me into a government-issue Mercedes outside Sheremetyevo's terminal 2. The chain hooked to an eyebolt in the floorboard, limiting the range of motion of my feet to a few links in either direction.

An accident on the M10 stalled traffic. Rykov sat in the front seat next to the small cop, who accelerated to close each opening, only to slam on the brakes two or three car lengths later. The bullet-headed cop who'd rapped my skull sat with me in back, cradling a shotgun aimed at my midsection.

Nobody talked. Occasionally the car radio squawked static, the sound turned too low to make out any words. City lights danced in and out of the car—whites, greens, reds, and yellows playing over the leather seats and across our laps and burnishing the blued steel of the shotgun barrel. We crossed the Moscow River and rattled over the railroad tracks to the east side of my warehouse and parked next to the loading dock. The metal door at the top of the dock was scrolled open.

Months ago the outside of the warehouse would have been dark and the inside brightly lit, with several videos being shot at once, the hectic filming schedule necessary to keep up with the insatiable demand for our products. This was where my most profitable enterprise produced and distributed Internet porn and then stole identities from the witless customers, part of a front created so that I could pretend to be a discharged veteran of the wars in Chechnya and still serve as the General's staff officer and enforcer in his many underworld activities. The idea hadn't dawned on me until recently that the money it made—millions of dollars, euros, and rubles—was more the point of the venture from the General's perspective. Russia is for sale, I once told him angrily. He was surprised by my naïveté.

Now, arc lights mounted outside the building painted circles of white on the asphalt and cast a phosphorescent glow on the concrete walls. On the other side of the roll-up door was only darkness.

After I was unhitched and we got out of the car, Bullethead pointed to the chain between my legs. "What about those?"

Rykov glanced toward my feet. In the artificial light his pointed features appeared waxen, bloodless. "Let him shuffle," he said, and ducked under the yellow crime scene tape to lead the way inside.

Darkness distorted everything within the cavernous studio area. Hanging wires, open crates, and a tripod listing on one broken leg all threw eerie shadows. The gloom lifted as I scraped ahead and around the false wall of a stage set, light coming from the mezzanine halfway up the far wall. Gutted of their faux furnishings and makeshift scenic arrangements, the familiar stage sets looked like derelict hulls. Most of the cabling and equipment had been sold months before. Only the bones were left—scaffolding, painted backdrops, and a wooden platform, along with isolated props. A canopy bed, a kitchen set, a casting couch.

Rykov picked his way over the remains of duct tape that used to secure cables on the concrete floor and led us up a set of metal stairs. Bullethead tromped behind me, breathing heavily, prodding me in the back to quicken my pace when the leg chain caused me to stumble between hops from one step to the next. The jolt of each landing sent pain spiking up my left leg. The stairs led to the mezzanine, which overlooked the floor of the warehouse on one side and held a suite of offices on the other. The far office, the largest, was mine. I couldn't remember the last time I had actually used it. A year? Fifteen months?

The crime scene lights inside were so bright that the doorway glared like a gigantic white eye. Two Moscow policemen stood guard while a coroner's assistant leaned on the railing of the balcony, reading through her notes. From here the floor of the deserted warehouse looked as if a giant hand had smashed the sets and swept them away, leaving behind scattered debris.

Rykov nodded at Bullethead, who shoved me through the door.

A dead man was sprawled between two chairs in front of a metal desk. He was on his back, face turned away from the door. Scarecrow skinny. Legs scissored apart, one arm unnaturally bent beneath his body, the other flung to the side as if he were reaching for something just beyond his grasp. Gray hair, most of it gone on top, blotchy age spots showing on the pale skin beneath. Tan windbreaker, blue knit shirt, brown slacks riding high enough to reveal pasty calves above drooping black socks. Scuffed shoes that said Rockport on the heel. Blood the color of maple syrup forming an oval pool in the area between his chest and the gap beneath his outflung arm. He appeared to have been shot in the back, but the entry wound wasn't visible from where I stood.

The smell was bad. Several days old, at least. I mentally pulled back from the body and swept my gaze around the office, trying to take in the entire scene.

Four lights mounted on metal stands in each corner of the room framed the real-world set. No stagecraft here. Metal desk, chairs, lamp, and bookcase all dusted with white fingerprint powder. Two techs carefully measuring a trajectory pattern, using a string stretched between them. Another man standing behind one of the lights with a pad cradled in his arm, apparently drawing a diagram, his brow knotted in concentration. Or maybe it was the odor wrinkling his nose. On the floor next to his feet, a handheld video camera.

I looked back at the dead man. American, maybe, but he didn't appear to be rich. Drab clothes, no jewelry, ordinary in every respect, except he struck me as being ancient, even without being able to see his face.

Rykov tapped the side of his nose. "When was the last time you were here, Volkovoy? Right before you left for Hong Kong, was it? I think the coroner will find the time of death fits nicely." He gave me his cold smile, waiting, watching for some kind of reaction.

Fishing, I realized. Something about the crime scene bothered Rykov enough to cause him to bring me here instead of directly to Lefortovo. He wanted information, but he wouldn't get it from me.

"Tell your boss to call General Nemtsov."

"Hah! The silent man speaks!" Rykov pursed his lips and blew an audible stream of air, shaking his head in mock sadness. "Too late, I'm afraid. The General was informed of your impending arrest more than four hours ago. Like any true patriot, he said . . . let me see"—he snapped his fingers in the air theatrically—"he said, 'Let Russian justice take its course.' Yes, those were his precise words."

From the moment these men pulled me from the debarkation line I'd known this was no ordinary roust, the kind sponsored by any of a dozen Moscow-area police officials bearing grudges or hoping for a payoff. Rykov wasn't the type of man who would be sent on that kind of mission. He was something different, alien, like a deepwater creature rarely touched by light.

And now my initial fears seemed confirmed. Whether the General had really succumbed to pressure to stay out of the way or whether Rykov was bluffing and didn't care about the General, either way, someone important was behind this murder. Whoever had that much influence could easily frame me based solely on the evidence I'd already seen, not to mention the many ways I could be falsely incriminated. Ballistics wouldn't tie to my Sig, but the prosecutor wouldn't need that; he could show I had access to all the weapons I needed. My trial wouldn't last a day.

"Make things easy on yourself," Rykov purred. "Tell me. Why did you kill this man?"

Bullethead shifted his weight behind me. He grunted something to the techs, and they hurried out of the room, all except the man drawing the diagram, who held his pad in front of his chest and started to say something. Before he could, the small cop pushed him out and slammed the door closed. Bullethead's truncheon made a steely rattle as he pulled it out of the slot attached to his belt. I remembered the breadth of his shoulders as he led me away from the arrivals line.

Shackled as I was I couldn't do anything except go with the blow when he clubbed my kidney. The explosion of agony dropped me to the floor. Another blow clipped my skull and punched my face into the tiled floor. Blood wormed down my neck. Bullethead rolled me over with his boot. Rykov's face loomed above me. His lips were moving, but I couldn't hear anything through the roaring in my skull. He scowled and repeated the words, talking slowly enough that I could read his lips.

Why did you kill this man?

chapter 6

Alfred Reese rolled his wheelchair over the travertine tile to the edge of the balcony outside his home office. The panoramic view overlooked the Pacific Ocean from atop the sheer cliffs on the western tip of Point Loma. Dawn was just beginning to break. A silver band glowed in the distance, bisecting the gray haze above and the slate-colored waves below.

To the east, on the other side of Coronado in the harbor at the end of a curved stretch of San Diego coastline, he imagined he could make out the familiar shape of the USS *Midway*, the mothballed aircraft carrier turned tourist attraction. The thought appealed to him, carried him back to the day she was commissioned in 1945, during his first years working as an aide to the Joint Chiefs.

He sipped coffee. Even through gloves the hot mug felt good in his arthritic hands. This morning wasn't particularly chilly, but his hands were always cold nowadays.

Strange how the years have melded together, he mused. He was one of the lucky ones. His mind was still intact. How many of his former colleagues had lost their intellect to age? Nonetheless, sometimes events that happened decades ago felt fresher, more real, than a conversation he'd had before breakfast. By any measure his post-military career had been a wild success, eclipsing anything he had ever dreamed for himself. He'd been one of the first men appointed to serve as Under Secretary of Defense for Policy, one of the highest-ranking civilian officials in the Department of Defense. From there to Lorelei Industries, a fledgling defense contractor when he started, now an aerospace giant. And he'd built Lorelei the right way. No shortcuts, no side deals, no off-the-books financing, no illegal bribes to crooked congressmen. He now served on the boards of eight international companies besides Lorelei, and except for his legs—his goddamn legs—he still felt strong on most days.

Yet somehow all those achievements collapsed in on themselves during his more contemplative moments, when the distant past cheated its way into his thoughts. Just now appeared the unbidden memory of a used bookstore in Rome on a rainy afternoon, when a young woman with flaxen hair and a shape that made his mouth go suddenly dry cast a sidelong glance at the slim volume of T. S. Eliot poems in his hands. "You like poetry, yes?" she asked in heavily accented English.

How does one become a spy? The stories of General Donovan recruiting the best and brightest from Harvard and Yale for the Office of Strategic Services, America's World War II intelligence agency, had become legendary. But Reese hadn't been one of those golden-boy recruits. He'd been a child of the military, born in Athens to a father who was gone more than he was home and a mother who struggled to fit into the regimented world of the Army Air Service and resented every day she spent away from their modest home in Escondido. Athens, Berlin, Prague, London. New schools, new languages, new cultures— never anywhere long enough to have real friends, or even unstrained relationships. All the usual childhood conflicts magnified. Every visit from his father a special occasion to be savored and then endlessly replayed, until Major General Gordon Reese had been polished in Reese's childhood imagination into a heroic figure—right up to the moment when Reese had learned the truth about him.

Reese stared out at the sea, thinking that those early years had birthed a rare hunger to succeed and made him deeply suspicious of people's motives. A profile, he reflected, that was easy to spot and would later prove useful to men like Donovan.

He downed another slug of coffee. The morning was getting on. He pictured the *Midway* in sharper focus now, her island superstructure limned by the rising sun. His house manager would be here soon to remind him of his morning appointments. In a few minutes Santori would whisk him in the Bell helicopter to the Lorelei building in Los Angeles, where Reese would preside over a boardroom filled with men and women hyper-driven to succeed. More power, more wealth—always more.

During the afternoon break he would wheel himself to one of the floor-to-ceiling windows and stare at the Century City high-rises from his usual spot. He had a decision to make about Colonel Allen Haynes, a good man who had served his country well as a soldier and a congressman before leaving public service to become a lobbyist. Sometime this afternoon after the meeting would be the time to decide, he thought. The time to weigh the cost of another life against the benefits of the JANUS project.

JANUS. Reese turned the word in his mind, drawing a mental picture of the two-faced god guarding the portal between the beginning and the end. Reese had chosen the code name himself because he liked how well it fit the final project of his long career. But he didn't like the way the price kept going up.

He scowled and pushed the button on the arm of his chair to signal Santori. Time to go, not waste away the morning on idle musings.

On the way home from the meeting, he decided, he would instruct Santori to fly the Bell on a course that would take them over the *Midway*. He'd never had anything to do with the old ship. Never served in her, never even walked her decks under his own power. But one day last spring on a whim he had told Santori to help bring his chair to the flight deck. Then he ordered him away and rolled to a spot above the LSO platform.

For the next two hours he had soaked up sun and breathed heavy salt air, remembering that rainy day in Rome and a time when everything seemed to matter so very much more.

chapter 7

I came to on my back, on a surface so hard it seemed to be pushing through my skin, digging into muscle and bone. I moved only my eyes, scanning for movement, trying to guess where I was while the memory of the warehouse flooded back. A dead American, Rykov looming over me while Bullethead worked the truncheon.

I was in a solitary cell. Two claustrophobic steps by three. Wet stone, the far wall punched with empty sockets that once held wooden pegs that secured chains and shackles. Perforated iron bench. Shit-streaked bucket. Everything coated with an eye-watering blend of urine, formaldehyde, and crawling black mold. The feeble bands of light between the bars in the Judas hole revealed fragments of words and symbols gouged into the rock wall. Scattered among the names and dates were a stylized representation of the hammer and sickle, the circular sign for peace, and an outline of hands pressed together in prayer.

Lefortovo prison, most likely, just where Rykov had said I would be. But not in one of the usual cages or in the holding pen where they shovel the dregs rounded up the night before. From the look of it, this place had been constructed decades ago, a secret dungeon to hold the people the Soviets wanted to deny knowing anything about.

I stretched, groaned, pulled myself to a sitting position. Waited for the waves of pain to recede to an aching throb, then hugged my knees to my chest, feeling the hard tubular titanium of my prosthesis dig into my forearm through its synthetic sheath and the leather of my left boot. I still wore the same clothes as before, now scuffed and soiled. My shoelaces and belt were gone. A gauze pad crusted with blood had been taped to the back of my head. My back felt like one continuous bruise.

While working my fingers and toes and flexing the muscles in my legs to get the blood flowing, I tried to draw a connection—a hint of recognition, a wisp of memory, *something*—to associate with the dead American in my warehouse.

Nothing came to mind.

Hours passed. The pain became more manageable. I moved to the bench, settled into a position on my side, and mentally replayed the scene in my warehouse over and over without any result. An old man by the look of the body. Shot in the back at close range. Not an easy way to go. Depending where the bullets had been placed he'd have had time to think about it as his life drained away. But I had no idea who he was.

My gaze fell on the wall engravings. Carved declarations and laments turned black with grime. How many had suffered in this place? So many holes like this in Russia. Wells of sadness and pain and misery, spreading through Moscow from here inside Lefortovo to the cells of the Lubyanka and so many other places, extending outward all the way to the Stygian darkness of the mines in Kolyma and the bone-deep cold of the camp in Arkhangelsk where my friend Vadim spent nearly a decade.

From Vadim my thoughts turned to Valya, who would be ragged with worry after I failed to show up on the May 20 flight from Hong Kong to Moscow. She was different now, after losing her foot. Her stride more of a rolling hitch instead of the confident glide she used to have. Only a month ago she had admitted that she couldn't stand to look at the stump of her left leg, and I could tell from the way she grimaced when she made a misstep that the prosthesis still hurt her.

I made it to my feet and stepped to the corner. Leaned one hand against the wall over the bucket and pissed blood. The dual sensations of discomfort and relief made me groan.

When finished, I settled back onto the iron bench, trying to find a position that didn't hurt, still thinking of Valya, of the changes in her since our fateful trip to Prague when she lost her foot. Watching her limp away not long ago, Vadim had told me about a long-running feud he'd witnessed between a prison doctor and another prisoner in Arkhangelsk. Food, drugs, a choice place to sleep—Vadim never knew the cause of the dispute. One day the prisoner caught his arm in a conveyor belt. Ripped it off at the elbow, splintered the humerus. During mealtime the next night the doctor bit into a chunk of black bread and announced, "When I don't scrape so well the bone ends up with burrs." His smile revealed a crosshatching of partially chewed black bread and brown teeth. "Means a lifetime of pain." Vadim said that he figured doctors in secret Prague prisons like the one who amputated Valya's foot tend not to be concerned with rounding and smoothing the severed bones of their patients, either.

But Vadim had it wrong, I decided. Even a dog knows the difference between a kick and a stumble. The doctor at Arkhangelsk wanted to inflict pain; the one in Prague simply didn't care. And that, I realized, was what struck me as strange about the body of the dead American. As brutally as he'd been killed, as much blood as he'd shed on the tile floor, his murder still seemed oddly bloodless to me. As if he'd been led there and dispatched by an indifferent killer who stood over his victim to make sure the job was properly done then disappeared into the streets of Moscow.

As if the dead American was less flesh and bone and more a message or a package to be delivered on a certain date and time.

chapter 8

The next day I jumped in place to loosen sore muscles. Completed a short regimen of push-ups, squats, dips, crunches—a fraction of my usual routine. Slept on the bench for a few fitful hours. Paced the cell, three steps and turn, do it again. Empty hours filled only with the monotonous rhythm of my movements and my thoughts. Time passed in achingly slow increments.

When I had been in the cell for at least two days by my reckoning somebody rattled a metal slide on a portal at the bottom of the steel door and slid a plate into my cell. Moldy bread, processed meat, and a tin of water. The Judas hole, divided into thirds by two iron bars, was cut into the door at eye level, but the person bringing my food took care to remain unobserved. That happened several more times in the coming days.

I was in the middle of a set of push-ups when a metal door boomed open in the distance. Mealtime was still hours away. I stood and faced the door as footfalls echoed toward the cell, the sound of one man walking. Then Rykov peered inside, his head a dark oval backlit by the weak light in the hallway.

"The medical examiner established the time of Walker's death." His tone was friendly, as if we were resuming an interrupted conversation. "Seventeen May, afternoon or early evening."

He chinged open a silver-plated lighter and held the flame to the tip of a hand-rolled cigarette dangling from his lips. The flare cast the contours of his face in half shadow, made his nose appear longer and thinner before he snapped the lighter closed.

"We have a witness, too, my friend. A machinist saw you leaving the warehouse. Three o'clock. He is quite sure it was then, because the train came only a minute or two later. Plenty of time for you to catch your flight to Hong Kong and concoct your little alibi."

He blew a stream of foul-smelling smoke through the bars.

"Funny thing about your trip. Macao police found a dead Russian shot in the head from close range. So they made some inquiries here. They discovered that this man was not just anyone, no, this man used to be a big player in the Kremlin." He gave his thin-lipped smile, eyes flat, cigarette drooping. "Quite a coincidence, you being there when he was murdered."

"Walker was the name of the dead American?"

He nodded, studying me through the bars. "Everett Walker. A famous cinematographer and occasional director. His camera was 'the eye of God,' or so the newspapers liked to say. And he was one of ours, a fellow countryman, although he denied it publicly. The American politicians refused to let him work for years. Do you know the story of the Hollywood blacklists?"

"How old was he?"

"Very old. In his eighties. He would have been dead soon enough even if you hadn't shot him."

"Why was he in Moscow?"

"That's one of the questions we want to ask you."

"I never met the man. Never even heard of him. I had no reason to kill him."

Rykov dug into a pocket inside his jacket to produce a photograph the size of a sheet of paper. He held it on the other side of the bars so that I could just reach it with my finger and thumb, then flared his lighter.

The photo showed my warehouse office as it looked the night they took me there, except from this angle I could see Walker's face more clearly. Blotched and gray, livid on the side where it had been pressed into the carpet. Gray mustache streaked with rust-colored lines of blood from his nose and mouth. Dark brown eyes, shocked wide. Exit wound in his chest the size of a wide-open mouth. More than one bullet, it looked like. Rykov flipped his lighter closed, and the photo went dark.

"I still don't know him," I said.

Rykov strode back and forth outside my cell, rippling the ribs of light between the bars. "Then why do you suppose he was shot in your office?"

I closed my eyes and brought the face in the photo back to life. Drew another blank. "No matter how many times you ask, the answer won't change. Give me more to go on."

He produced another photo and put the lighter in my hand so that I could hold the flame close and keep it lit. This one had been shot from above, looking down on a white dropcloth covered with Walker's personal effects. Brown leather wallet, open and apparently empty, driver's license and passport displayed on the cloth next to the wallet. The picture on the California license bore little resemblance to the dead man. The photographer appeared to have caught a younger version of Walker with his head tilted back. His haughty gaze gave him a patrician air. I lifted my thumb, and the flame guttered and died.

"He looks better here. Rich. And alive."

"We've looked into his finances. He owned enough credit cards to make a big spender proud, but he didn't have any of them on him when he died."

I thumbed the flame back to life and looked at the picture again. A whitish, rectangular shape bulged the leather of the wallet from the pressure of Walker's weight against the cards he must have carried inside.

"He paid cash for everything," Rykov said. "Exchanged dollars for rubles at Sheremetyevo, used the rubles to rent a room at a cheap hotel. He paid for one month in advance. Got around on the metro, sometimes a gypsy cab. In three days he never once accessed the Internet or used a phone. The man left the same kind of mark you leave when you pull your finger out of a pool of water."

Once again I flicked on the lighter. The passport next to the driver's license lay open to the page showing the visa stamp. The name on the visa was not Everett Walker. "False papers?"

"Probably cost over thirty thousand American dollars. The money impresses me less than the fact that he knew who to bribe and how to make contact with that person."

For many years the KGB ran a phony ID operation out of the Russian Consulate on East Ninety-first Street in Manhattan. Passports and birth certificates were copied or stolen from people applying for Russian visas or other travel papers, then altered to be used by intelligence officers entering the United States illegally, many of them posing as Eastern European immigrants looking to marry Americans and find jobs in government or sensitive U.S. industries. Once in place with their synthetic identity—their legend—the officers burrowed in, sucked information, and passed it back to Moscow for years, sometimes decades.

The process to create a forged passport and visa for Walker was probably similar to the method used to plant illegal intelligence officers, operating in reverse in this case, America to Russia.

"He had help."

"Brilliant. You're not making things better for yourself, Volk."

Rykov motioned for me to return the pictures and his lighter. He fired another cigarette, one hand cupping his mouth. Captured in the light from the flame, he reminded me of a Soviet-era propaganda poster that I'd seen posted on a wall in a juvenile detention center years ago, one showing the silhouette of a figure lighting a cigarette. Bad memories, all of them from those days, beginning when I was cast adrift in St. Petersburg's Orphanage No. 15.

The orange glow from the cigarette turned Rykov's eyes into dark hollows beneath the dome of his high forehead as he inhaled greedily. Prison time opens your mind. Hours of reflection yield a crop of ideas, some right, some wrong. One that had come to me—when I recalled thinking in the warehouse that Rykov seemed strangely out of place, even alien, in the middle of a murder investigation—was that he might be a member of a rare strain of the secret police virus that has prowled Russia's bloodstream for centuries, the kind that makes sure its host isn't infected by outside powers. A spy who hunts for other spies. I lowered my voice.

"The question is, help from which side?"

Rykov stilled, half his face illuminated by the overhead lights in the hallway. The one blue eye I could see in the bar of light narrowed.

"*That* is a far better question. Who arranged for him to travel this way? Who taught him what he needed to know in order to get around without leaving a trace?"

"The Americans."

"Maybe. Or maybe the same people who made your false passport so beautifully, Mr. Vasily Pravdin? The ones who ordered you to ventilate Lachek's skull?" He started to say more, then clamped his jaws and looked over his shoulder down the hallway as though expecting someone.

I kept my face impassive, trying not to reveal that he had made a mistake by saying Lachek's name after pretending not to know him. *A big player in the Kremlin*, he'd said before, implying that Lachek was one of many faceless power brokers. Now I knew for sure. Somehow, some way, Rykov was tied to Lachek.

"Why did Walker bring his driver's license into this country?" I said.

Rykov returned his attention to me. Gave me a look that said what difference does it make? "Habit? Ineptitude?"

"He changed everything else but not that?"

He dropped his cigarette, dipping his head to track its fall. The sole of his shoe grated over concrete as he ground it out. He took a deep breath, let it out slowly.

"You don't understand what's happening here, Volk. All this talk, but you won't tell me what I need to know. Why was this man killed in your warehouse? I need a simple answer to a simple question." He shook his head and looked toward the door again, restlessly shifting his weight from side to side. "What good are you to me if you won't tell me that?"

"Do you want me to make something up? I'm sure plenty of confessions have been beaten out of prisoners in this very room."

My answer seemed to enrage him. Growling, he reached beneath his jacket and pulled out a 9-millimeter Gyurza. An ugly cannon of a gun, black with a polymer grip and scarred steel slide. He chambered a round and aimed through the bars, holding the weapon at eye level with two hands.

"Step back, face the wall, and kneel."

I held myself as still as stone. "I never heard the name Walker until you said it ten minutes ago."

He snorted. "You've treated me like a fool from the moment we met. You don't get it, do you?"

"What? What don't I get?"

"That it's easier to blame a dead man than a live one. Enough talk. Back up, turn around, get on your knees."

chapter 9

"**N**o," I said.

I made no effort to move to the back of the cell and kneel as Rykov had ordered. He stared at me over the barrel of the Gyurza from the other side of the bars of the Judas hole, face contorted, knuckles white from the pressure of his grip.

"You think it bothers me to shoot you in the face? I'll kill you the same way you did the man in Macao."

His model of Gyurza was built in the '90s. More modern versions exist, but he hadn't bothered to keep pace with the changes. Nor had he bothered to clean it lately. Somebody had blocked the grip safety with clear plastic tape, now yellowing and curled at the edges, but I didn't think it was him. He wasn't the type to worry about getting into action fast. He was a thinker.

"You're not going to kill me."

Anger rippled his features, and in that instant I thought I had misjudged him. All in one motion he shifted aim a fraction and the Gyurza jumped in his hand with a deafening roar of fire and smoke. The bullet struck stone somewhere behind me and sprayed fragments all over the

cell. I reeled back, hands over my ears, the reverberations ringing inside
my skull. Smoke filled the room and blotted the Judas hole, then a disembodied hand waved it away and Rykov's face appeared again. The
rosette birthmark above his left eye seemed to have spread, a growing
stain mottling his features. He took aim, drawing down, making a show
of it.

I didn't move, just waited, letting several seconds tick away.

"You're still not going to kill me."

We stood facing each other through the bars for a long time. Then
he slowly lowered the Gyurza and slotted it into its holster. He took a
deep breath and wiped his brow with the back of his index finger, the
trembling in his hand noticeable even in the dim light. When he finally
began talking again, he spoke quietly, deliberately.

"The American embassy is making inquiries. We think the diplomats are shilling for the NSA. Behind the scenes they're saying that
Walker was giving information to Unit forty-four three-eighty-eight."

Unit 44388, the military designation for the Fourth Department
of the General Staff, also known as the GRU. Military intelligence.
"You're saying that Walker was a GRU agent?"

He ignored my question. "You're the perfect person to blame for
his death. Ex-military officer gone bad. A criminal. You see how easily
your cover can be used to convict you? But we also want certain questions answered. There's the problem."

A metal door clanged at the end of the hall. Rykov glanced that
way and motioned with his left hand. With an electrical whirr, a row of
fluorescent lights on the ceiling in the hallway began a loud buzzing.
An instant later they popped to life. After so many days of murky darkness, the harsh light burst against my retinas. I stepped back, covering
my eyes. When I opened them in slits, Rykov was lighting another cigarette.

"From the moment he arrived in Moscow, all Walker did was look
for you." His voice sounded as though it were coming from a long way
away, lost in the ringing in my ears. My left ear, the one closest to the
Gyurza when he fired it, felt like it was full of water.

"Why?"

"Who knows? All we have is an old photo we found in his hotel room. A picture taken in America. A picture of your father and Walker together."

I stiffened, ever so slightly, but I could tell that Rykov noticed.

He took a palm-sized photo from the inside pocket of his jacket and speared it through the bars. No need for a lighter anymore. I could see well enough. But the image itself was less clear. It showed two people standing in front of a wall made of white stones next to a large vine with reddish-pink flowers spilling out from its protective cage of rebar. One of the men appeared to be Walker, older than in his driver's license photo, but younger than he looked on the floor of my warehouse. The features of the second man were in shadow.

"That's the Getty Museum in Los Angeles," Rykov said.

I turned the photo over. Nothing written on the back. "The man next to Walker is supposed to be my father?"

"Yes, according to our technical people. Even stranger, this photo was taken in 2002. What do you make of that? Walker travels to Moscow with a photograph of a man who was supposed to have died in 1974."

Time slowed. I still held the photo, but I wasn't looking at it anymore. I smelled the bucket in the corner. Saw the hands carved into the wall, glazed white by the light coming from between the bars. Heard my left boot creak loudly when I shifted my weight.

"Died how?"

"Lost in a plane somewhere over the Baltic Sea. A frantic call over the radio, engines failed, a death spiral, reports of an oil slick and debris in the water, nine men lost—all documented by air force records. So what is this photo? And how does it come to be found among the possessions of a man murdered in your office?"

Rykov blew a noxious cloud of smoke above his head and watched it trail away. "We need answers, Volk. And somebody needs to hang for this. You're as good as anybody else."

"You know who I am? What I do?"

He nodded warily. He couldn't possibly know all the details. Moscow Military Academy, two years' special operations training at Balashikha-2, five years of service in Chechnya and the surrounding republics—the Southern Cauldron—and everything that implied. Deep penetrations. Shakedown schemes. *Mokriye dela*—wet work. Six months a captive, during which I lost my foot, then a year of diplomatic training and five more performing covert operations all over the world, always on behalf of the General. Lachek was personal, after what he did to Alla, but in most other ways he was no different from nearly a dozen others from Tokyo to London. Rykov would have seen glimpses of those things in whatever files he was able to access, sufficient to understand my point.

"Let me loose," I said. "I'll find out who killed Walker and why. Then you'll know why the Americans are applying so much pressure. You'll have the leverage you want."

Rykov studied me, chewing the inside of his cheek, tapping his nose. "You'll turn on me the second you're out."

I don't know which of his mannerisms tipped me. Perhaps some telltale sign registered at an unconscious level. But suddenly I saw with utter clarity that he had already decided to let me out. Or maybe he had been ordered to do so. Beating me in the warehouse, threatening to shoot me, all of that was his way of seeing if I knew anything about Walker. But it was also part of a stratagem, his way of trying to make *me* offer to help *him*.

"You're going to let me go, aren't you?"

The flesh on his face seemed to tighten against his skull, but he remained perfectly still, never breaking eye contact. Self-discipline was probably one of the most basic skills a man like Rykov learned to master. "There must be more to this, Volk. Walker didn't come all the way to Moscow just to exchange family photographs."

I moved closer to the bars. "Where do I start?"

Rykov studied me for a moment, then nodded. He signaled with his hand and the door at the end of the corridor boomed open again.

"Walker stayed at the Hotel Zolotoy. We already searched the room and found nothing interesting other than the photo of your father. But there has to be more."

Boots clicked on concrete in the hall, approaching us. Rykov held up his hand and the sound stopped. He stuck his nose between the bars, his features drawn back and hard. "You let me know anything you find out, Volk, or I'll have you in here again," he whispered. "The next time I tell you to kneel, you'll do it."

He spun away and disappeared, replaced seconds later by another figure darkening the Judas hole, someone I didn't recognize. The new man wore a business suit and looked like an accountant. He worked a large key in the lock on the cell door for a long time, wrinkling his nose at the odor when it finally opened. Led me through a maze of gloomy catacombs made of thick granite blocks inset with steel doors. Behind the bars in one of the doors a pair of eyes hovered in the darkness like white marbles; incoherent babbling carried from behind another. After many turns we climbed several flights of rough-hewn steps and pushed through an iron-latticed oak door to a hallway made of painted concrete and flaking plaster.

We stopped in a room that contained a filing cabinet, desk, one wooden chair, and a cardboard box. I stood while my escort wordlessly filled out a form, then locked a copy into the cabinet and put the original into a file folder. Once that was done he shoved the box toward me with his foot. Inside were some of the things taken from me when I was arrested. Dead cell phone. Wallet. Belt. Shoelaces. No watch, no rubber-banded wad of cash, no passport.

My disinterested escort tapped his foot impatiently while I laced my boots. Then he pushed me along more labyrinthine corridors, up more stairs, and finally to a windowless steel door layered with thick coats of paint revealed in its scratched surface. He unlocked it and shoved me out of the building and onto the top of a row of concrete steps, swinging the door closed behind me.

chapter 10

The streets outside Lefortovo prison glistened from a recent rain. A flushed hint of pink, the birth of a new day, colored the bottom of a fanlike formation of gray clouds above the row of buildings across the street.

Valya was waiting at the foot of the steps. Dressed in ripped jeans and a tight, sleeveless black T-shirt emblazoned with a silver cross, she stood with her hands at her sides, searching my face for a sign as I descended. I stopped when we were almost touching.

"No," I answered her unspoken question. "They held me, nothing more."

She closed her eyes, slipped into my arms, and melded her body to mine.

A year ago she left me for six months. Or maybe it's more truthful to admit that I drove her away. However it happened, she went to Paris, Milan, London, Vienna, and many other places I don't know about. World travel is hard for her, given her status as a Chechen refugee and the precarious relationship between Chechnya and Moscow. She managed it only because the General obtained the travel documents at my insistence, although he was never willing to meet her face-to-face. One night over vodka in his subterranean headquarters he'd explained to me that the commander of the notorious Fifty-eighth Army could never expect forgiveness from a child of the mountains. "You've made your bargain with the White Chechen, but she remembers, and so do I." When I encountered her next she was back in the Caucasus, the place of her worst horrors, working with the Red Crescent and others to ease the suffering caused by the simmering conflict there.

Holding her on the rain-slick steps outside Lefortovo, the great mystery to me was how that hellish war in a country churned by conflict for hundreds of years had somehow given birth to this mystical spirit.

"You forgot to shower," she said in a muffled voice, and she tried to laugh.

She smelled like warm vanilla. My shirt was wet where her cheek was touching it.

"Six days, Alexei," she said. "I didn't know what to think. How many more times must we do this?"

On the way to the metro she told me how she had bribed Aeroflot officials for information about the passengers on my flight, then questioned those she could find, several of whom recalled seeing a man led away by two policemen. She'd also gotten word to the General, a difficult proposition given his wariness toward her.

"The General says he tried to help," she said. I thought of the quote Rykov had attributed to him. *Let Russian justice take its course.* I didn't repeat it to Valya. True or false, it would only harden her more against him. Just as Rykov intended, however, the words had tunneled wormlike into my subconscious.

Valya punched a button on her phone, then held the screen for me to see. "He sent this text a few hours ago."

WAIT FOR VOLK EAST SIDE OF LEFORTOVO. TELL HIM DO NOT DISCUSS STEPAN. MAKE NO MOVE BEFORE TALKING TO ME.

So the General had known I was going to be released. One way or another, he had gotten to Rykov. Forced his hand, cut a deal, or however it happened, I was glad to be out of that hole.

Valya frowned, searching my face for clues. "Is he talking about Stepan, your father? He has been gone for thirty-five years. How can anything he did matter today?"

I told her about the dead American, Walker, and the picture Rykov claimed to have found in his hotel room. I described Lachek's last minutes, how he gleefully told me that my father had defected in a spy plane.

She frowned. "Is it possible your father is still alive after all these years?"

"I don't know."

We took the concrete steps down to the metro tunnel. Valya stumbled on the cracked edge of one and winced, and her limp became more pronounced. We both pretended nothing had happened.

"Rykov," she said. "Is he FSB? SVR?"

Two KGB offspring, both created by Gorbachev after the failed coup attempt in 1991. The FSB handles internal security. The SVR fills the void left by the KGB's First Chief Directorate, the intelligence arm that spied on other countries. They differ from each other in much the same way as the American FBI and CIA.

"Neither," I said. "I think he's GRU. And I think Walker was a GRU asset."

We stepped onto the boarding platform. Valya stared at me, processing what I had said. "If Walker was one of theirs then they should know what he was doing here and why he had a picture of your father."

"Apparently it's not that simple."

The train arrived and rocked to a stop, brakes screeching, and we boarded, standing close among the press of bodies. Her hand found the blood-crusted bandage on the back of my head. She turned my head to see the wound.

"Oh, God."

"It's nothing."

Valya's eyes were enormous, gray, soulful. Looking into them, I experienced a sensation akin to vertigo. She leaned into me as the train rolled down the tracks. She was tense, all corded muscle.

"I thought once Lachek was dead, things would change," she said. "I imagined we would travel, enjoy the world like tourists, all the evil safely tucked away in the dark places we would never go back to. Now . . ."

The train rumbled along the tracks. We swayed together in a close embrace.

"I always pictured Hollywood as the magical place where all the movies come from," Valya said.

"I think Hollywood is one of those places that are better in the imagination."

I felt her nod, but she didn't answer. We stayed quiet for several minutes. I put everything else out of my mind, enjoying the scent of her hair and the feel of her body while she clung to me, thinking her private thoughts.

"Where are we going?" she asked after several stops, lifting her head from my chest.

"The Hotel Zolotoy, on the north side."

"You're going to work for those people? What about your injured head? What about the General?"

"Later."

She stared through a window, where there was nothing to see except the periodic lights shining on the tunnel wall as we rolled past. "You are relentless."

"I don't have a choice, Valya. Not if I want to learn the truth."

"You never seem to have a choice."

She kept her gaze averted, her pearly features washed of emotion, drifting away while standing still.

I am haunted by a recurring dream. I'm on a balcony, looking down on a wide boulevard teeming with people. Valya stands beneath me in the crowd. She radiates her usual white light, a pale beacon among the dark throng. She motions to tell me that she's coming up the stairs. I leave the balcony to open the door. I wait for a long time, but she doesn't appear. I go back and look down again upon all the bodies in motion, shades of gray and black, darkness without light. She is nowhere to be seen.

chapter 11

The Hotel Zolotoy typified Soviet-era architecture—a blocky monolith of gray limestone. But in recent years somebody had added spice to the place. Yellow trim on the window casings and bas-relief carvings of the hammer and sickle interspersed along a stringcourse of brick halfway up the building, red steel columns framing the entry.

An addict lay curled around one of the columns. He opened one bloodshot eye to watch us as we entered the hotel. The manager looked from Valya to me, his glance taking in my soiled clothes and week-old beard. The sight caused him to set his pen aside and back away from the scarred wooden countertop. His back thumped the wall, where a crooked shelf pushed his head forward at an uncomfortable angle.

"We need to see the register," I said without showing any identification. In Russia, not telling a man who you are often sends a more powerful message than any ID badge. He pointed to a vinyl-covered book on the counter behind a black phone that was new when Stalin prowled the Kremlin. I told Valya the name on Walker's false passport, and she thumbed open the register, finger-walked back through the days, grunted, and turned the register so that I could see it written in a crabbed scrawl: Room 312. I motioned the manager closer and pointed to the name.

"Did this man leave anything here?"

"The police took everything."

"Is anyone staying in the room now?"

The manager scratched a hairless patch in his scruffy beard so hard that his fingers left angry red trails as he looked at the numbered cubbyholes behind him. "He's out now."

Responding to my gesture, he plucked a key from one of the slots. Dull brass, dark from years of handling. Valya stayed in the lobby while I took the stairs two at a time. Room 312 was two doors down from the stairwell. Inside, the décor was Soviet-chic. Worn lime-green throw rug tacked to the floor. Corroded metal TV stand holding a 1980s TV and VCR combo. Listing nightstand. Tiny closet. Rust-stained sink beneath a mirror screwed to the wall. A deodorant stick, a disposable razor, and a frayed toothbrush rested on the chipped porcelain ledge of the sink.

Tacks popped into the air as I ripped away the rug to reveal the rippled wood beneath. The joints held under my probing fingers. No loose planks hiding secrets beneath the floor. The closet contained a pair of slacks shiny from wear and a jacket that reeked of mothballs and body odor, probably the property of the current occupant, but I searched the pockets and the linings anyway.

I tore the sheets off the bed and pulled the mattress off the box spring. Ran my fingers over the stained fabric of the mattress, searching for holes or signs it had been cut and stitched back together, my only reward a swirl of dust. Traced the wooden frame of the box spring, got a splinter stuck in my palm for my trouble. Felt along the length of the metal frame. Something sticky coated the metal—the remains of a spilled drink, I hoped. No sign that anything had been tampered with.

The nightstand held underwear, socks, and a flier advertising the services of an escort agency, one of my former competitors. Nothing tacked beneath it or taped inside the drawers.

I stood in the middle of the room and turned in a slow circle, trying to see things from Walker's perspective. He was traveling to Russia on expertly forged papers. Needing to make contact with a man he'd never met, a hard man to find. He had the photo as a calling card, an introduction to earn a step up the ladder of trust. But the photo was only the ante. He still had a hand to play. After he earned my trust he would show me—*show*, not tell—the real reason for a Hollywood cinematographer to fly halfway around the globe.

So where would he hide his prize while he looked for me? I'd searched all the obvious places. What about somewhere peculiar to him? An accountant might carry a ledger book, a lawyer a legal pad. What might a man who worked with cameras and film bring with him?

I thought of a lesson from a course in tradecraft. Microphotography. Old technology, yes, but still a proven way to conceal documents. Maybe antiquated enough that Rykov and his cohorts wouldn't have thought to look for it.

One method used a positive-type film to bleach an image so that the microdot appeared as clear cellophane or plastic. Called "mikrats" by the Germans, who employed them extensively during World War II, they were perfected by the Soviet intelligence services during the Cold War. Almost as soon as the thought came to me, I dismissed it. Walker had carried the photo of my father in the open among his things. His behavior didn't suggest he had the sophistication to hide something else. Besides, what would an American be doing with a mikrat?

Still . . . Walker was a cinematographer. He would have had access to the special photographic equipment required to reduce documents. Assuming the idea was even remotely possible, where would he have hidden his little secret? A modern mikrat would be less than a square millimeter. If it was clear, it could be hiding in plain sight.

I scanned the room. Saw the mirror over the sink from a different perspective. Approached it slowly, head angled to one side. Less than half a meter square. A few dried flecks of shaving cream and spattered toothpaste. Streaks, stains, smudged prints.

I bent down to look at the mirror from an angle where it caught the reflected light from the bulb in the ceiling, hoping to spy an odd wink or mysterious shadow. Nothing unusual except a faint distortion in the upper right corner, more than head high for the average person, the least likely place to be wiped with a towel to remove steam. Sure that I had found something, I gently ran the tip of my index finger over the spot.

It was as smooth as polished glass should be.

I was on a fool's hunt.

I returned to the middle of the room and took a last look around, cursing myself for having wasted time. But even as I did I felt a churning in my gut that told me I was missing something obvious. Walker's passport and visa were professional grade. True, his methods were not faultless; otherwise, Rykov and his men wouldn't have been on top of him from the minute he set foot in Moscow. But they weren't amateurish either. There had to be something more than the photo.

One more turn around the room. Still nothing. What was I missing?

Rykov would have searched everywhere. Compulsive by nature, the man would have been thorough. But except for the photo he found nothing extraordinary.

I forced myself to look at the problem from a different perspective. Assume that the same person who helped Walker obtain the visa and told him how to blend into Moscow so seamlessly also helped him to hide his secret document. This person knew the old Soviet tradecraft, wanted a message delivered, and found the perfect vehicle in this American so anxious to meet the son of his friend, or acquaintance, or whatever my father had been to Walker. He or she taught Walker how to microphotograph his document and instructed him where to hide it. A Russian knows that the best place to hide something extraordinary is among things that are ordinary.

The photo of Walker's personal effects sprang to mind. Brown leather wallet, empty, with only the driver's license and passport next to it.

Could something have been hidden in plain view?

I went down to the lobby and called the General. He made no mention of my arrest. Instead, he listened while I told him what I suspected, snorted derisively, then remained silent while I explained my reasoning. At first the only reply was the sound of him breathing. I visualized him with his stubbed fingers hovered over the computer keyboard, eyes out of focus while he mulled the idea.

After a minute or so he said he would see if he could get his hands on Walker's driver's license. Then he told me to meet him on the steps of the Cathedral of Christ the Savior in two hours.

chapter 12

After leaving the Hotel Zolotoy, Valya and I went to the loft, where I showered, watching the dried blood from my head and the filth from Lefortovo prison sluice into the drain while I tried to scrub away the stain of Lachek's last words and make sense of everything I'd learned from Rykov.

The loft takes up the fifth floor of a mostly deserted industrial building. Renovated several years earlier as part of my cover, it serves as a sanctuary for Valya and me. High ceilings, exposed ductwork, modern furniture, an abundance of security devices—it cost a small fortune, even by Moscow's exorbitant standards, all of it paid for by my former illegal operation. Done right, crime pays.

Valya sat on the edge of the bed and watched me dress, her expression pensive. "Why are you rushing into this, Alexei? Let the GRU play its games without you."

"It's not that simple. I don't know if whoever is pulling Rykov's string will *allow* me to walk away. And that picture, the story of my father's plane crashing in the Baltic . . ."

From the time I was old enough to know what a father is I have always felt the same emptiness whenever that subject comes up. My father existed in the scar tissue of my mind, a figment haunting my thoughts. Sometimes I hated him, sometimes I longed for him—or for the idealized image of him—but always I had a hole inside. My earliest memories are of a series of work farms outside of Leningrad on the leaden edge of the Baltic, where I was put to work to "pay my way," a euphemism for the sale of my labor for profit. But no matter what my circumstances, the same empty pit threatened to swallow me when talk turned to my disappeared father. All these years later, I should have been past that, but I wasn't.

"I can understand simple curiosity," Valya said. "But your father was nothing to you."

I finished buttoning my shirt, then logged on to my computer and e-mailed the General, asking what he knew about Rykov. Valya chewed the inside of her lip, absently massaging her left leg as I closed the computer, then checked the action on my spare Sig and slapped in a full magazine. She started to say something more, stopped, and looked down at her hands.

"You must be starving," she said.

I looked at the digital clock on the nightstand. Still an hour before I had to meet the General. "Let's go."

Vadim's Café is squeezed into the jam of buildings in the Kitaygorod district, a short hop east of the Kremlin and north of the Moscow River. The entrance looks onto a crooked street that bustles at all hours. The alley in back serves as an access for delivery and trash collection trucks, as well as a late-night meeting place for prostitutes and johns, drug dealers and addicts. Things were busy, so one of the waiters served us. Vadim joined us halfway through the meal, settling into a wooden chair and looking at me curiously.

"I'm fine," I said.

He wore a red bandanna tied over his head and a white shirt with the sleeves rolled up to reveal rail-thin wrists. When he glanced at Valya, the dangling end of his bandanna and the hooked profile of his nose reminded me of a pirate.

"What is this I hear about your father?"

"If you talked to Valya, you know everything I know."

He picked up the salt shaker and turned it in his hands. Long and thin, ridged with a network of sharply defined tendons and veins, Vadim's hands were dark from exposure, scarred from the bite of too many shovels, adzes, and pickaxes to count. A furrow of puckered skin ran from the third knuckle on his right hand to his wrist, the trail of a homemade shiv, he'd told me.

"Fathers are trouble," he said.

I stuffed the last of my whitefish into my mouth and chased it with a slice of bread. "Uh-huh."

"Mine was killed in Hanoi."

"Hanoi?"

"He was one of several hundred specialists sent to train and equip the Vietnam People's Army. He disappeared during an exercise there when I was sixteen. A month later my family was on a train to the camp in Arkhangelsk."

When Vadim reached for the pitcher to pour himself a glass of water, the rolled-up sleeve of his shirt hiked up his forearm, revealing one of the faded blue numbers tattooed there, a permanent reminder of his time in the camp.

"My mother, my sister Jaelle, and me," he said. "Terrified. Packed into a shivering bundle in the back of a railcar reinforced with steel bands and wrapped in barbed wire. When the train left the temporary camp, our car contained three-dozen people. A few Gypsies, including a family we knew from our village in the steppe. All the rest were rough-looking men. I learned later they were criminals sent north to purge Moscow's jails, draining the bad blood into the bottomless bucket of the gulag."

Vadim drank. Valya's sad gaze caught mine. She looked as though she were hearing this story for the first time, too.

"The men argued," Vadim said. "Two of them fought like I'd never seen men fight before. The one who gained the advantage hooked a thumb into the eye of the other one. I heard his anguished cries echoing in my head for days. Then those same two men copulated in full view of everyone else in the car. I averted my eyes and tried to close my ears against the catcalls and laughter and grunts while my mother hugged my sister to her bosom and cupped her hands over her ears to block the sights and sounds."

The noise of the café seemed to have faded to a dull hiss. I thought of the lonely cell in Lefortovo and the bits of stories told in the carvings gouged into the rock there. Vadim lowered his voice, talking with his gaze pitched down at the top of the table.

"I didn't understand the society of the *urki*, the professional criminals. I thought the man on the bottom was a willing participant, not a victim of rape. Later, I learned the customs and language of the thieves—*blatnaya muzyka*, thieves' music—so I understood that the loser had been forced to submit to the humiliation, just as weaker men were sometimes passed from bunk to bunk based on the results of a card game. But on that night I was still an innocent, shocked by the *urki*'s coarse ways and utter lack of inhibition.

"Some of the men shared a bottle they got from one of the guards. The train took on coal, then rolled for hours, drumming its beat along the steel rails. The wooden toilet bucket overflowed. One flat-faced *urka*—the top half of the copulating couple—hacked a hole in the floorboards with a hand ax he'd smuggled on board. The men swayed around it in groups, carelessly splashing each other's boots with urine . . ."

Vadim folded his hands on the table in front of him, rolling his head as if to shake off thoughts of the past. "Yes, fathers are trouble."

I glanced at the clock over the door. I needed to go now to make my meeting with the General. "What does that story have to do with fathers?"

"When the old Soviet files were opened I looked and found my papa's. They accused him of desertion. They said he left his family to live there in the jungle. We were punished for his sin."

"You can't believe he deserted," Valya said.

"At first I didn't. How could a man who loved his family so much leave them to suffer? Now I know the truth." He paused, looking me in the eyes. "Whether he did or didn't doesn't matter. We couldn't escape his legacy either way. You can, Alexei. Turn away from this. With the General's help you can face the GRU."

I stood to leave. "I already told Valya. It's not that simple."

Vadim looked at Valya. "Like I said, fathers are trouble."

chapter 13

"Stepan Volkovoy's air force service file was wiped clean of everything except the most basic information," the General said fifteen minutes later. "We've talked about that before."

He had been waiting for me outside the Cathedral of Christ the Savior. As soon as I arrived he led the way toward the crowd at the entrance, already talking in his clipped cadence.

"He disappeared in 1974, the file was purged. Nothing strange about that. But here's the odd part. *Nothing* exists—no record, report, or note—from 1967 forward. Something odd happened in 1967, seven years *before* he vanished."

"We never talked about that part before."

He glanced up at me. "No, we didn't. Why be distracted by things you can't change?"

The colossal bulk of the cathedral dominates the skyline along the Moscow River. The original structure took twenty-one years to build in the mid-nineteenth century, then another twenty for scores of artisans and painters to embellish the interior with polished granite, Carrara marble plaques and statues, inlaid precious stones, and wooden galleries. In other parts of the world it would have been a national treasure. But in Russia all of it was reduced to rubble in a single day in the 1930s, during Stalin's orgy of secularism. For the next fifty years it was the world's largest swimming pool.

How long had I been searching for news of my father? For more than a decade the General had been helping me. Or so he had said. The news that the General had been concealing information from me, if not outright lying to me, came as little surprise. Who tells the dog they're taking him to be neutered? Just snap on the leash and go.

"What happened in '67?"

"He was recruited," the General said. "I don't have a document saying so, but I can tell. Someone spotted talent and plucked him away."

"KGB or GRU?" I said.

"Not KGB."

I didn't ask how he knew that. The General's ties to Soviet and Russian intelligence had long been a mystery to me. I had always assumed, however, that he had been attached in one way or another to the KGB's First Chief Directorate, and his certitude that my father had not been recruited by the KGB seemed to confirm it. The possibility that my father might have been enlisted by the GRU—the Soviet military intelligence agency—tied in with what Rykov had told me about Walker. I also saw it as a hopeful sign that my father's defection had a higher purpose.

The crowd at the entrance parted as we approached, herded aside by members of the General's security detail. The General rarely ventures outside his subterranean headquarters. Buried in the river rock beneath the towers, cathedrals, and palaces of the Kremlin, accessible only via secret tunnels and protected by layers of security, his chambers are the locus of his power. A sanctuary for a man hated by the enemies of Russia for his former command of the Fifty-eighth Army and a stone fortress against his rivals in the Kremlin, resentful of the power he has amassed over the years. The General stands just over one and a half meters tall, and yet he has achieved mythic proportions as the *vozhd*, the iron-fisted leader, of his multi-tentacled organization.

Inside the cathedral three of the General's uniformed bodyguards opened a path before us, while several more, both in and out of uniform, patrolled the crowd. Only a handful of people noticed us, and without fail their eyes turned to me. Lean, latent ferocity, something wild in my eyes—those were the things that drew their attention, I knew. As most people tend to do, they missed the real danger in the form of the General tottering by my side, the top of his head barely reaching my breastbone, shapeless in the lumpy business suit he had substituted that day for his uniform with all its medals and service ribbons.

"Once I had the file I sent it to a former KGB illegal officer," he said. "She was stationed in the Los Angeles *rezidentura* during the seventies and eighties. Now she calls herself Isadora. A pretty name, don't you think?" He said the name again, under his breath, so quietly I almost missed it. "*Isadora.*"

We entered the gallery surrounding the lower church, and he led the way to the museum. Icons. Paintings. Vestments. Photos and drawings of the cathedral, most of them gaudy salutes to the two-year rebuilding process and its champion, Moscow's self-aggrandizing mayor.

"Trash," he said, waving his hand to take in the entire building. "Erected too quickly at a price too high. Remember when this was a swimming pool?"

I told him yes, I did.

"I used to come here when I was a child. It was a place of many happy memories. Once I saw Stalin. I nearly peed myself I was so excited. Then my mother told me it was not him, only a look-alike—a double. The same build and mustache, those black Georgian eyes. For years I refused to believe her. I saw what I wanted to see."

He moved off again, this time heading toward the rear of the cathedral. By the time we arrived, his men had already cleared the area. Several of them stood in a rough semicircle with their backs to us. Over the shoulder of one I thought I saw a darting shape, a tall, familiar form that bisected the colored light from the stained-glass window for a moment, then vanished.

"What do you think?" the General said. "Was it Stalin?"

"No."

"Of course not. Later I understood how the mind distorts reality. How a certain kind of person can change shapes and identities as easily as the rest of us change socks. But most people never lose the childish belief that their physical senses don't lie."

The General clasped his hands behind his back and swung his gaze in a slow circle, panning the gilded dome, the balconies, and all the statuary. He looked unnatural out of uniform, like a man in disguise himself, but his features were steady and familiar. Granite visage, ridged forehead cantilevered over icy green eyes, flesh thick as armor plates. I tried to picture the General's reptilian lineaments as they would have looked when he was a child splashing in the swimming pool, but my imagination wasn't up to the task.

"It seems Rykov watched Walker from the moment he arrived in Moscow," he said. "Three days the man spent roving the city, always asking questions. Most of his questions were about you."

What was I supposed to say to that? I was through denying I knew Walker. "Rykov implied that Walker was a GRU agent. Is that why he had him under surveillance?"

"Good question." The General pulled at the lobe of his right ear, grimaced. "Here's the problem, Volk. Walker was keyed in on you, or your father, which amounts to the same thing. Somehow he'd figured out your public persona and knew where to look, meaning he had help from someone."

I thought of the familiar form I'd seen among the milling crowd on the other side of the room a few minutes earlier. Tall and angular, just like NSA agent Brock Matthews. "The Americans?"

The General shrugged. "Walker went by Vadim's Café several times to ask about you. Lurked outside your warehouse. That's where Rykov's men lost him. They say he was out of their sight for less than an hour. They're probably lying to protect themselves, so let's suppose they lost track of him for as long as two or three hours. The fact is that somebody *else* was watching him at the same time, and *they* seized the opportunity. After Rykov found Walker's body, he searched his hotel room. That's when they found the photo of your father. But they missed the most important clue. They didn't think about old technology. You didn't miss it."

He tugged his earlobe again. Gestured to one of his men, a chubby lieutenant named Golko, who I'd worked with during the aftermath of the bombing of the American oil company's headquarters by Lachek and his men. Golko scurried over and handed the General a folded document, then backed away, avoiding my gaze.

The General snapped the paper open and held it between us. "Your hunch about the mikrat was right. This document was reduced using a sophisticated camera and positive film. Right out of the old KGB handbook. Somebody affixed it to his driver's license, where it was nearly invisible under the lamination."

That was what I'd told the General. Walker's driver's license was the one thing he had carried that didn't make sense. The mikrat was probably placed there before he had the phony passport and visa, and Walker must have decided to bring the license with him rather than risk damaging it by moving it from one place to the other. I rubbed the bone between my eyes, peering between my fingers toward the gift shop to see if I could spot Matthews again. Nothing looked to be out of place.

"Where did you get the license?" I said.

"The evidence room at Tverskaya station. As far as the outside world is concerned, Walker's murder is being investigated as a routine police matter. Simple enough for one of my people to stop by and take what we needed."

I took a moment to digest that. Decided that a trip to the Tverskaya station might be worthwhile, both to find out whether the evidence collected there might offer a different angle on the case and to settle a score with Bullethead, the big cop who was so free with his truncheon.

The General studied the document in his hands. My gaze followed his.

"What does it say about my father?"

"Walker could have learned how to make the mikrat easily enough," he said, musing out loud. "The techniques are well known."

"What does it say about my father?" I repeated.

He raised his eyes to mine, obviously curious to see my reaction. "Not a damn thing."

chapter 14

The General's words seemed to echo around me. *Not a damn thing.*

I looked around the cathedral, trying to hide my disappointment. Scattered among the tourists were the usual contingent of babushkas wearing their colored scarves, there to worship, to use the church for its intended purpose. Old beliefs die hard.

Then I shook my head free of delusions, angry at my own weakness. What had I expected to find? Was I so needy that I would harbor silly hopes about a man I had never known?

The General was frowning. "The question is why anybody would have bothered with all that spycraft. There's nothing secret about this document. Not anymore. It can be found in any number of places, including the Web site of the American National Security Agency."

"They have a Web site?"

"Yes. Hard people to understand sometimes, the Americans."

He cocked his oversized head to one side, appraising me.

"Have you heard of an American project called Venona?"

"No."

"A secret program developed during World War II. Code-breakers gathered to decrypt diplomatic and intelligence cables sent by the Soviets, many of them from New York and Washington, to Moscow. Look it up if you want to know more." He brushed lint off the front of his jacket, dismissing that part of the story.

"The point is this," he said. "The document Walker went to such pains to conceal was a decrypted cable. Sent during the Stalin years from the head of the KGB's illegal station in New York to Fitin, the head of KGB foreign intelligence. The goddamn thing dates all the way back to 1943. What the hell could have happened in '43 that would be important now?"

He thrust the papers into my hand. Two pages, stapled together, already wrinkled and dog-eared from handling.

"Read it. See if it jogs anything loose. Then go talk to Isadora."

I memorized the address he gave me for Isadora's dacha, a few hours' drive northeast from Moscow. "What can she tell me?"

The General blasted air between his lips like a warhorse. Started to say something, then gestured for me to follow him back into the rotunda. Once there he returned his gaze to the cupola for a minute or so while his men repositioned themselves. One of them whispered something into his ear, probably saying that his car was ready.

"Isadora is an odd one," he said. "She held the post of deputy *rezident* in Los Angeles for a long time, but . . . well, you know how it works. She came under scrutiny, something more than the usual First Directorate paranoia. I saved her, so she owes me."

"Saved her from what?"

"In a word? Russia. Accusations of treason. Rumors circulated that she had adopted the lifestyle in Los Angeles, that her contacts were working *her* to spread disinformation instead of the other way around. It didn't help her cause that several of her reports contained faulty intelligence. Not just off on the details. Wide of the mark by a long shot, in ways that meant covers were blown and people died. First Directorate ordered her hauled back to Moscow in the hold of a freighter. They put her in a Lubyanka cage for more than a year and asked a lot of questions. I vouched for her."

"Why?"

The General gazed up into the cupola as though answers to

imponderable questions were written there. He held the pose for a long time before he rocked back on his heels so that his gaze met mine cleanly.

"Do you know how many Red Army officers Stalin purged? Three of five marshals, fourteen of sixteen senior army commanders, and thousands more. Shot in the cellar of the Lubyanka, the execution yard on Dzerzhinsky Street, or the basement of Lefortovo prison. Poisoned in the *Kamera*, the death chamber—they say the drug paralyzed you first, then took twenty minutes to tear you up from the inside. The questions didn't stop when Stalin died. They never stopped. Khrushchev, Brezhnev, Andropov, Chernenko—they ruled *in* fear, and so they ruled *by* fear. The secret police were always there, Chekists by one name or another.

"One day I was put in a cell. 'Your father was a bourgeois landowner, wasn't he? A trader? A provocateur? An enemy of the State. You are the son of a *kulak*. You plot against the Motherland.' Over and over, the same questions, and many others. My case wasn't unusual. We were all suspect."

The memory of that time weighed on him still, evidenced by his lowered head and hushed tone. A side of the General I'd never seen before.

"Isadora was the case officer assigned to investigate me," he said in his quiet voice. "She was young then, passionate and idealistic."

"But there was nothing to find," I said, trying to keep the question out of my voice.

He gave me a scornful look and swept a hand across the front of his thickset form. "Look at me and look at where I am. With what I've had to do to come this far, do you really believe they needed to *find* something?"

I didn't respond.

"I've given Isadora the parts of your father's air force file that we could uncover. She agreed to look it over as a favor to me and because of her prior relationship with Stepan."

"She knew my father?"

"I'll let her tell you about that. I've already been briefed, but you need to see the file and hear what Isadora has to say for yourself. Read, listen, observe—but not as a child. Remember that things are not always as they seem, and bear in mind that on some days Isadora loses touch with the difference between what is real and what is not. Hers is a distorted world, but it's one you are going to have to make sense of if you're going to find out about your father."

The General never did anything without profit. One way or another every breath he took was all about power. I still liked to believe that he wielded his power for the benefit of Russia and her people, but whether that was true or not, he certainly wouldn't use it just to help me satisfy my curiosity.

"Where's the payoff?"

He drew back his thick lips in the shape of a smile to show that the question pleased him. "Rykov's boss is a man named Captain Oleg Bassoff. Don't be fooled by the rank. He's a captain because that's what he chooses to be. He was a protégé of Petr Ivashutin, the GRU foreign intelligence director who lasted almost twenty-five years in the post. Bassoff picked up his spy networks in Europe and America ten years ago and he's been running them ever since."

I nodded to say I understood. Bassoff would be one of the few men in Russia able to operate in the same league as the General, assuming Bassoff had a desire for personal wealth and power on par with his. And now the General smelled opportunity. He wanted leverage, something to use against Bassoff or somebody else.

Still wearing his satisfied expression, he gestured for me to walk with him and we moved toward the exit with his security detail all around us.

"Let's assume that Walker was one of the agents in Bassoff's stable, one who strayed off course. Why? And what does that mean for Bassoff and his network?"

We passed through the door into the sunlight. He paused there and looked at me.

"You see how the answers to those questions might be useful?"

chapter 15

After the General and his entourage departed I glanced down at the document in my hand. Two pages, folded in half lengthwise. Held together with a staple meant to secure a thicker packet, prongs looped back through the front of the page and sticking up like thorns. The top of the back page was beginning to curl where it overlapped the front page by a few millimeters.

I found a concrete bench near the gift shop. Sat and absently pressed the ball of my thumb into the staple until I'd punctured the skin and drawn two globes of blood, then sucked them away. Nobody paid any attention to me. I leaned back against the cold marble wall behind the bench. Squeezed my thumb and index finger together, drawing more blood. Licked it away and then unfolded the document Walker had brought to Moscow at the price of his life.

VENONA.

Beneath that, the words TOP SECRET had been crossed out. Breaks between the paragraphs showed where certain word or phrase groups were "unrecovered." Seven footnotes identified those present or referred to in the cable. According to the second footnote, the unidentified Soviet spy who was the source of the information went by the cover designation "19."

The cable described a meeting among Roosevelt, Churchill, and other Allied war leaders discussing whether to open a second front against Germany in 1943, one of the most important questions of the war at that time. I read the cable start to finish several times, trying to remember my history lessons to put the words into context. The Battle of Stalingrad was over, Germany's Sixth Army trapped and destroyed. The Siege of Leningrad was broken. The tide had turned and Stalin was already planning his push west, plotting how to remake postwar Europe. Six months after the meeting referred to in the cable, Stalin met with Roosevelt and Churchill in Tehran. In return for their promise to open a second front and make a cross-channel invasion into occupied France, Stalin committed to enter the war against Japan after Germany surrendered, a promise that later had little value because the Americans bombed Japan into submission with Little Boy and Fat Man.

I set the cable aside, then picked it up again. Decided that it was a remarkable document for many reasons, one of them being that it illustrated how deeply Stalin's officers and their agents had penetrated the American and British governments at the highest levels. Stalin would have leveraged information like this at every step during the war years and after, from Tehran to Yalta to Potsdam. How different the world might have looked if he hadn't known so much about his negotiating partners.

But what did a cable dated 29 May 1943 have to do with Walker or my father?

I lifted my head and swept my gaze around the nave. Nobody seemed to be interested in me. The pinprick holes in my thumb had stopped bleeding. They looked like tiny red eyes staring at me. My father would have been a toddler when this cable was sent. It didn't—couldn't—have anything to do with him.

A wrinkled babushka plumped down next to me on the bench, rummaged through her canvas bag, and methodically extracted a paper napkin, a tomato, an avocado, two pieces of black bread, and a plastic knife. She wordlessly offered me a chunk of her bread and a slice of tomato. I told her no thank you, and she ate her meal delicately, staring straight ahead, someone who had learned long ago that only trouble can come from prying.

I turned the pages of the cable in my hand, studying the manner in which it had been formatted. Remembered learning in a training course at Balashikha-2 that the KGB had a rule designed to limit the damage if a cable was intercepted: "One cable, one topic." This one fit the pattern.

I recognized the name of KGB officer Iskhak Abdulovich Akhmerov, the man who prepared and sent the cable. The head of the KGB's illegal station in the U.S. during the war years, later deputy chief of the KGB's illegal intelligence section in Moscow. Two-time recipient of the Order of the Red Banner, along with many other commendations. A Russian hero, not unlike thousands of other Russian heroes stationed abroad, among the waves of deep-cover officers sent over the decades to infiltrate the "main enemy"—the United States.

How many thousands of cables like this one were sent during those years? How many are still being sent? A long-ago conversation with NSA agent Brock Matthews came to mind. We were sharing drinks at a blues bar in Washington at the end of a joint intelligence meeting sponsored by the Americans. The year was 2003. The bar was jammed. Sweaty, smoky, loud.

"You fucking guys never give up," Matthews said, making wet circles on the table with his glass. He drank in gulps, cheeks sucked in.

The lead singer of the band onstage looked like a sad Buddha. His deep, mellifluous voice crept into my head and lodged there, impossible to displace.

"What is that supposed to mean?" I said.

"Russian intelligence operates more *rezidenturas* in this country today than they did before Yeltsin climbed onto the goddamn tank outside parliament and told the KGB its job was to defend the country, not attack its leaders. More *rezidenturas*, and more officers and agents, too. One CIA old-timer told me he feared for his job in '91. 'Where will all the spies go?' he wondered. What a joke."

Matthews downed the last of his drink and signaled the cocktail waitress for another, eyeing her legs as she swished away.

"You fucking guys never give up," he repeated.

The babushka sitting next to me carefully repacked her bag, thanked me needlessly for letting her share the bench, and left. I stared at the pages in my hands until the individual letters seemed to smear together. I imagined Iskhak Akhmerov drafting it, sending it within hours of the meeting between the two most powerful men in the world. He must have known the value of the information it contained. Maybe not the specifics of how Stalin could use the information in his ongoing negotiations with Roosevelt and Churchill about supplies, troop movements, and diplomatic intrigues designed to change the fate of nations. But he at least would have known the importance of such real-time knowledge. Did he allow himself a moment of reflection? Of pride for a job well done to have recruited an agent with the access of source 19? Or did he live his life in fear, terrified of what the next knock on his door might bring or worried that his enemies in Moscow might be hatching a plot against him?

I shifted my weight. The chill of the concrete wicked through the wool of my pant legs. The cathedral was even more thronged than before, but I looked without really seeing the shifting crowd.

The cable was an interesting bit of history. A record of a moment in time that could have been lost in some dusty Soviet archive, now a part of Cold War history. But so what? Why did Walker think it was important enough to conceal in a microdot?

chapter 16

Reading the Venona cable again in the loft later that day, and researching what we could find on the Internet, Valya and I still couldn't figure out why it had been so important to Walker. Or why it might be important to Rykov and his boss, Bassoff.

Venona was an arbitrary code word applied to the cryptanalysis of telegraphic cables sent by Soviet spies to their Moscow handlers during the years 1940 through 1948. In total, nearly three thousand cables were decrypted and the information they contained exploited, but never used openly. The Americans jealously guarded their success.

The Venona project ended in 1980. But it wasn't declassified by the U.S. government until 1995—and then only after references to the program were found in the Moscow archives of the Communist International and the American Communist Party, opened after the Soviet empire collapsed.

This cable obviously dealt with a serious issue—whether and when to open a second front against Germany. It also proved that the meeting between Roosevelt and Churchill—called the Trident Conference, according to Valya's research—harbored a high-level spy code-named

"19." The presence of a Stalinist informer at a wartime meeting between Churchill and Roosevelt was momentous, not only then but at any time during the Cold War. Historians still wonder how it happened and who 19 was, but to them the question would be an academic exercise. Not to me. I needed to find the key to what the events of 1943 had to do with a dead American in a warehouse on the banks of the Moscow River.

The identity of source 19 seemed a logical place to start.

I pointed to the second page of the cable, footnote [ii], which stated that 19 was an "Unidentified cover designation." Next to the note an analyst had written, "Beneš Czech delegation?"

"What about that?"

Valya Googled the name and read out loud that in 1943 Eduard Beneš was the president of the Czech government in exile, living in London. Before that he was one of the men who had planned the Prague assassination of Reinhard Heydrich, head of counterintelligence for the SS and a key architect of Hitler's final solution. "They killed Heydrich," she said somberly. "But the Germans razed the villages of Lidice and Ležáky in retaliation."

She clicked through several more screens, brow furrowed.

"Beneš and a delegation attended the conference with Churchill."

"So Beneš was 19?"

"I haven't found anything to suggest that, except for this note." She tapped the photocopied pages the General had given me.

Footnote [vi] identified Zamestitel, deputy, as "possibly" being Henry Agard Wallace, Roosevelt's vice president, although apparently Wallace was later given the cover name "Lotsman," suggesting that he was not Zamestitel. An analyst with different handwriting than the one who made the note about Beneš wrote that Zamestitel was "More likely to be Harry Hopkins??" I didn't recognize the name.

"Hopkins was Roosevelt's diplomatic advisor during the war," Valya said after another Google search. "An 'unofficial emissary' to Churchill and Stalin." She navigated through several more screens. "In other Venona cables Hopkins's name appears 'in the clear,' meaning he probably hadn't been assigned a cover name, Zamestitel or any other. Some researchers believe *he* was 19."

Valya made a copy of the cable and gave the original back to me.

Feeling frustrated, I folded the pages and put them into the front pocket of my jacket.

Valya continued to peck at the keyboard, occasionally calling out tidbits she found interesting. During the Cold War many of the American and British spies identified in the cables couldn't be prosecuted, or, in cases like the Rosenbergs and others, the Venona evidence against them couldn't be used in court for fear of compromising the breakthrough. Some historians speculated that leaks from the Manhattan Project, which the Soviets had code-named "Enormoz," advanced the Soviet bomb program by ten years and—among other things—emboldened Stalin to allow North Korea to invade the south.

"Did you know any of this?" she said.

"Bits and pieces. Not so much from the American point of view."

"Me either. Every one of the decrypted cables is on the NSA's Web site. At least all of the ones they've released, nearly three thousand of them. They show hundreds of Americans working against their own government."

"Pull it up."

"What?"

I tapped the pages folded in my pocket. "This cable, 29 May 1943. Pull up the NSA's copy."

She stared at me for a moment, then her eyes widened, and she turned back to the computer and started clicking. The screen changed color from white to blue as the NSA/Venona Web site popped up. She clicked the link to "Document Images—Dated," and on the next screen entered May 1943. Another page appeared. She scrolled down to May 29, and there it was: "'19' reports on Roosevelt/Churchill meetings." One more click, and the first page of the decrypted cable filled the screen.

It was identical to the one in my hand.

Valya's gaze met mine. "The next page is the one that matters," she said, and I nodded tensely.

She hit the Back button, then clicked on the link to the second page. We both stared. In every way except for one this page of the NSA document was identical to ours. It even had the analyst's handwritten note speculating about whether Zamestitel might be Harry Hopkins.

But it did not have the note about Beneš and the Czech delegation.

Somebody other than an NSA analyst had drawn a connection between 19 and the Czechs and written it on Walker's copy of the cable.

Valya let out a low whistle. "So for that the man goes to so much trouble to hide this document and gets shot? It must be important, but why?"

It was nearly 3 P.M. I needed to go talk to Isadora, the former KGB officer who had been given my father's file by the General. If I drove fast I could be at her dacha in two hours. I grabbed a set of keys.

Valya watched me, saying nothing, but her question hung in the air between us. *Why?*

"I don't know why they do, but I'm sure the GRU cares about that document," I said.

Then I thought about Matthews lurking about in the cathedral while I was with the General, and I thought again about him in the D.C. bar, drawing wet circles on the table with his sweaty drink, and I decided that what I should have said to him then was that his people never gave up, either.

"And the Americans. The Americans still care, too."

PART III

The wilderness of mirrors is that myriad of stratagems, deceptions, artifices and all other devices of disinformation which the Soviet bloc and its coordinated intelligence services use to confuse and split the West . . . an ever-fluid landscape where fact and illusion merge.

—James Jesus Angleton,
former chief of CIA
counterespionage

chapter 17

"You studied at Moscow Military and Balashikha-two?"

Former KGB officer Isadora talked with a tremor. Her quavering voice gave the impression of weakness. So did the sluggish way that she had admitted me to her dacha. A long look through a peephole in the unpainted wooden door, the wearied rattle and scrape of chains and bolts before she opened the door, and her measured steps to a dinette adjacent to a small kitchen overlooking the leafy trestles of her garden. Summer colors abounded among the flowers and leaves there, attesting to the attention she lavished on it. The dacha itself was a single-story wooden cottage still unfinished inside, tucked away in a wooded vale about a hundred kilometers northeast of Moscow; a compact Toyota was parked under an attached awning.

I didn't bother to answer her question about my training. Whatever the General had told her about me was all she needed to know as far as I was concerned.

The late afternoon sun shone brightly through the big windows, warming the room, but she wore a cable-knit sweater with the sleeves pushed up to reveal naturally dark-skinned forearms, and a skirt that brushed the floor when she walked. Black hair streaked with gray, loosely held back by a tortoiseshell clip. Dark eyes tilted up like the wings of a bird, obscured but not hidden entirely by reading glasses perched on her nose.

Age is a slow-developing mask, I mused. The person we used to be disappears behind sagging skin and graying hair, then becomes lost in a wasteland of failed mental connections and fading recollections. Isadora appeared to have embraced the physical changes, perhaps even accentuated them with her choice of clothes, her downcast eyes, and her tremulous voice. Even so, there among nature's vicissitudes— and the persona she had chosen to adopt—still lingered a trace of the beauty that once was.

After offering me a seat at a metal dinette she walked around the built-in breakfast bar to the kitchen. Her hands shook as she struggled to open a plastic bottle of *kvas*, a fermented drink made from rye, waving away my offer of help. Some of the brown liquid spilled onto the countertop when the cap finally surrendered. She wiped away the mess, then set two glasses on the table and gurgled a bit of the brew into each glass. Went back into the kitchen, retrieved a wire basket of hard-boiled eggs and two paper plates and napkins, and put them in the center of the table next to a salt shaker.

Once the task was done she settled into the chair across from me, folded her arms beneath her breasts, and continued talking, citing details of my career, looking everywhere except into my eyes. She had focused on her work as she prepared our small meal, her head pitched down. Now she seemed to be contemplating the basket in the center of the table while she talked. She plucked an egg from the pile, turning it in her hands.

"So you *think* you know everything," she concluded.

"I know nothing. Whatever you have to say, tell it to me like I'm nine years old."

She nodded thoughtfully. Tapped the egg on the edge of the table and started peeling. She tried neatly stacking bits of shell into a pile on her napkin, but some fell onto the table and the floor. She pretended not to notice.

"The KGB operated the most effective foreign intelligence organization in history. When I say KGB I include its many predecessors and successors, you understand? The Cheka, the NKVD, the KGB, and now the FSB and SVR. From before the revolution to today—it is a long history. You might say we are a nation of secret police, with conspiracy bred into our DNA."

Her gaze caught mine briefly, then darted away.

"The first directive of the Cheka was to exterminate counterrevolution and sabotage. Right off they started their show trials, and they butchered anyone suspected of being counterrevolutionary. Rounded up thousands and put them to work as forced laborers. You see, the Bolsheviks never stopped their intrigue even after they killed the Tsar and gained power. They *defined* themselves by it. They wrapped their government in the poetry of the proletariat, embracing the people to achieve their aims, but theirs was a revolution of beautiful rhetoric, brutal policies."

She salted her egg. White crystals bounced and scattered across the tabletop.

"They used the Communist Party apparatus to bind the people, not empower them. Party loyalty was paramount, the linchpin of their control. You know that, you lived it as a child in the orphanages.

"After the revolution, Communist fervor spread around the world. These people were motivated by *ideology*, not fear or money or power. They believed in the moral superiority of communism. They were the perfect foil for the spawn of the Cheka."

Isadora ate her egg like a rabbit, nipping the white with her lips and tongue, and then nibbling delicately at the exposed yolk. She pointed to the basket. "Are you going to eat?"

I picked one, still warm from boiling. Peeled it fast and popped it into my mouth whole. Through the window over her shoulder I watched a flock of birds pirouette in the sky, unfurling like a black flag in the orange light of the early evening sun to land as one in a leafy oak tree. Soon more joined them until all the branches were dotted black. Isadora's voice was musical, periodically varying pitch and modulation between long bridges of the same monotonous inflection.

"The *remnants* of the KGB, what's left of it today, are poor imitators all. But still they are superior intelligence gatherers compared to the CIA, MI5, and MI6, and even the Mossad. And we were always far better at spreading *disinformation*. The nonexistent missile gap, bogus troop and armor numbers, misleading claims of technological breakthroughs—we excelled at creating false impressions. After *Sputnik* the space race was laughably one-sided, but we led the world to believe it wasn't.

"We did the same thing on the intelligence front. You know the story of the CIA during the sixties? We sent one defector after another to the West, mixing truth and lies, giving up enough actionable intelligence to attest to their veracity, but always casting suspicion on those who came before. The KGB crippled the CIA during the time it was most needed. The CIA's counterintelligence unit didn't know what to believe or who to trust, even in their inner sanctum. The most troubling revelation—was it the truth or a horrible lie?—was that the CIA had a mole at the top. Just that alone, the credible *suggestion* of such a thing, tied them in knots for decades."

"Did we?"

"CIA counterintelligence chief Angleton believed we did. He obsessed over it."

That wasn't an answer, but I let it go. She probably didn't know one way or the other. Very few people would know.

"The KGB stationed two kinds of agents in foreign countries," she said. "So-called *legal* officers were those who operated under diplomatic or official cover. They worked at Soviet embassies, consulates, or other recognized agencies or organizations, such as TASS or Intourist. Although they posed as diplomats, journalists, trade officials, or some such, the legal officers were openly Soviet officials or representatives, known to the local governments, tracked and accounted for.

"*Illegal* officers operated without diplomatic status or any other official connection with our government. They almost always used a false identity, often pretending to be from another country altogether. Because they had no visible connections to legal Soviet establishments, they were far more effective—or dangerous, depending on your point of view—than legals."

She wiped each corner of her mouth with a napkin. Drank from her cup, then set it gently aside.

"I was an illegal. Posted in London during the late sixties, then transferred from station to station for several years, an *artist on tour*, to use the old KGB parlance. In 1972 I was assigned to the *rezidentura* in Los Angeles, and three years later I became deputy *rezident*, second to the chief of the illegal station. I held that post for thirteen years. Longer than any other officer.

"Now people in America like to pretend such things no longer exist, or that they no longer matter." She paused, regarding me thoughtfully, her gaze suddenly steady. "Is that how you feel, Volk? Is that why you find the sparrows in the trees so fascinating? Forget the past, your expression says, tell me about *now*. 'Why is this man Walker dead in my warehouse? What are these silly papers he carried?' "

She licked her fingertip and used it to transfer loose grains of salt from the table to her tongue, her head cocked to one side in a silent query like one of the birds framed in the petals of the flowers in the window box over her shoulder.

"Isn't that what you want to know?"

chapter 18

I didn't respond to Isadora's question. I would let her tell it her way. Let her dance around with words for as long as she wanted, just so we got to the heart of things eventually.

After nearly a minute of silence, she gave an elaborate shrug. "Fine, let's talk about your precious cable. The man identified as the sender, Iskhak Akhmerov, was the KGB's chief illegal officer in the United States during the war years, and one of the most productive we ever had. He had networks everywhere, funneling information to him from the highest levels of government and private industry."

I leaned forward at her mention of the cable, my gaze intensifying. As darkness approached outside, the contrast of light and shadow flattered her face, removed years, allowed me to see the younger woman beneath the wrinkles and unkempt appearance. My scrutiny seemed to make her nervous, uncertain.

"Gathering information is one thing, of course," she said quickly to cover her discomfort. "*Communicating* those findings back to Moscow is something else entirely. In the old days, diplomatic pouch and courier were too slow for time-sensitive material. The Soviets had to choose between radio and international cables, neither of which was secure.

"So they devised a multilayered system. They converted messages into four-digit numbers using a code book. Then they changed the four-digit numbers into five-digit groups by moving the first digit of each successive number to the end of the prior number. And, finally, they transformed those groups into a *second* series of five-digit numbers by adding the first group of numbers to random sets of five from a 'one-time pad' to create an entirely new set. The one-time pads eliminated the risk of finding repetition, the heart of all cryptanalytic attacks. Done correctly, each message was a unique cipher, impossible to break."

She broke off and lifted her hands in a helpless gesture.

"But, indeed, the code *was* broken. By the Americans, with some help from the British, who were always very good at such things. The wall of secrecy cracked in 1941, when Hitler invaded Mother Russia. Our diplomats, soldiers, and intelligence officers produced so many ciphered messages that our cryptographers couldn't make enough one-time pads to meet the demand. Creating pads of pages each with sixty random five-digit numbers—without the hidden patterns created by a phenomenon known as the 'psychological random'—was a complex undertaking, you see. Several thousand pages were duplicated and *reused* during the crazed days of the Wehrmacht's march toward Moscow. *That* compromised the integrity of the system. That stupid mistake created the potential for repetition.

"Imagine. Some low-level functionary makes a decision to copy some of the pads. How bad could the security breach be? he must have wondered, if he thought about it at all. How many *other* layers of protection were in place? What were the odds of someone breaking such a complex code with a few duplicates? Before sophisticated computers?"

Isadora dropped her gaze to the tabletop. "The Venona project was a *singular* counterintelligence achievement. But from our perspective it was a gross, *fundamental* failure."

She drank the last of her *kvas* and dabbed her lips with the napkin while I pulled my crinkled copy of the cable from my pocket and spread it on the table between us. She barely glanced at it.

"The General already sent it to me. I'll tell you what I told him. This particular cable means nothing to me."

I made no effort to hide my disappointment. "Read it again."

She adjusted the glasses on the end of her nose and read the first page, then held it in the air while she read the second before letting it drop when she finished. She shook her head.

"What about source 19?" I said.

"Why is that important?"

"Because that's the only unanswered question. All the people present at this meeting have been identified, except one. The one who gave the Soviets the information they wanted."

She stared at me, not agreeing or disagreeing. "Probably a GRU source," she said finally. "They liked to use numbers. But he might *also* have been a KGB source. In those days it wouldn't have been unusual for the KGB and GRU to have overlapping networks of agents. Later, during my time there, we took more care to assign one officer to an agent."

"Look again at the names and the handwritten notes."

She did it with a sigh, her expression bored. This time when she finished she pushed the papers to my side of the table. "This isn't why the General sent you to me."

I returned the cable to my pocket, still disappointed, but now I could feel my heart thudding in my chest. As much as I tried to remove my emotions, I'd been anticipating this moment from the time the General told me that Isadora had had a relationship with my father. I kept my features flat, devoid of expression.

"He said you knew my father."

"Yes, I did."

I swept a few grains of loose salt off the tabletop. "When? Before your posting in London?"

"No, I met him in 1985." She said the words casually, but I could tell she was watching for my reaction. This time she must have gotten one, because a fleeting look of satisfaction crossed her face. "In Los Angeles. According to my legend, I was a Czech writer who'd fled Prague during the Soviet 'normalization.' I even had sufficient credits to qualify as a member of the Writers Guild of America. I met your father, however, through my *real* work."

Isadora stood and walked to the far wall and fumbled among the books and papers in a cluttered bookcase. Most of the books had English titles, but the one she opened was a collection of short stories by Chekhov. She slipped a black-and-white photograph from the book and handed it to me.

"The resemblance is quite remarkable," she said. "Starting with those eyes—those terrible, amazing eyes."

chapter 19

Reese powered his chair closer to the bed in the V.A. hospital on Wilshire Boulevard and peered between the steel rails at the broken body of Colonel Allen Haynes. A decorated Vietnam veteran and four-term congressman, Haynes had retired from public service to join the ranks of defense-contractor lobbyists in 1984, just when Reese and Lorelei needed such a man. Now, after a one-car accident on Mulholland Drive, arranged by Santori to occur at the top of a steep curve on a spine of the Santa Monica Mountains, Haynes was a broken figure near death.

"Excuse me, Mr. Reese," a doctor said, an internist according to the laminated badge attached to his pocket. He was the last of several physicians to visit Haynes in the past hour.

Reese rolled away from the bed. He despised hospitals, told all who would listen never to go near one unless bone or metal broke skin. Hospitals were incubators for infection, surgeons and neurologists no more than glorified plumbers and electricians. And internists like this one were the most useless of the lot.

"You're nothing but a chin-scratcher," Reese told him. "Your kind is always thinking, never doing. If Haynes could talk through the tubes he'd tell us to put a bullet in him. Come time to die, we treat animals better than we do people."

The doctor read the chart, unfazed. "With a little luck, your friend has another twenty years in him, thanks to us chin-scratchers." He checked the glowing green screen of the heart monitor and made a note.

Reese felt the first stirrings of alarm. Haynes was a good man, one of the best. A former University of Iowa wrestler, he would "take it to the mat," as he liked to say, when he really believed in something. All of which was fine as long as his sights were aimed in the right direction. That was the problem, of course. At their last meeting Haynes had confided in him that he'd discovered a security problem related to a missile system Lorelei was contracted to build.

"Let the experts at NCIX chase phantoms, Allen," Reese had told him, referring to the Office of the National Counterintelligence Executive, the agency responsible for preventing foreign countries from obtaining U.S. military and nuclear secrets.

But Haynes simply stared out the window at the lights of L.A., visible from the top floor of the Lorelei building, and shook his head. "This isn't even a close call, sir," he said, and that was the end of that. The information Haynes had discovered didn't point directly to Reese. Very little did anymore. But it was one of those things that would start too many people sniffing down a trail Reese couldn't afford to let them follow.

The doctor tore a strip of a printout from one of the machines, scanned it, and jotted something else on the chart. "He needs rest now, Mr. Reese," he said on his way out the door. "Give it five, then leave him be. It'll be a few days before he's ready to talk to anyone."

As soon as the doctor was gone, Reese rolled forward again. Haynes appeared to be more vital now that Reese knew he wasn't dying. A tube through his skull terminated in the ventricle of his brain, according to the neurologist, placed there to monitor the intracranial pressure and drain fluid. Both legs in traction, bandages on his face and head hiding the most serious damage done by the impact. The parts of his face that Reese could see had the bluish, washed-out aspect of the severely injured.

But he no longer looked ready for the grave.

Reese was prepared. He hadn't become the man he was, he hadn't fulfilled his vision and achieved so much in his life by failing to plan. The crash should have killed Haynes—*would* have killed him if Santori had done his job properly—but sometimes one needed to give things an extra nudge. He removed a syringe loaded with fentanyl from a case hidden beneath the blanket on his lap, checked to make sure the door was still closed, and slid the needle into the injection port on one of the IV tubes.

Then he froze.

Not because he was afraid of being caught. Haynes was already doped to the gills on morphine. Toxicology would reveal only more of the same chemical cocktail that was already surfing his bloodstream. What stopped Reese for an instant was a flare of conscience. Haynes was too good a man to die this way.

But he pushed the idea out of his mind, despising himself for his temporary weakness, for revisiting a decision already made. That was the very reason Haynes had to die—because he was too good a man. No way would Haynes let go of facts he suspected would lead to a ring of industrial spies, not even if they led all the way to the commanding officer he had called "the quintessential American patriot" on the day Reese received his Congressional Medal of Honor. Reese briefly tried to recall how many more like Haynes had paid the same price over the years, then dismissed that thought as well.

JANUS was too important. His final project, one last cargo of lies meticulously wrapped in protective layers of truth. The decision to protect JANUS at all costs had been made a long time ago. It was the right one. It had to be, because if it wasn't then many more just like Haynes had died for nothing. Too many to think about without feeling sick.

Reese depressed the plunger.

chapter 20

The face staring from the picture that Isadora handed to me was so much like my own that I might as well have been looking into a mirror. A white, half-centimeter border framed my father's head and squared shoulders. The epaulettes and insignia on his dress uniform identified him as a major in the Soviet Air Force. The photo must have been folded in half for a long time, because it was deeply creased, the emulsion cracked all the way through like a gash beneath the stern line of his mouth.

His features and the outline of his head were faded, hazy, overexposed. What struck me were his eyes. Not the color, for no hint of their color remained on the photo, which was so washed out that his irises appeared translucent. The strangeness in them emanated from more than their familiarity, just as Isadora had said. Piercing and bottomless at the same time.

This photo was not taken by the Soviet Air Force. Inscribed in gold letters along the bottom was the name of a photography studio with a Leningrad address and the date, October 15, 1974. I would be born, and my mother would die, less than a month from when he posed for this picture. Staring at his face, I wanted to believe that my mother had asked him to sit for the portrait. "A remembrance," she might have said. "For a time when our son asks what his father was like as a younger man." Little could she have known that within weeks she would die giving birth and he would disappear.

Isadora cleared her throat. I startled at the sound, something I rarely do. Seeing a picture of my father for the first time—one that showed him when he was close to my age—had disoriented me. She slid a dark brown file across the table in front of me. The outside was worn, stained by water and spilled coffee, and edged with a frayed strip of green canvas. The whole thing felt thin and light in my hands.

"Stepan Volkovoy's service file," she said. "The General had it couriered to me a few hours ago. From what I can see, most of its original contents were removed a long time ago. Read it, then I'll tell you what I know and what I think."

Every document in the file was stamped "Top Secret." The first group of papers told the story of his life before joining the military, at least from the state's point of view. By age eight he was a Son of October, by eleven a Young Pioneer. He became a member of the Komsomol, the Young Communist League, at fifteen. Entered university when he was seventeen, then full Party membership followed four years later, an extraordinarily young age. Family contacts might have helped him, but all references to his father and mother had been expunged. The file made no mention of me or my mother.

The first few pages of his military file were a log that tracked his time in the air force, beginning with the date of his enlistment in 1962. One advancement after another, most of them referencing outstanding fitness reports, four a year until the winter of 1967. He could "fly anything with wings," according to a senior officer in a memorandum attached to the last fitness evaluation, the one that marked his promotion to captain. After that, nothing until 1974, when an air marshal whose name had been redacted placed a notice that the contents of the file were "top secret" and that Stepan's military commission had been "terminated."

End of file.

Sometime in December 1967 my father ceased to exist in the eyes of the Soviet Air Force. He became a phantom. Seven years later even the phantom was gone, erased by the word *terminated*.

Affixed with glue to the inside of the back flap of the file was a smaller, passport-style photo. In that palm-sized window he appeared as a buzz-cut teenager, and the light failed to catch his eyes, so I couldn't tell if the feral intensity was already there or if it lay dormant, marking time until circumstances summoned forth his piercing gaze.

The dried glue cracked as I gently pried the photo away from the flap. A stick-on label had been affixed to the back of the photo. White turned yellow, two centimeters by three, with lines for a number, date, and name. Someone had written the number *V0362*, and beneath it the date *January 13, 1975*, and beneath that the name *O. Bassoff*.

"Good," Isadora said, startling me again. "I didn't think to look behind the photo. Neither did the people who were supposed to purge the file."

She rounded the table and peered over my shoulder.

"The letter *V* stands for Volkovoy, of course," she said, pointing. Her arm brushed mine, surprisingly firm. She smelled like flowers—the real thing, not a manufactured fragrance. "The numbers zero-three-six-two must be the date the photo was taken, March 1962, since that coincides with the date when he was inducted into the military. And O. Bassoff, if I had to guess, would have been KGB or GRU. Probably a nobody."

I slipped the photo into my pocket without mentioning that the General had already briefed me about Bassoff. Bassoff might have been a low-level GRU operative in 1975 when he placed this label on the back of the picture, during the investigation of my father's disappearance—or, most likely, my father's defection—but he wasn't anymore.

"So tell me what you think," I said.

Isadora eased back into the chair opposite me and steepled her slender fingers. "Your father joined the air force during the height of the Cold War. Spies all around us, or so everyone thought. Here, there, everywhere, even overhead, the American U-2 we shot down being the most famous example of that."

She poured more *kvas* and took a sip.

"Surveillance from above was the new religion. Russia was first with *Sputnik*, followed by even more sophisticated satellites, while the Americans raced to catch up, so fearful of the 'missile gap' and the 'technology gap,' the products of Soviet deception and misinformation. But soon the tide turned. Our scientists worked round the clock simply trying to keep pace. Meanwhile our intelligence operatives tried to steal what the scientists couldn't create."

I glanced at the picture in my hand, wondering, was he a traitor as Lachek said, or was he a patriot?

"What we stole supplemented their work, occasionally allowed them to push ahead. During one of those rare times when we had an advantage, your father disappeared in a spy plane, and he took our newest technology with him."

"He was flying a prototype?"

"No, the plane itself wasn't important. By American standards the Bear E was antiquated, even in 1974, and both countries had satellites by then. We were gathering aerial intelligence and testing radar installations all the time. *Videmus omnia*: We see all. But we didn't, not really, and neither did the Americans. The problem was the *quality* of our intelligence. For both countries, but especially the Americans, detailed photos couldn't be taken, because—"

She broke off and raised an eyebrow, slowly smoothing her paper napkin flat on the table with her fingertips.

"Can you guess, my new friend? A little test for the son of our famous pilot. After we both had all those orbiters, what could have stopped us from obtaining all the pictures we wanted? Something so common we usually don't even notice it. Something that would have presented even more problems for the Americans than it did for us?"

I imagined a spy plane kissing the dome of blue sky, the curve of the earth in the distance, the horizon softly drawn by an eggshell band of whiteness.

"Clouds."

She slapped her hand on the tabletop. "Ah, yes, the *clouds*! The Americans caught glimpses of our planes and defenses and ballistic missiles, but those insufferable cloudy Russian skies prevented them from seeing more. Sometimes months would pass like that, and by the time the clouds were gone so were the missiles and whatever else they wanted to see. Let's try another question. Tell me, what was the answer to that damnable cloud problem?"

I shook my head, no idea.

"Imaging radar. Radio waves that pierced the overcast and the darkness. And for once we had this technology first. But somehow the Americans managed to put a synthetic aperture radar into orbit in June 1978. Where do you suppose they got the prototype?"

For the first time Isadora's gaze met mine and held.

"The *camera* on Stepan's plane was what the Americans wanted," she said. "His was one of the first test flights with the new equipment, you see. *That* was what he gave them when he broke off his flight plan and flew north above the Arctic Circle."

The balance tipped. Like a butcher with his thumb on the plate of the scale, I had been considering all the evidence in the way most favorable to my father. But now things looked bleak. The word sliced through my mind like a shard of glass.

Traitor.

chapter 21

Isadora led the way along a narrow path between the trees. Our feet sank into moist earth covered with leaves and twigs. The sparrows stood watch above us, silent sentinels framed by the moonlight. Isadora talked in her singsong voice as she led the way with small, carefully placed steps.

"The early years of the Reagan administration were heady times for defense contractors in the United States. Nervous times in Moscow. As pressure mounted for information, I became even more demanding of my agents, especially those who were well placed in defense industries.

"I paid out thousands of dollars a week, but it was never enough. The days of ideological agents were over. No one believed in the Communist dream anymore. Cynicism ruled the day. Most of the information I got came from *chuzhoi*." She grimaced when she used the KGB term for foreign agents who spy against their own country for money.

"I had assets among all the big contractors. Lockheed Martin Marietta, Boeing, Northrop Grumman—name any one of them, and I had an agent in place there. My information was accurate, but the *quantity* was lacking, according to Moscow. They sent reams of questions, most of them so technical I could hardly describe them to my agents. 'Give us an avalanche,' my controller told me. 'Drown us in data.'"

We paused on the edge of a meadow blanketed with flowers like a pale carpet. A fallen log, chopped and planed, made a crude bench. Isadora sat and stretched her legs in front of her.

"I was on the verge of being replaced. That's not unusual. My posting had already lasted far beyond the norm, and the longer I stayed the greater the risk that I would be turned. Then one of my agents approached me with an opportunity to recruit three employees from one of the bigger firms, all of them strategically placed. You remember the lessons of *konspiratoria*, basic tradecraft? Never trust anybody. It is the first law of agent recruiting."

She absently spun a serrated oak leaf by its stem between her thumb and forefinger.

"So there I was, overwhelmed with a string of potential recruits. KGB paranoia required baby steps. At least half a dozen meetings and a Form 21-A completed with all the personal data we could find. If everything checked out we began the first stage of operational development, probing every weakness, every vulnerability. Drugs, alcohol, money, sex. Even something as mundane as a sick mother in Baltimore who couldn't afford the surgery she needed or a daughter in trouble with the law."

I listened with half an ear as she talked. I knew the basic tradecraft. Once the KGB bureaucracy was satisfied, an agent like Isadora would complete a dossier of recruitment, and the new agent would be given a KGB number that would stay with him for the rest of his life. Then he would be asked to steal something, anything, top secret or not, just to set the hook.

"We insisted that all the *chuzhoi* be paid for the first thing they produced," Isadora said. "Gifts and money changed the nature of the relationship once and for all. No longer a courtship, now it was a business arrangement. The source was committed, or could be forced to stay committed. But we never dropped our guard. We never forgot the first rule—never trust anyone.

"After ten years as the deputy illegal *rezident*, I had thoroughly absorbed those lessons. I tested and retested the information those prospective agents provided and found it to be authentic. In some cases, spectacular. An agent working on the latest military satellite communications technology provided designs that changed the way our antiaircraft systems operated. Another agent passed along a secret theoretical paper about the role of lightwave technology in electronic warfare systems. At one point I was the top source of industrial intelligence from anywhere in the world. I had my *avalanche*.

"And then I was hauled back to Moscow, quite literally in chains, accused of deliberately falsifying my data. Imprisoned for a year, questioned relentlessly until your General came to my defense and I was finally released. The next years passed in a haze. I lived in a dilapidated communal flat and survived off a meager pension and the sporadic generosity of former colleagues. And then the Wall crumbled, the Union shattered before our eyes, and Yeltsin and his cronies put our country up for sale. The entire KGB infrastructure fell into disuse and neglect. The best and brightest of the KGB, the party's 'sword and shield,' went into business for themselves and became rich off the sweat of the Russian people."

A light wind riffled through the leaves and branches above us. Isadora closed her eyes and lifted her face toward the blaze of stars in the night sky.

"But you don't want to hear ancient history. You have enough war stories of your own, don't you, my young friend? So many successes and failures. Do they cancel one another out?"

I thought of the dispirited plane ride back to Moscow after my last operation in Chechnya, a joint Russo-American action four months ago. NSA agent Matthews had remarked during the bumpy takeoff from Budennovsk air base that we kill people in the name of our governments because we believe in something bigger—something nobler, I think he meant. In some ways, listening to Isadora was like hearing an echo of Matthews, the same words traveling back and forth between the shadow warriors of two cultures that are not as different as they like to believe.

Isadora opened her eyes and tilted her head forward to face me, waiting for an answer. She sighed when I didn't give her one.

"I'll cut to the chase, as the Americans are so fond of saying. It turned out that your father had developed a ring of spies at one of the largest defense contractors in the world. Somehow he had tapped into the richest vein of high-grade intelligence we received during my whole time there. Beginning in 1982 he turned the ring over to me, one agent at a time. He insisted on dealing only with me. Otherwise, I would have been sent back to Moscow long before I was. He single-handedly extended my tour in Los Angeles by six years."

This should have been good news to me, but it wasn't. I didn't like the implication buried in Isadora's tone that the story had a bad ending. "How was he able to do that?"

"I'll tell you what he told me. After his defection he spent four years under arrest at various military and intelligence facilities all over the United States. The imaging equipment was everything the Americans had hoped it would be, but some in the CIA still believed he was a false defector. They locked him in a safe house without contact with the outside world.

"By 1978 the issue was moot. Nothing he could tell them was actionable anymore. The CIA established a new identity, and they obtained a job for him that was worthy of his talents. And from the moment they cut him loose, he began putting together the network he later turned over to me. At least that's what I believed."

Isadora placed her hands on her knees and took a deep breath.

"It's beautiful here, isn't it?" she said.

"My father was the reason you spent a year in the Lubyanka."

She nodded. "Stepan used me. He played me beautifully. So much good information, like the satellite and lightwave technology, but so much of it sprinkled with tiny kernels of destruction. Schematics for equipment with microscopic tolerances that we couldn't make work. Test results we couldn't duplicate even after months of trying. He hurt us badly for six years, maybe as much as any other single source."

"What motivated him?"

"Money? Ideology? A woman? Who knows?"

The glade had turned into a gloomy cavern of green and black. Deep lines etched Isadora's careworn face. Her eyes gleamed in the moonlight. She is a trained and practiced liar, I told myself, mentally sifting through her words and body language to try to sort truth from fiction.

"What happened to him?" I said.

"That part of my life died during the year I spent in a dungeon. Never-ending interrogations. Days without sleep, always under a bare bulb. Do you know what it's like to never get a respite from the light? To never rest? Some days I would be marched to a wall that was pocked with bullet holes and splattered with blood. One of the guards would pull a hood over my head. On one occasion a guard pressed a gun barrel against my skull, but usually I just heard the sound of a pistol hammer being drawn to full cock. Each time I believed the moment for my execution had finally come. Sometimes I wished it to be so."

"You never heard from him again?"

"Not directly. A few years back one of my former handlers called to say an L.A. police detective was trying to track me down using my old cover identity. The matter involved your father, I was told. The inquiry triggered the usual response that the person he was looking for was deceased. In a way, she was."

"What was the name of the detective?"

"I can call and try to find out."

I nodded. The night had turned cold. Crickets chirped.

"Who was my father's original CIA handler?"

"Stepan never said. You're a lot like him in that respect. Not much of a talker."

I peppered her with more questions, but she claimed that Stepan had no personal life to speak of.

"He had a wife for a short time, but that ended in divorce. After that, his work was his life."

"Where did he work?" I said finally.

Isadora stood and brushed a leaf off the back of her woolen skirt. "One of the big aerospace firms, you've probably heard of it. Lorelei Industries."

chapter 22

The drive back to Moscow from Isadora's dacha took almost three hours because I got caught in the tail end of the Sunday-night crush of cars returning to the city. A police roadblock on the M8 slowed traffic even more. The cops directed every fifth car to the side of the road and threatened to hand out speeding tickets unless a "fine" was paid on the spot. Usually five hundred rubles, more if the driver looked like he could afford it or if tourists were in the vehicle.

I used the stop-and-go time to mull what I had learned from Isadora, still wondering about the father I'd never known.

When I finally arrived in Moscow it was after midnight. But I figured the two cops who picked me up at Sheremetyevo airport with Rykov were the type to work the night shift, since more money could be made under cover of darkness.

I parked a couple of blocks from the Tverskaya police station and walked the rest of the way to it along quiet streets. A hunched figure carrying a briefcase hurried past. An old man jerked his Scottish terrier by the leash when it strayed too far. Two babushkas pushed a shopping cart, bent to their task like Repin's Volga barge haulers.

Most district police stations are falling apart from neglect, but not the Tverskaya station, a modern building made of smoked glass and steel located close to the tourist center. A showpiece in the shell game we play so well, one of many false fronts designed to cast Moscow in a favorable light and comfort the tourists. Built during the decade when oil money poured into Russia's coffers, although even during those years the money was sticky: most of it stayed at the top.

Inside, the station was brightly lit. Fresh paint, clean gray commercial carpeting, smooth Formica counters, cubicles bright with primary colors. The reception area thrummed with the sound of clicking keyboards, low voices, muted ring tones from cell phones and landlines. A radio crackled with electronic voices. The female officer behind the counter flaunted hair dyed a flaming orange. I told her I was looking for a man to thank him for helping me a few weeks ago. "Big man, bald, with a dented skull," I described the bullet-headed cop who had used a truncheon on me so enthusiastically.

"Zubko," she said immediately. "I'll let him know you're here."

"Tell him there's a reward." I patted my pockets. "But I left it in my car. I'll be right back."

I went outside and found a dark corner. Less than five minutes passed before Zubko emerged, looking worried that his reward might have walked off. I waited until he strayed away from the well of light in front of the building, approached him from behind, and kneaded the barrel of the Sig into his lower back.

"Payback sucks, Zubko."

He stiffened and twisted his head around, careful not to move too suddenly. "Fuck yourself, Volk. A beating's the least you deserve. Kill a man, pay the price. Or have you forgotten that?"

"What if I didn't kill him?"

"You did it."

"Make the case."

He tried to turn around, but I didn't let him, just pushed him ahead into the gap between the station and the brick wall of an electronics store.

"Go on," I said.

"The vic was looking for you all over the city for three days. His body was found in your office in your warehouse. He had a note on him with the address of the café where you like to hang out. Ballistics were consistent with a Sig Sauer Navy, your weapon of choice. You did it."

I didn't like that Walker had been killed with a Sig. It meant the frame went deeper than merely shooting him at my warehouse. Somebody had thought things through, and I didn't have a good candidate for who that might be.

"Show me the things Walker had on him when he died."

"No way."

"Then I drop you right here. Or maybe I wait a few weeks. Catch you coming home one night after a few drinks and paint your flat red. Your choice."

The artery in the side of his neck jumped. He twisted his bald head around, trying to get a clear look at me. "You're a fucking animal, you know that?"

I said nothing.

"You'll have to come inside the station."

I gave him a shove, gripped the Sig in my pocket, and followed him into the brightly lit station. He hesitated in the reception area in front of the metal detector, eyeing my hand in my pocket. I knew he was wondering if he could make an arrest stick. But he'd already arrested me once for Walker's murder, and here I was at the station. If he did it again and I walked again, well, I'd already told him what would happen.

Watching him work things out in his mind, I couldn't tell which way he would decide to go.

chapter 23

Zubko and I stayed frozen in time for several seconds. All activity in the station seemed to stop at once. Just as I decided he was going to take the chance and arrest me on the spot, a passing cop said, "Hey, some of the guys are going for food," and Zubko straightened and told him to go on ahead. He motioned for me to follow him around the metal detector.

"I think maybe you got lucky this time," he said under his breath as he led me upstairs and into the squad room.

He shared a desk with someone, probably the parakeet-faced cop who had helped him arrest me at Sheremetyevo. The desktop was cluttered with paperwork, the wreckage of his last meal, a glossy magazine opened to a page showing a falling-down-drunk starlet with her skirt hiked up to her waist, and an iPod with tinny music leaking out the earphones. He dug through the mess and found a file too thin to have been worked very hard. Slapped it onto the desk in front of his partner's chair.

"It won't do you any good."

The top page was an activity log. Zubko and his partner had been dispatched to my warehouse at 6:55 P.M. on May 17.

"Who sent you to the warehouse?"

Zubko gave me the name of his station commander, someone I'd never heard of before. "He told us to meet a man there named Rykov. That's all he gave us, just the name."

I played it out in my mind. Rykov's men had been following Walker for reasons I didn't know. These were likely the same men Valya told me about when she phoned me in Macao. When they lost Walker they frantically searched the area where he went missing. Actually, that description probably doesn't do justice to what they did. More likely they tore that corner of the world apart looking for him, because bad things happened to those careless enough to lose their quarry. They broke into the warehouse, found the body, removed anything they didn't want anyone else to see or have, then brought in the police to smear a layer of legitimacy over the whole mess.

"Who is Rykov?"

"How the fuck do I know? Some spook with a line to my boss's boss. Whatever he tells me to do, I do. Nothing confusing about that."

"What happened after you met him at the warehouse?"

"Nothing. You saw what I saw. We called in the techs. They bagged everything and brought it here. We talked to a few of the locals while Rykov worked his cell phone. The goddamn thing never left his ear. Few hours later we headed for Sheremetyevo to pick you up."

I glanced through the file, starting with Walker's autopsy photos. One of them showed him laid out on a table in the morgue. Pudgy, pasty, piebald—white skin with gray hair matted and clumped with blood on his chest and shoulders. Exit wound the size of my fist in his sternum. Another picture showed three entry wounds in his back, numbered 1, 2, and 3 on little cardboard squares. The wounds were arranged in a triangular pattern, the first one at the top of the pyramid, the next two forming the base.

Scattered throughout the file were ass-covering reports showing activity but no results. Witness interviews were clipped together in a separate section. One summarized the statement of a machinist who was working near the building across the tracks from my warehouse on the afternoon of the murder. This must be the man Rykov claimed had identified me leaving the warehouse. The summary was neatly written, so I assumed Zubko's partner had prepared it, but he surprised me.

"Yeah, I talked to that guy," he said, looking over my shoulder. "Pavel. Strange breed. I showed him your picture, and he piped right up, said he'd seen you there on the seventeenth, a few minutes past three o'clock, just before the last afternoon train."

That was true. I'd gone there to pick up a computer for Valya. The part that gave me pause was a different line in the summary. "Witness ⇒ two men entered ⇒ after the noon train (1–2 P.M.), too far to ID."

I tapped my finger on the line. "What did you do to follow up on this?"

"What was I supposed to do?"

"Did the witness describe the two men?"

"One was tall and thin, the other fat."

"You didn't think to write that down? Too busy kissing Rykov's ass and planning dinner to worry about police work?"

"If policing mattered, you'd be in jail, asshole."

Pavel the machinist lived in the building where he worked, a stone's throw from my warehouse. I decided to make him my next stop after I finished with Zubko.

"Let me see the things you bagged and brought here."

Zubko heaved himself out of his chair and plodded to an elevator. We rode it two stories below street level to an evidence room, where an eager trainee sat behind a door made of wood on the bottom and steel bars on the top. When Zubko told him what we wanted he gestured toward a room with nothing in it except four chairs and a table, then disappeared deeper into his steel cage.

Ten minutes later the trainee pushed into the room and thunked a cardboard box onto the table. I looked over Zubko's shoulder while he signed for it. His name was the only one that appeared on the sign-out sheet. It showed up twice. The first time on May 21, when he deposited the evidence, the second time on May 28, yesterday, when, presumably, he'd pulled Walker's California driver's license at the request of one of the General's surrogates.

"Really been working this one, I see."

"You're a hard man to find, Volk, but when whoever's protecting your sorry ass steps out of my way I'll have you back in the basement at Lefortovo."

The box contained the things Walker had on him when he died and the items from his room at the Hotel Zolotoy. His driver's license was gone, of course, removed by one of the General's men at my request. So was the photo of my father and whatever else Rykov might have taken. I pawed through what was left.

One change of clothes. Toiletries. Prescription pills—bottles of Ambien and Zoloft, both empty now but probably not when the police found them. Metro pass. Key ring with several keys on it. Rolaids with the foil crimped down over the remaining tablets. Alligator-skin wallet, worn in the places where credit cards used to be stored, just as I had seen in the photo Rykov showed me. Phony passport and visa. A plastic ballpoint pen with dried blood speckled over the name of a company inscribed on it. Several hundred rubles in notes of various denominations, what little remained after Zubko and his friends skimmed off a few for their time and trouble.

I palmed the pen while Zubko talked to the trainee about a soccer tournament in Finland. Then I walked away.

"Where do you think you're going, Volk?"

The elevator doors dinged open, and I stepped inside.

"Hey, wait a minute!"

Zubko rushed toward the open doors, face flushed with anger, but skidded to a stop when he saw the outline of the Sig in my pocket. The doors closed, and I started up, but I could still hear his voice.

"I was just doing my job! We're square now, asshole!"

I didn't respond. I was too busy staring at the pen in my hands. I scraped away some of the dried blood to make sure I hadn't misread the name there.

LORELEI INDUSTRIES, it said.

chapter 24

The industrial building across the tracks from my warehouse seemed an unlikely place for a residence, but I was nobody to judge. When Valya left a year ago, I spent six months living in a room barely bigger than a closet in the basement of Vadim's Café. Maybe Pavel the machinist had his own special reasons for choosing to live here.

The building had been secured for the night with electronic locks, impossible to pick with anything I had. I pried off a wrought-iron window cover screwed into the brick, broke the window with my elbow, and climbed inside. If the alarm system worked, I couldn't hear it.

Starlight filtered in through the skylights, coating everything silvery gray. Machinery crowded the first floor. Presses, drills, grinders, lathes, and whatever else draped in dusty plastic sheets. An elevator shaft rose in a central column. The numbers indicated four floors above and one below ground. The place reeked of oil and dust mixed with the metallic scent of curled metal shavings overflowing a row of bins lining the far wall. I located the stairs and took them down. The door at the bottom was propped open with a cylindrical chunk of milled metal, an engine part turned fancy doorstop.

The opening led to a narrow passageway lit by a bare bulb, crowded with pipes, loose wires hanging from gaps in the ceiling where tiles were missing, and grease-blotched boxes filled with more metal parts. Empty doorways gaped along the tunnel. Metal hinges screwed into the casings marked where the doors used to hang. The openings looked onto a series of storage rooms filled with jumbled machine parts, scavenged motors, copper wire, leaking drums.

I followed the passage to a room lit by fluorescent tubes, most of the space taken by an enormous boiler that heaved and clunked in a cacophony of sound and steam. A shorter hallway led away from the back of the boiler room. At the end of it was a steel door painted dazzling purple. The door hardware looked fit to withstand a battering ram.

I drew the Sig. Knocked. Waited.

Knocked again, louder.

"It's open," someone shouted through the door.

The friendly tone made me even more uncomfortable. Anyone who lived in a place like this valued his privacy. I figured I was as likely to walk into a trip-wired shotgun as anything else.

"I just want to talk."

"So what's with the gun?"

I looked around for a camera. Didn't see one, meaning that I wasn't dealing with anybody's fool. I holstered the Sig and raised my hands, palms out.

Within seconds the door opened with a hydraulic hiss. Sweet-smelling smoke billowed out. Behind the smoke a man covered me with a Tokarev pistol so old that it might have been carried by a Hero of the Soviet Union during the Battle of Stalingrad.

"What do you load that thing with?" I said. "Rocks?"

Pavel the machinist was short, round, and freshly scrubbed, wearing a bathrobe and a towel draped over his shoulders. Drops of water fell from his threadbare scalp to the towel as he turned the gun in his hand to study it.

"Seven-six-two millimeter," he said defensively. "I could find something newer, but I like this one. Besides, nobody ever bothers me down here."

"My name's Volk. I own the warehouse across the tracks."

"I've seen you around. Used to see you more often." He scowled. "Why did you have to break a window? Guess who's going to have to fix it?"

Without waiting for an answer he put the gun into the pocket of his bathrobe and disappeared around a corner. I followed him into a room that had been converted into a studio apartment.

The marijuana smell was more powerful here, smoke leaking from a bong on a table made of boards laid across milk crates, partially covered with a pink blanket. Next to the bong was a computer monitor that showed various views outside and inside the building, including one on the other side of the purple door. The rest of the furnishings consisted of an office chair with a keyboard on the floor in front of it—I figured he typed with the thing in his lap—two beanbag chairs, a mattress made up with a tightly stretched sheet, a microwave, a rust-stained sink, and a miniature refrigerator. Rough board shelves filled with books completed the decor.

Everything was used, jury-rigged, but clean.

He offered me a hit, and I declined, whereupon he clinked open a Zippo lighter and settled in front of his makeshift table. While he smoked I wandered over to the shelves. The books were an eclectic mix of old and new. Mostly Russian authors—Tolstoy, Dostoevsky, Paster-nak, Akhmatova, and a few newer writers like Viktor Pelevin—along with some of the popular Brits and Americans, several Spaniards, one Irishman, all of them in Cyrillic. Set on top of one row of books was a rubber-banded bundle of pamphlets that turned out to be mimeo-graphed samizdats—manuscripts denied official publication but clan-destinely circulated. I thumbed through the stack and saw dates from the 1930s and '40s.

"You told the cops you saw me leaving the warehouse in the after-noon on May seventeenth," I said when he finished smoking.

"Yeah, so?"

"Did you see me go in?"

"Nope. But a brigade could have paraded in and out and I might have missed it. Depends whether I was outside at the time."

A jacket hung on a hook behind the door. It bore the insignia of the 205th Separate Motorized Rifle Brigade. "Chechnya?"

"Yeah." His gaze slid to the boot that covered my prosthesis. "You too?"

I nodded. Neither of us said anything for a moment. I picked up a samizdat pamphlet and turned it over in my hands. Dated June 1937, a month before NKVD Order number 00447 was issued during the Great Purge, aimed at "former kulaks, criminals, and other anti-Soviet elements." The author of the pamphlet wanted freedom to speak and publish. I thought about his likely fate and swallowed the bile in my throat.

"Before me you saw two men go inside."

"Uh-huh. Big change from how it used to be. Mostly beautiful women before, flocks of them. What did you do, fire all the help?"

"Did you see the two men leave?"

"Uh-uh." He got up and opened a cupboard, rummaged until he found a plate, loaded it with crackers piled with white cheese from the fridge, and popped the whole thing into the microwave.

"Describe them."

"One was tall, built like a soccer fullback. The other one was short and fat. Can't do much better than that. I was busy fixing a coupling on one of the cars." He nudged his chin in the direction of my warehouse. "Out on the north spur. I wasn't paying much attention."

"What were they wearing?"

"Nothing that stood out. Casual clothes. Not suits and ties."

I decided I was wasting my time. Except for his sketchy description, Pavel couldn't add anything new to his statement in the police file. He worked the bong again.

"The guys that came after *that* were wearing the suits and ties," he said on the exhale. "Then a half hour later the cops swarmed the place."

The ones in suits and ties would have been Rykov's men, panicked after losing Walker. Too late to save him. The microwave chimed, and Pavel removed his impromptu meal. When he offered me some I realized just how hungry I was. I shoveled a load into my mouth, burning my fingers and tongue.

He went to the fridge and peered inside. "I got one Coke left. Split it with you."

We finished the last of the crackers and cheese and Coke in companionable silence. He ran the back of his hand across his mouth, crushed and tossed the empty can into a garbage bag, rattling the cans already there, and began washing the plate.

"You speak English, Volk?"

"Yes. Why?"

"Those guys—you know, the fullback and the fat guy who went inside the warehouse before you did? I heard them talking, but I couldn't understand what they were saying. They spoke English, too."

chapter 25

Valya was asleep in the loft when I arrived home after my visit with Pavel the machinist. The loft was dark except for a pool of light on the desk where she kept her computer. She'd taped a note to the screen telling me to watch select scenes on the four DVDs she had left on the desktop.

All four were films by Everett Walker. *Sign of the Times*, *Nightscapes*, *Age of the Tsars*, and a documentary about the rise of the U.S. military-industrial complex during the Reagan years called *Lost Innocence*. Clicking from scene to scene on Valya's list, I realized that she had tagged the scenes in each film that appeared as if a Soviet propaganda minister had directed them. Themes of American imperialism, warmongering, global meddling, alliances with dictators and quasi-fascists, and nuclear winter were all juxtaposed with vignettes describing Soviet advances in space, collective farming, and medicine, along with newsreel footage of Soviet diplomatic, technical, and charitable aid to Third World countries.

The task of reviewing the scenes took a fraction of the time I would have needed if Valya hadn't already done the research. When the job was done I removed the pen I'd stolen from the evidence locker and looked again at the name of the company printed on the plastic casing over an address in Century City, California.

Lorelei Industries.

The company where my father worked. A company mentioned no less than seven times in *Lost Innocence* alone, always unfavorably.

After a few minutes I put away the pen and e-mailed an update to the General, including the information that two English-speaking men had been at the warehouse the day Walker was shot. I described them the same way Pavel did. That done, I surfed the Web for news about Walker, found a brief mention of his death in the *Moscow Times*, but nothing in the Russian-language papers. The story in the *Moscow Times* mentioned his wife, Sasha Tovar, a woman many years his junior who was an accomplished director of documentary films. I watched several YouTube clips of one of her films, mostly disturbing images of war, and a brief interview shot in her home in Los Angeles. By the time I navigated back to my e-mail page the General had replied to my message.

Bassoff is built like a hog. From a distance one might think him short and fat.

I logged out and went into the bedroom.

Valya slept curled on her side, white hair fanned over the pillowcase, one bare leg, curved and gleaming in the moonlight, drawn up over a comforter that wrapped her like a cloud. I shed my clothes, lay down beside her, and woke her slowly. We made love for a long time, and during those hours we were back to the way we were before—before I was called on to steal a lost painting, before she lost her foot, before I returned to Chechnya.

But we couldn't stop time.

Lying in bed afterward, I felt like a spectator watching the past snatch me from the present. Valya had it right when she talked about wasted days spent chasing ghosts. Now that Lachek was dead, I was pursuing new apparitions in the form of my father and Source 19. The pursuit was both irresistible and foolish. I was drawn by my desire to know more about my vanished father, and impelled by the General to search for the reason why Walker had carried the hidden Venona cable with him to Moscow. But I was a fool because the chase was taking me away from the ghostly presence already by my side.

Later, Valya told me she had spent most of the day researching Everett Walker and going through the archived records of the Communist International, known as the Comintern, the organization that once controlled Communist parties worldwide. "Stalin used the Comintern to set up intelligence networks all over the world," she said. "He merged the party with espionage, political propaganda actions, and state-sanctioned violence. The Communist Party U.S.A. became a vetting and recruiting agency."

She paged through a leather-bound book and stopped on a page marked with a torn strip of paper.

"Do you recall the name Willi Münzenberg?" Without waiting for an answer she ran her finger down the page, reading the text and interspersing her own comments.

"German. An entrepreneur and propagandist. Stalin gave him financial backing because his work attracted writers, artists, and journalists—the kind of people Lenin called 'useful idiots.' He formed the Münzenberg Trust with Soviet money, then founded a variety of Communist-front organizations—the International Workers' Relief Fund and International Labor Defense, to name just two. Eventually the Trust included companies that published books and newspapers and produced films and plays."

I knew Münzenberg's story. He ended up swinging by his neck from a tree, probably hung there like an ornament by the NKVD after he fell out of favor with the Great Leader.

What does that have to do with Walker?

She let the book fall onto the bed near our feet, then stretched the full length of her supple body against mine, her head resting in the crook of my arm, palm flat on my chest.

"The Communist Party U.S.A. maintained more than four thousand files. Some of them indexed by year and sorted alphabetically, but most of them classified haphazardly." She wrinkled her nose. "Everett Walker's file was buried in that mess. I wouldn't have found it except for help from a friendly staffer. She allowed me to read it, but not make a copy.

"He was a film student at a California university in 1937. He traveled with a student group to Paris, where he met Münzenberg. Walker would have been just sixteen years old then, and according to the CPUSA report, his instructors had already identified him as an extraordinary talent. The report described him as 'sufficiently well-developed politically' for recruitment and was personally signed by the NKVD's deputy chief of foreign intelligence at the time."

I shrugged. "According to Rykov, Walker admitted his Communist past. He claimed he joined the Communist Party to fight fascism."

"Not an easy argument to make considering Stalin had crawled into bed with Hitler and only jumped out when German panzers rolled onto Russian soil." She dragged a short fingernail down my chest, pressing hard, etching a white line on my skin. "Anyway, Everett Walker was more than a casual participant in the KGB's games. His movies confirm it."

"To find out how much more we'll need access to the KGB's archives."

"Those will be hard to come by."

I reached for my phone. Held it in the air above us to punch in the numbers to the General's special line with my thumb. Valya shifted her body while I thumbed the keypad, angling her face toward the glow of the tiny screen. After I left a message we made love again, this time roughly, with an unspoken sense of urgency. Hungry, desperate—Valya untamed, the way I most like to think of her.

The General called just after dawn. My time in the Lefortovo hole had caught up with me. I was bone-weary, my eyes glued shut with fatigue when I picked up the phone and croaked something that resembled a greeting.

"Rykov wants a meeting. I'd told him you'd be at the metro entrance to the Lubyanka at eight o'clock. Call me when you're finished with him."

chapter 26

At seven o'clock I leaned against a pillar in the rush-hour madness of the Lubyanka metro station, across the tunnel from the window of a stall selling CDs, DVDs, books, magazines, cigarettes, and snacks. Many of the products were pornographic. I could tell from the labels that some of them had been produced by my former company at the warehouse where Walker met his fate. From my post I could see the mouths of three tunnels emptying into the area.

A beggar plied her trade in front and slightly to one side of the window, sitting cross-legged on a drugget made of worn hemp. Head bowed, gray hair hanging in long braids like iron bars. All the time I was there she never looked up. The inside of the stall had barely enough room for its proprietor and the merchandise on display, so customers were forced to stand at the window with one foot on her rug while making their purchases, but nobody seemed to mind the arrangement, least of all the beggar, since her tin cup received some of the loose change.

A dented metal door stood just to one side of the window. For the last several years—and probably even during the KGB era—it had been used by FSB officers to access the bottom floors of the Lubyanka.

A woman tinkled change into the beggar's cup. Two men bumped shoulders. One of them muttered an oath, and they both hurried on. I checked my watch: 7:35 A.M. Still early, but Rykov struck me as the early type.

Sure enough, he emerged from the central tunnel a few minutes later. He carried a briefcase in his left hand, his head bent over a mobile phone in his right. Rumpled blue suit, a net of thinning blond hair, he walked fast, a man in a hurry. I fell in beside him.

"Not here," he said without looking up. "One hour, the pharmacy across the street."

He turned toward the dented door next to the beggar, and I continued straight ahead.

I climbed the tile steps out of the metro. My left leg throbbed, still aching from the wet coldness of the Lefortovo hole. I crossed to Dzerzhinsky Street—named after the former head of the Cheka—and trudged all the way around the foreboding Lubyanka. Walls of rough gray brick, from which the cast-bronze features of Yuri Andropov stared in perpetuity from a plaque commemorating his service to the KGB. One more secret policeman who was made the leader of our nation. The building reminded me of Isadora, her trip back from America in the hold of a freighter and the year she had spent in this place afterward.

I went to the pharmacy on the other side of a parking lot and waited.

Forty-five minutes later a woman pushed open the glass door and peered around. Mouse-brown hair, pursed lips, and round, wire-framed glasses gave her a prudish appearance. She carried a tote bag slung over her shoulder, her right hand buried inside of it. She spotted me and approached warily.

"Volk?"

There was nothing mousy about her eyes. Forest green, burning with so much anger that I tensed, ready to grab her wrist if she pulled a gun out of the bag or tried to shoot right through it. I'd expected Rykov to send a surrogate, but she wasn't acting like a disinterested intermediary. This looked personal.

"Do we know each other?"

"I know all about you, *Colonel*. You think you are above the rest of us. Go anywhere, kill anyone. As if we won't find out when a Russian hero is murdered in Macao."

chapter 27

With a disapproving scowl, Rykov's surrogate motioned for me to follow her from the pharmacy. She clipped along the street outside the
Lubyanka with dainty steps, her back ramrod straight, taking an occasional peek over her shoulder to make sure I was still there as we headed
across Lubyanskaya Square.

Outside a coffee shop she pointed toward the door and then gave
me one last malignant look before scurrying away. I watched her go,
disturbed by the brief meeting. Lachek's tentacles stretched everywhere when he was alive. I didn't like the idea that they might still have
the power to seize and grasp.

I gathered myself and went into the coffee shop. Rykov sat perched
on a high stool at a counter overlooking the street. A soft-brimmed hat
hung over his eyes, leaving his long nose and his jaw as my only frame
of reference. As far as I could tell he was alone, but I assumed watchers
were stationed nearby.

"You wouldn't start shooting in a public place, would you, Volk?"

"Would you?"

He grunted.

I pulled up a stool. "Has the M.E. narrowed the time of Walker's death?"

He took off his hat and set it on the counter next to a steaming mug of coffee, an obvious signal. He looked relieved that I wanted only to talk. "Walker died between one and six on the afternoon of May 17."

That meant he might have been dead already when I went to the warehouse to find a computer for Valya. Rykov studied me while I processed this information.

"That means something to you, Volk?"

Four months ago the warehouse hummed with activity day and night, but all that changed when Alla died. Besides me, only three people had access. Valya, Vadim, and the General each had an electronic key that deactivated the security devices and unlocked the door.

"Who went in and out that day?"

"The administrator's key card had been used at 3:03 p.m."

"I'm the administrator."

"I know. That's one of the reasons I thought you were the killer."

"Who else?"

"Only one other authorized key was used. The security company assigns numbers, not names, so they couldn't identify the user. Only the administrator can do that. How much do you pay for that level of security?"

We both watched the morning traffic through the window for a few beats while he rubbed his thumb on the brim of his hat, his palm flat on the counter.

"So, are you going to help us match the number to a name?"

A bus squealed to a stop outside the window. A boy maybe all of twelve stepped off, casting a predatory gaze around him before starting down the street, limbering his fingers at his side. A pickpocket in search of a mark. Rykov poured half a packet of sugar into his coffee, stirred, then folded the wrapper to seal the unused portion and put it into his pocket. He took a sip and then set down the mug with a sour expression.

"Didn't think so," he said.

I tapped out a text message to Valya, asking her to go online with the security company and use my administrator password to check their logs. I hesitated before hitting send, then added: STARBUCKS. LUBYANKA SQUARE. WATCH MY BACK. Rykov eyed my phone, obviously wanting to ask if my text meant I was going to help him, but he didn't. He looked older today. Bags under his eyes, etched lines around his mouth, thin red veins beneath his nostrils.

"Why did you have someone take Walker's driver's license?" he said. "I missed something, didn't I?"

I nodded, still preoccupied with the question of who could have entered my warehouse.

He lit a cigarette and burned it halfway to the filter with a single greedy inhale. "You have no idea what you're dealing with here, Volk. This is an international problem involving a GRU source. You need to tell me what you learned from the driver's license. Something that means nothing to you might be significant to me."

I looked directly into his eyes and switched to English. "You lost your chance when you left me in that hole under Lefortovo prison."

"Get serious!" he said, also in English. "I squeezed you, so what? This is too important to waste time worrying about things like that. And if it makes you feel any better, I no longer think you killed him."

"Who did?" I said, switching back to Russian.

He threw up his hands in exasperation. "I can't believe we're going in circles like this."

He was right. The time had come to move past my arrest and detention. I didn't trust him, but maybe I could make use of him.

"We found a microdot," I said, watching his face for a reaction. "A reduced photocopy of an old Soviet cable, decrypted, translated into English. Dated May 1943. It discussed a meeting between Churchill and Roosevelt."

He stared at me, waiting for more. "So what? We knew they broke those cables decades ago." He sucked his cigarette to death and stabbed it out in a tin ashtray. "What makes this one important?"

I told him about the substance of the cable and its description of Source 19 as an unidentified asset, deliberately omitting the handwritten note about Beneš and the Czech delegation. Since it was the one part of the cable Walker carried that differed from the version posted on the NSA's Web site, the note must be important, but for the moment

I decided I would rather find out why for myself rather than risk that Rykov would get ahead of me. But the omission didn't appear to matter. His eyes lost focus while he worked things over in his mind, and a few seconds later he shook his head.

"That doesn't mean anything to me."

"Research it. See if you can connect it to Walker. Try to identify Source 19, for starters. We've already looked at the declassified Comintern files. They don't contain anything useful." I angled my chin southwest in the direction of the KGB's former center at Yasenovo, now the headquarters of the foreign intelligence service. "Why don't you dig through the old First Chief Directorate files, see what the KGB had to say about Iskhak Akhmerov, the officer who sent the cable. Who were his contacts, who was he running, who might he have known that had high-level access to Roosevelt or Churchill? Then dig through your own GRU files, see what they say."

"What difference does any of that make now?"

"We won't know until we look."

My phone buzzed, displaying Valya's number. I moved away from Rykov and answered with a grunt.

"I'm on my way," she said. "What's the problem?"

"Maybe nothing. Rykov's here, along with at least one other agent."

"Ten minutes." A horn blared on her end of the line, and she swore.

"What did you find out?"

"According to the security company's records," she said, "the building was entered four times on May 17. You entered at three-oh-three P.M."

"That's right."

"After that, the records say 'access granted, state security' at six-ten P.M., then 'access granted, Moscow police,' at six-forty P.M. The police deactivated the security system a few minutes later."

Six-ten would have been Rykov and his men, followed half an hour later by Zubko and the rest of the forensics team from the Tverskaya station, after Rykov called them in.

"Number four?" I said. This would be the tall footballer and the fat man who may or may not have been Bassoff.

"According to the records . . . somebody entered at one-fifteen that day."

"Somebody?"

"They say that the person who went into the warehouse at one-fifteen was me."

Valya hadn't gone inside the warehouse since Alla died. Not because she was afraid of a place where violent death had happened, although she did believe that such places absorbed something intangible from the terrible things that occurred within their walls. Her reason for avoiding the warehouse was simply that she was "done" with that part of her life—that part of our life together. That was why she had asked me to go there to pick up a computer for her that day.

Standing near the window of the coffee shop at that moment, with Rykov now talking on his own phone and watching me expectantly, I could only think of one possibility. "Someone stole your card."

She didn't say anything for several long seconds. "That's not possible. I just checked. It's in my backpack."

"Then the security company's records were falsified."

"That's what I think."

I looked at Rykov. "Who would be able to do something like that?"

"That's what worries me, too."

chapter 28

"**W**ho was that?" Rykov said when I returned to the counter next to him. He'd ended his call and returned his phone to the pocket of his jacket as soon as my call ended with Valya.

"Do you know your Shakespeare, Rykov? 'Misery acquaints a man with strange bedfellows.' From *The Tempest*."

"Does that mean you're going to cooperate with me?"

"No, it means you're going to cooperate with me. I want to know what's in those old KGB and GRU files."

He didn't answer. I picked up his hat. The price tag was still attached to the sweatband. He probably intended to return his prop and get his money back. I set it back on the counter.

"The people who killed Walker spoke English."

He narrowed his eyes. "Was that the reason for your little language test earlier? You thought maybe I pulled the trigger?"

"You would have known the two men spoke English if your pet policeman Zubko had done his job properly when he interviewed the machinist. The guy's the only witness to anything, you'd think Zubko would have kept asking questions. Did you order him to be so sloppy?"

Rykov shook his head in a way that could mean either yes or no. Fatigue weighed down the corners of his mouth. Sitting on his stool, watching the bustle on the street outside the window, he seemed like an exhausted runner with his hands on his knees in the middle of a long race.

"Lachek was an important source for me," he said. "He gave me vital information countless times. Did you know that?"

I tensed. "How could I know something like that?"

"He disappeared four months ago. Dropped off the edge of the earth. Then he turns up dead in Macao, and, big surprise, you happened to be there right at the same time."

I casually slipped my hand in my pocket and gripped the Sig. Rykov tracked the movement with his eyes.

"Relax. Lachek had it coming. That's not my point. The point is that I got a box in the mail today from a lawyer in Macao. Filled with files. Very incriminating files."

Like a photographic still burned into my mind I saw Lachek, face covered in blood, snot seeping out of his nose. *You, the General, Bassoff, all of you will pay.* I kept my face impassive, but inside I was thinking of Lachek's prehensile tentacles reaching for me. How many others would feel the same way when they learned of the existence of his files?

"What do those files have to do with me or the dead guy in my warehouse?"

"I don't know yet. I'm still going through them." He gave his thin-lipped smile, then lit another cigarette. "Lots of names over lots of years—it's not a job I can delegate."

I stood to leave. "Let me know when you find something I care about."

"You can't leave, Volk."

I didn't wait for him to say more, just stepped in close and pressed the barrel of the Sig against his lower back. "Why not?"

"Look at the countertop."

I did as he said. Saw his coffee mug, scattered crystals of sugar surrounding it like a moat. A folded napkin tossed to one side. And a small red dot that skittered over the counter and jumped to a spot in the center of my chest.

"It won't do you any good to kill me," Rykov said, just as the woman with angry eyes came through the door and stood behind me. "Besides, maybe he just wants to talk."

"Who?"

"Bassoff. Captain Oleg Bassoff."

chapter 29

Rykov and his angry partner took my Sig. Loaded me into a white BMW, cuffed my hands in front of my body, and drove toward the old Khodinka airfield, then through a maze of turns that led to the main GRU complex. The largest building was nine stories of blued glass, called the Aquarium by westerners and *Steklyashka*, piece of glass, by the officers who worked there. To me it represented raw authority, no different from the Lubyanka or Lefortovo, though newer.

Rykov and the woman flanked me on the way into the complex. Two men walked behind us. We stopped at a guard station, where I was told to surrender the knife hidden in my prosthesis even before they searched me.

"Bassoff knows everything," Rykov said in response to my raised eyebrows, watching as the guards searched me from head to toe.

"Does he know about Lachek's files?" I whispered in English, but he didn't answer. When the guards finished we entered through the side doors of the main building, passed through another guard station—another search, a metal detector, more questions—then up nine flights of concrete stairs and into a nondescript office with a window overlooking the Khodinka arena.

Rykov stopped me just inside the door. Four paces separated us from the front of a metal desk. The man seated behind the desk overflowed his chair. Not fat so much as thick and bloated, as if slabs and rounds of muscle were bulging out his skin from the inside. Captain Oleg Bassoff reminded me of a baby pig. Mean eyes scrunched by folds of healthy pink flesh. He pointed to a wooden chair with the barrel of a Yarygin Pya pistol, the standard military-issue sidearm.

"Put him there," he said, and Rykov pushed me into the chair and attached the chain between my cuffed hands to the chair arm using another set of handcuffs. Once it was done, Bassoff gestured him out of the room and he left, closing the door quietly behind him, leaving the two of us alone.

Bassoff set his pistol on top of the desk and regarded me in silence for a moment, sucking a mint so hard it dimpled his fat cheeks. I stared back.

"You've worked for the pygmy general a long time," he said. "That must be difficult. The man is . . . how should I say this? Elliptical."

When I didn't respond he resettled himself in his chair with a grunt.

"You saw the picture of your father? The one outside the Getty Museum in Los Angeles?"

I nodded.

"He worked for me. Nearly thirty years. We spent three years preparing him before he defected. Or I should say, pretended to defect. Once in America he had a bad time of it for several years. He did what he was supposed to do, spreading disinformation, but they made things difficult for him. Quite a remarkable man, really, because long after I thought his usefulness was at an end he resurfaced and became a productive agent again. Most of this you learned from Isadora, yes?"

"She said he betrayed her. Mixed lies with truth."

"Maybe."

"You don't know?"

"How can anyone *know* something like that? Maybe he turned on us and cooked his reports. Or maybe somebody gave him bad information. Somebody who is still there, still active. You understand why that question might still be important to me? Important to Russia?"

I nodded. He leaned forward and made a slurping sound as he sucked saliva around his mint. The peppery smell of it mixed with the sharp scent of cologne and watered my eyes.

"So you found a microdot," he said.

"I told Rykov about it."

"Yes, I'm aware. And it turned out to be an old KGB cable. 1943. An old cable indeed. My, my, that must mean something, don't you think?" Bassoff's eyes glazed briefly. "Did it have writing on it, this cable?"

"Yes."

"What kind of writing?"

"English."

"What did it say?"

"Something about a man named Harry Hopkins."

"Anything else?"

"No," I lied.

His expression soured, like a teacher disappointed by a once-promising student. His chair creaked as he leaned back.

"Your friend, Valya. The White Chechen. She is dangerous, that one. Lermontov said it best. Do you remember the verse? 'Over the rocks the Terek streams, raising a muddy wave / Onto the bank the wicked Chechen crawls, sharpening his dagger as he goes.'" Bassoff sucked his mint and flourished his pudgy hand in the air. "She is always sharpening her dagger, that one."

I scrubbed my face of emotion.

"Yes-s-s," Bassoff said wetly. "She is very dangerous." He rubbed his forefinger along the matte finish of his pistol. "And always busy. Did you know she built a safe house in Mytishchi? Near the train station on the other side of the Yauza River."

I did not know that, but I wasn't surprised. Valya had time and money. I hadn't been around very much and spent little money when I was. Mytishchi is an industrial city of less than two hundred thousand people on the northeastern edge of Moscow, its skyline dominated by factories, smokestacks, and power lines. She could make it there from the loft in about an hour on her scooter.

Bassoff watched me absorb this information, his lips twisted in a small smile. "She joined three basement flats and constructed common areas and ten rooms, enough for twenty people. Young women, mostly, siphoned away from the stream of human cargo trafficked through Moscow."

Whitish crud lined the corners of his small mouth, either dried saliva or dissolved mint, I couldn't tell which.

"What's your point?" I said.

"I think you know."

Valya could take care of herself against almost anyone. But this man could come at her in a thousand different ways. He could order her sniped from fifteen hundred meters away. Arrange for a garbage truck to run her over on her scooter. Drop poison in her drink.

Bassoff squinted. Slurped. Scratched his gleaming scalp through its thin covering of coppery-gray hair.

"I want the mikrat. I need to see the original photograph of the Venona cable for myself. You'll get that for me, won't you?"

I looked down at my left boot, filled with a complex mechanism of titanium alloy and a rebounding spring. No flesh, no blood, no bones. Empty of life.

"I will get it for you," I said.

chapter 30

Valya wasn't in the loft when I returned from the *Steklyashka*, GRU headquarters, nor did she answer her phone. I left a voice mail, then e-mailed the General an update on his secure server, telling him about the meeting with Bassoff and his demand for Walker's mikrat. While waiting for him to respond I inserted the DVD of *Lost Innocence*, Walker's documentary of the U.S. military-industrial complex, and watched the whole thing again. The narrator named a laundry list of multinationals, from Boeing to Lockheed to Microsoft, but he mentioned Lorelei more times than any of the others.

The film lasted seventy-six minutes. Still no word from Valya when it ended. I drummed my knuckles on the computer stand. Checked the e-mail and saw no new messages. Called Valya again, and this time she answered.

"How was your visit with the GRU?" she said.

"I'm still in one piece."

"I know, I saw you leave. I followed you there and waited. So did Brock Matthews."

She gave me a moment to consider this.

"He didn't see me," she said. "When you left he went inside. That's why I stayed. Fifteen minutes ago he came out and drove to the American embassy."

Matthews and Bassoff. Matthews was tall and looked like a soccer fullback; according to the General's file, he'd played American football at the Naval Academy. He and Bassoff were a perfect match for the two men Pavel the machinist saw entering my warehouse.

"The last time I saw Matthews was four months ago in the mountains," Valya said. "I didn't trust him then, and I don't now."

A new e-mail message arrived. The General, summoning me to his subterranean quarters with a curt text message.

"I need to see the General," I told Valya. "Keep the Walther ready." Her Walther P22 was an assassin's weapon, best for close work, where the bullet could pinball inside the skull and do the most damage.

"Always."

The portly lieutenant named Golko led me to the General's quarters, down stairs made of river rock, and past a security checkpoint. Four months before, Golko had helped me investigate the brutal slaying of another member of the General's secret cadre, and he seemed to think we had formed some sort of bond, because he asked me how I was. I told him "Busy," and that was the end of the chatter.

Golko admitted me to the General's office, then stayed outside as the door hissed closed behind me. The door was made of steel clad in aged wooden planks. It had been designed like everything else there to hide all the technology behind a primitive facade.

The General sat behind his wooden table, bathed in the glow from several different computer monitors. Without looking up, he pointed to something on the corner of his desk.

"You'll need those."

A phone capable of making international calls and a charger. Next to the phone was a passport issued in my name. Tucked inside were a tourist visa that gave me thirty days to stay in America, beginning the day after tomorrow, and a California driver's license and credit card issued in the name of Geoffrey Rogers.

"How solid is this ID?"

"It won't stand up to real scrutiny. Use it sparingly."

He finished whatever he was doing on the computer and swiveled his chair to face me. "Your flights have been arranged. You'll leave tomorrow afternoon. Moscow to L.A., then L.A. to Albuquerque."

"Why Albuquerque?"

"A Soviet-made Bear E bomber is stored there. Is that something you might be interested in seeing?"

I didn't reply, just stared over his shoulder at channeled stone that seemed to be weeping from the moisture of the nearby Moscow River.

"You'll be met in Albuquerque by a NCIX agent named Elizabeth Rhodes. Do you know about NCIX?"

"No."

"The Office of the National Counterintelligence Executive. Bush started it in 2005, part of his preemptive action strategy. It replaced NACIC, the national counterintelligence center. NACIC waited for foreign-sponsored agents to act. NCIX doesn't. Its job is to prevent other countries from obtaining U.S. military and nuclear secrets.' "

"Why does NCIX need to know I'll be there?"

He leaned back in his chair to stare at the soggy wooden beams above his head. "Bassoff called. I met him once in Afghanistan. He had a full head of red hair then. Saw him again a few times in Chechnya, looking even more swinish than before. But he was effective. Still is."

"Does that mean you're going to give him the microdot?"

"Not right away, but yes. More than that, I'm going to give him you."

"To do what?"

"He wants you to retrace your father's footsteps. Find out whether the man betrayed his country. He says he needs to know in order to evaluate another one of his sources."

"NCIX has agreed to let me do that?"

"Yes. Strange, I know. Part of your job will be to figure out why."

"What else?"

"Learn what you can and report it to me. Let me decide what to do with it. This isn't about revenge or redemption for your father, despite what you might think. It's business."

He started to dismiss me, but I held up a hand to stop him and told him about the box of files Lachek had sent to Rykov. His face turned grave, and after I finished the silence stretched into several minutes. I think he was toting up the years and the operations, legal and illegal, that a man like Lachek might have known about. Especially after the Caspian Sea oil play, Lachek would have hated the General enough to harm him any way he could. The silence was finally broken when he looked up and appeared to remember my presence.

"Okay," he said absently. "Dismissed."

I hesitated. "I still don't understand why NCIX has to be involved."

"They're your entrée, Volk," he said, tone curt and abrupt, obviously ready to get on with his next order of business. Probably a phone call to SVR headquarters in Yasenovo to probe—quietly, carefully, mindful of sticking his hand into a nest of vipers—for answers about Lachek's files. "NCIX gets you in and gives you information. They say they're willing to cooperate with us because of the 'thawed' relations between our countries. We both know that's nonsense. But I don't know their real reason."

I pocketed the phone, the charger, and the driver's license and credit card. Flicked the corner of my new passport with the ball of my thumb, thinking about how I could obtain a weapon as soon as I arrived and how I would lose NCIX if they started to get in my way.

The General scrutinized me from the darkness beneath his brow. "If you cross the wrong line over there, you can't look to me for help."

chapter 31

Early the next morning, hours before first light, the buzz of an incoming text message awakened me. VISITOR HERE, was all it said, followed by the letter v for Vadim.

Valya's side of the bed was undisturbed. She hadn't come home yet. I pulled on clothes and headed for the café.

Rykov was standing on the narrow sidewalk outside the painted window, smoking a rolled cigarette. When he spotted me, he dropped the butt, ground it out with the toe of his shoe, and followed me to the back entrance. Inside was dark. Without turning on a light, I took two of the upturned chairs down from one of the tables in the rear, sat on one, and stretched my legs to rest my heels on the other. After a moment Rykov took down another chair and sat, leaning forward with his elbows on the table.

"You're off to America, then," he said.

When I didn't answer, he offered a faint smile.

"I have sources, too."

He rolled and lit another cigarette, then drew on it so hard that his cheeks collapsed as he sucked as much smoke as he could. He blew it out in a column above his head.

" 'Strange bedfellows,' right?"

"That's right."

"Okay, then. I give you something, you give me something."

"You start."

"Your father was murdered in Los Angeles in 2004. Somebody smashed the back of his head with a club."

"Who?"

He took another greedy drag, pinching the cigarette between thumb and forefinger against his lips. The glow fired the birthmark on his cheek, made it look like a bloodstain.

"You know what the GRU does with pigs. It slaughters them."

"Bassoff had him killed?"

"That's my guess. The police there sniffed around. Even our friends at the CIA took a peek, or so I'm told. Now it's the kind of file they call a cold case." Smoke spiraled up from the ashtray as he ground out the butt of his cigarette.

"Why are you telling me this?"

"Because I want something from you."

"What?"

"Lachek's files have over forty years of dirt on people scattered across Russia. Politicians, oligarchs, journalists, crime bosses." His breath smelled like stale tobacco and coffee. His eyes looked even more tired now than they did before. "Not to mention military personnel and intelligence officers. These files could hang Bassoff. And they could hang the General, too, but I don't want him. Tell him I said that. I want Bassoff."

"What happens then?"

"Someone has to fill the void."

I waved away the smoke between us to see him more clearly. "I'll need to see the files."

"No. They're locked away. Safe. You'll see them after I have assurances that the General is on board with me."

"I'll tell him."

He nodded. Reached into his shirt pocket, pulled out a slip of lined paper, and slid it across the tabletop.

"Call that number, day or night."

After Rykov left I sat in silence for a few minutes, still cloaked in darkness, the sounds from the street muffled. I still wasn't any closer to answers about Walker or the Venona cable, but now I was closer to the truth about my father. The General and Bassoff might have their own reasons for sending me to America, but for me it meant an opportunity. A cold case means a file. A file means leads—names, addresses, witnesses, physical evidence. Everything about Los Angeles would be foreign to me, but one thing I was confident I could do was follow up on leads.

"Did you hear all that, Vadim?" I said, and the words seemed to fall away and die among the gloomed clutter of the café. I had meant for them to come out with more force than they did.

Vadim materialized from the darkness of the kitchen, carrying two bottles and two shot glasses. We drank the first round in silence, vodka for me, arrack for him. He poured another.

"That man is as good as dead."

"I know."

Rykov had stepped into waters too deep for him. The General, Bassoff, or somebody else connected to Lachek's files would kill him as surely as night follows the day.

"I'm sorry about your father, Alexei."

"He's been dead in my mind for a long time," I said, lying, thinking of the holes that I can't seem to fill. "People can't die twice."

"He wasn't a traitor." Vadim said the words with such conviction that my glass stopped halfway to my lips.

"How do you know that?"

He downed his drink, grimaced, and swiped the back of his scarred hand across his mouth. "Because you are his son. A man like you could not be the child of a pig."

chapter 32

Valya was at the loft when I got home. Music played softly through the wall-mounted speakers. Violin, cello, the velvety swish of brushes on a snare drum, and a mournful, smoky voice singing a song I didn't recognize. She stood with her back to me, lit from one side by the light from a sconce mounted on the wall. The glow crowned her in a nimbus of white gold. I thought about my dream, standing on the balcony, searching the crowd for her pale, mystic form.

She shifted her weight to her good leg and turned to face me. "You have to go."

"How did you know?"

"The General called me." She gave me a wan smile. "First time ever. Probably the last."

From where I stood I could see into our bedroom. Her suitcase was open on the bed.

"I just talked to Vadim, too," she said. "I hope you remember that your father's decisions were his own. You're an honorable man no matter what kind of person he was."

"It's a hard thing to live with, thinking he betrayed Russia."

She rubbed her thumb into the palm of her other hand, an unconscious gesture, I think. I took another glance at her suitcase in our bedroom.

"Why did Brock Matthews follow you today?" she said.

"I think Bassoff and Matthews killed Walker. I don't know why, but maybe I can find out while I'm in America."

"That's bad, Alexei. It reminds me of the worst days in Chechnya, when everyone suspected that everyone else was giving the Russians information or spying for a rival *teip* or both. Crosses and double crosses, so many that nobody could remember who was on which side."

"I'll feel right at home," I said lightly.

Valya stepped closer and rested her hand on my chest. "Tomorrow I leave for the Caucasus, for South Ossetia and Abkhazia, where Putin's tanks pushed across the border. I can help there, working for the Red Crescent again."

I nodded.

"When this is finished, you'll call me. We'll walk along Hollywood Boulevard and see the stars on the sidewalk. We'll swim in an outdoor pool under palm trees on a night when the moon is big enough to touch. Everything will be magical like it is in the movies."

She touched her fingers to my lips. "I'll be all yours again, then. Just as I am tonight."

PART IV

Double, triple the guard in front of this tomb,
Lest Stalin should ever get out.

—Yevgeny Yevtushenko, *The Heirs of Stalin*

chapter 33

United Airlines Flight 6436, a Bombardier CRJ-200, made a bumpy descent into Albuquerque International Airport, kiting through the thermals over the Sandia Mountains and bouncing to a landing on the high plateau above the sprinkled lights of the city. The stewardess announced the time: 10:53 P.M., twenty hours since I'd departed Moscow for LAX.

My four-hour layover in Los Angeles hadn't been a total waste. On the approach I saw the L.A. basin for the first time, framed in the miniature window of the airplane. My first impression was of contrast, darkness and light—the inky blackness of the ocean, the mountains like a golden chalice cradling cut gems of white, red, and green. But as we descended, the mountains and the lights resolved themselves into just another busy airport that looked the same as a hundred others.

Courtesy of the clean passport provided by the General, I'd breezed through customs. As soon as I crossed to the domestic side of the terminal I spotted two tails, neither of them very good at their job. I pretended to stop in a bathroom, doubled back and then down another concourse to the street level, and caught a cab to Century City.

During the ride I rolled the pen from the evidence locker at Tverskaya station in my fingers, examining the white lettering beneath the rust-colored streaks.

LORELEI.

That was the name on the pen, beneath the bloodstains. And that was the name inscribed in stone and steel on a monument sign outside a monolithic edifice rearing into the smoggy sky just off Olympic Boulevard. Each letter as tall as a man, carved into stone slabs and backlit in crimson that shone brightly, even in the afternoon sun.

The cabbie wore his hair in blond dreadlocks randomly sprinkled with red and white beads. He drummed his thumbs on the steering wheel to the beat of the reggae music thumping from the boombox on the seat next to him as we drove in a square around the granite-and-steel high-rise, a mini city unto itself. We cruised the same circuit twice, and then I told the driver to park in a delivery lane while I took a last look around. Nothing special, just a large commercial building among many just like it, a few smokers milling about the plaza, cars exiting the underground garage.

I directed the cabbie to pull closer to the monument sign in the front so I could read the names of Lorelei's subsidiary companies, listed in smaller letters. Some of the names offered no clue about the work the company did. Others indicated the nature of their business. Pharmaceuticals, aerospace, software development, and—snagging my attention— one called Spotlight Studios.

I pulled a crumpled airline napkin from my front pocket. On it I had written the title of Everett Walker's documentary about the 1980s military buildup, and, beneath the title, a list of credits. Spotlight Studios had produced and distributed *Lost Innocence*. I wondered how a subsidiary could be allowed to make a film so critical of its parent. No matter how compartmentalized a multinational company like Lorelei might be, someone at the top had to know and allow the film to go forward.

On the way back into LAX, I had the cabbie drop me at the desk of one of the smaller car rental companies. Using the California driver's license and credit card in the name of Geoffrey Rogers, I rented a Prius and drove it around the airport circle to a long-term parking garage. I stashed the license and card in the glove box, hesitated, then pulled the Venona cable from the inside pocket of my jacket and studied it one more time before placing it next to the license. I locked the car and hid the key—a rectangle of plastic—on the metal lip beneath the left front wheel well, and hopped on a shuttle bus back to the terminal. An hour later I caught the connecting flight to Albuquerque.

Now the plane was parked at the gate in Albuquerque, all the passengers bumping down the aisle in their hurry to leave. The woman in the window seat nudged my elbow to get me moving. I pulled my duffel from the overhead bin and followed the line to the jetway, keeping myself hidden behind a large man as we neared the boarding area. Looking over his shoulder, I saw a woman eyeing everyone suspiciously. The giveaway was how she angled her head toward the gate while pretending to adjust the straps on her shoulder-slung bag. I skirted behind the gate counter and approached her from the rear.

"Hello, Ms. Rhodes."

She stiffened. Took her time turning around, tucking a strand of shoulder-length hair behind her ear as she did. Light brown eyes hovering over dark circles, cleft chin, pallid skin sprinkled with freckles. The face of someone who worried a lot.

"You didn't manage to sneak a gun through security, did you, Colonel?"

I lifted my left leg and rapped my knuckles on my prosthesis. "Only a knife. Call me Volk."

She didn't seem surprised by my missing foot. Just pursed her lips and motioned for me to follow and took off down the concourse, clipping along in her flat shoes.

"In America we call someone like you a cowboy."

"In Russia, a Cossack. Do you enjoy movies, Ms. Rhodes?"

She ignored the question. We parted to pass a slow-moving traveler. When we met again she glanced at me and picked up the pace. "Why did you leave the terminal at LAX, Colonel?"

"You thought I should buy a book and a bagel and sit in a coffee shop to make things easy for your men? Jeans and a blue windbreaker, row fifteen, seat F. He makes a thirteen-hour trip from Moscow, gets help from his friend at the arrivals gate—red track suit and sneakers—and between them they can't tail a guy who stops to take a piss?"

"Your English is good."

"I watch lots of American movies. Everett Walker was my favorite director."

That caused her to tighten her lips again and toss her head, but she didn't say anything. We reached the end of the concourse.

"Luggage?" she said.

"Just this." My duffel was made of tattered canvas, scuffed leather reinforcement at the seams, scarred brass fittings.

"How many wars has that been through?"

We went out the automatic doors into a hot wind. Rhodes led the way along a covered walkway to a beige sedan that chirped when she disarmed the locks. She drove out of the lot and paid the attendant. The sticker on the windshield marked the car as a Hertz rental.

"Where are you from, Ms. Rhodes?"

"D.C."

"Tell me about NCIX."

In profile she reminded me of the woman who had led me to Rykov in the coffee shop outside the Lubyanka. Lips clamped, eyes narrowed as she turned north onto I-25, clearly uncomfortable in my presence. But the comparison wasn't fair, I decided. Rhodes wasn't angry. She was tense, edgy, tightly controlled, but she didn't want to shoot me. Not yet, at least. She had a dark aura about her, the kind exhibited by people who have depth of character, in my experience. Those who see the world in shades of gray.

"What's there to know?" she said. "Our job is to stop foreign governments from stealing our secrets."

She swung us into the fast lane and accelerated until we were passing every other vehicle.

"We're in a hurry?"

"I would like to get this over with as quickly as possible."

"Because of my charming personality?"

"I stop spies, Colonel. I don't usually escort them through our military bases and research facilities."

From what I could see of the nighttime city from the freeway, Albuquerque consisted of McDonald's, Chili's, 7-11s, a Walmart, and auto dealerships. We passed two tattoo parlors and a dance club the size of a warehouse, Spanish words graffitied on the walls. In the places where the lights weren't so bright I glimpsed strip malls, motels, Mexican diners, and low-slung stucco houses with red tile roofs. The dashboard clock said 11:25 P.M.

"Agent York is meeting us at the hotel," she said.

We looped along a concrete ramp onto I-40, our rented sedan one particle in a huge mixer sending people to all four corners of the city, the state, the country. She cut her eyes toward me, then back ahead.

"Some people thought things would be different after the Wall crumbled," she said. "I was fresh out of college then. So my opinion didn't mean anything. I'm not sure I even had one." She pondered those words for a bit, then shook off the memory of that younger version of herself. "We all should have known better."

"Everything changed."

"Not from our perspective. My boss put it best a few years ago. 'The new Russian economic system is capitalism strained through the filter of a police state. That means they'll be *more* aggressive about stealing our secrets.'" She glanced at me. "You guys love your secret policemen, don't you? And you never stop trying to steal what you can't create. I have job security in spades."

She exited I-40 to the access road, made a left beneath the freeway overpass, then another left onto the surface street going the other direction, and pulled into the parking lot of a Days Inn.

"Agent York is a twenty-five-year CIA veteran, specializing in the Communist Party U.S.A." She cut the engine. "I imagine the two of you will have lots to talk about."

chapter 34

Reese listened to the breakers crash against the cliffs beneath the balcony outside his home office, waiting impatiently for Santori to finish
his report. So far it had been ten minutes of nothing. Rambling, dis-
jointed, not Santori-like at all. A cool breeze blew in off the Pacific. The
gibbous moon painted the water platinum. Reese felt the buildup to a
migraine starting behind his right eye. He swallowed two Imitrex tablets
to blunt the inevitable pain.

"Bottom-line it, Santori."

Santori wore his sandy hair clipped close to his skull. His heavy-
lidded eyes made him look sleepy all the time. A manila folder lying
open on his lap held several loose-leaf pages, one of which he'd just
finished reading. The gist of it was that, with the help of a powerful
patron—General Nemtsov, a man Reese knew by reputation—Stepan
Volkovoy's son had built an impressive résumé. Extensive military
training augmented with diplomatic and espionage instruction. Service
in Chechnya followed by dozens of special assignments around the
world, including a recent trip to Macao that Santori had just finished
briefing him about. Reese had heard half a dozen reports from his

American handler, NSA agent Brock Matthews, chronicling Lachek's excesses. He figured the world was better off without him. But the point of Santori's babbling was that Colonel Alexei Volkovoy—"Volk," according to Santori—was not a man to be taken lightly.

Santori turned to another page.

"The CIA reports that Volk is on the ground in Albuquerque, ostensibly to ask questions about his father. But we have to assume that Walker got to him in Moscow. From the look of this"—Reese held up the summary of Volk's career—"he's unlikely to give up until he finds what he came here to get."

"Bassoff should have kept a tighter leash on things over there," Reese said, but what he was really thinking was that Bassoff had fucked up. Bassoff had taken the bait, just as Matthews had predicted. He'd killed Walker, as expected, and by now he should have gotten his hands on the cable. It might take him a few days, but Bassoff would figure out the meaning of the words *Beneš Czech delegation*. Then, if Reese and Matthews had read him properly, he would hold his precious new discovery in reserve, anticipating the perfect moment to bring down the hammer.

"Sir?" Santori was looking at him strangely, and Reese realized he had been staring into space for a long time.

"Who did NCIX send to Albuquerque?"

"Elizabeth Rhodes. Yeah, I know. Not good."

Reese had met Rhodes once. She'd been holed up in one of Lorelei's cavernous conference rooms surrounded by walls of stacked banker's boxes and a table piled with documents, a notebook computer in her lap. He was rolling past her in the hall when she called out his name. "I just wanted to introduce myself," she said. Reese had cut their conversation short, but it lasted long enough for him to know that Santori was right about her. She was smart, resourceful, and dedicated. She could be a problem.

Reese popped the lid on the bottle of Imitrex. Two weren't going to be enough. "The CIA?"

"They dispatched York."

York was a different animal from Rhodes. York hadn't been bought yet, but he was for sale. Just like Santori was for sale, Reese mused. Reese had known for several years now that Santori was selling information to Bassoff. He'd taken pleasure turning Bassoff's planted spy back on himself. Indeed, Santori had proven to be an unexpected but ideal conduit to deliver selected bits of information to the piggish GRU man—including the name under which Everett Walker had been traveling in Moscow.

Reese dry-swallowed another pill. "Good. Let's see what York comes up with, then decide what to do about Volk."

Santori stood to leave. "Now I get to pretend to be an air force major for a few days." He rolled his well-muscled shoulders and grinned. "Working for you isn't easy. Lieutenant, major, colonel—sometimes it's hard to remember what I'm supposed to be from one day to the next."

As he started out the door, Reese raised a hand to stop him, intending to offer a warning. Something along the lines of don't underestimate Volk just because you had an easy time crushing his father's skull. But Reese didn't say it. He thought through several possible outcomes in a split second and decided to let events unfold for now. A slew of variables might change things, but for now the JANUS project was still on track.

"Dismissed," he said.

chapter 35

CIA agent Scott York met Rhodes and me in the lobby of the Days Inn. He eyed me silently for several seconds, his gaze dropping from my face to linger on my left foot.

I used the time to study him. Big, fat around the middle, wrinkled shirt, rumpled hair, brown stubble darkening his heavy jowls. He nodded curtly and led the way to a ground-floor room next to the elevator. Except for a laptop computer and a yellow legal pad on the writing desk next to the phone, the room looked unoccupied. Despite the No Smoking signs everywhere, it still smelled of stale cigarette smoke and disinfectant.

"Tom Arnold," York said, studying my reaction to his appearance. "I get that all the time. Fine with me. Guy makes tons of money, hangs out with Schwarzenegger."

I didn't understand the reference, so I kept my mouth shut.

He settled into an upholstered chair that looked too small to hold him. A dresser and a king-sized bed took up most of the rest of the room. Rhodes sat in the chair next to the computer. The bed was the only place left to sit, so I remained standing.

"So you like Everett Walker movies, huh?" York said.

Rhodes watched for my reaction to the news that she had been wired for sound when she picked me up. I didn't show any.

"Which film was your favorite?" York said.

"The documentary, *Lost Innocence*."

"Why?"

I pulled the crumpled airline napkin from my pocket and smoothed it out on the table next to Rhodes, who leaned back and arched her brows.

"It's a list of names from the film," I said. "People interviewed or credited—the ones who said something interesting or worked somewhere sensitive." I tapped the edge of the laptop. "How soon can you download their NCIX files?"

York flushed. "Hold on a minute, Volk. How long a chain do you think we're giving you? You're here to get information about your father. We're prepared as a matter of courtesy to give you what we can about him. Period. Anything else is off-limits. We're not about to allow a foreign agent free rein in our backyard."

I ignored him. He was either a blowhard or he was pretending to be one. Instead, I watched Rhodes study the names on the napkin, her eyebrows knitted together. The illumination from the computer screen flattered her, erased the worry lines and softened the angles of her cheekbones. She didn't look up for nearly a minute.

"Unlike your country," she said finally, "we don't investigate people for making documentaries critical of our government."

"Believe that if you want. But tell me, what happened to Everett Walker and his friends and family?"

York snorted and heaved himself out of his chair. "They were marched to the camps, where they starved or froze or got worked to death. No, wait, that's what happened in *your* country. Here, they might not have gotten easy work for a couple of years. I'm sick of hearing simple-minded comparisons from the architects of the most murderous regime in history."

I could have made a point about his shredded Bill of Rights. Talked about illegal wiretaps and surveillance. Secret prisons and torture and "extraordinary renditions." Fifty years of covert actions in

Vietnam, Cambodia, Indonesia, Guatemala, Cuba, the Dominican Republic, Chile, Greece, Nicaragua, Afghanistan, Syria, Lebanon, Iran, Iraq, and many other places, often with the aim of assassinating or overthrowing foreign leaders. But nothing I could say about the misery spread by all those quiet wars would amount to anything with York.

Rhodes ignored our exchange. She turned the laptop so that the screen faced away from me, her back to the drawn curtain. The whooshing sound of cars on the elevated freeway beyond the window accompanied the soft clicking of the keyboard, her fingers moving so fast that the sound of individual keystrokes blurred.

"I don't think this is a good idea, Elizabeth." When York tugged his waistband away from his gut, his hand flipped back the front of his jacket to reveal a holstered automatic.

"These are NCIX files, Mr. York, not CIA. Any one of these people you're particularly interested in, Volk?"

"Sasha Tovar. One of the writers and co-producers."

Still clicking keys, Rhodes angled her gaze at me for a split second, then dropped it back to the screen. "Did you know that she and Everett Walker were married?"

How stupid did she think I was? "Really?"

She glanced at me and shook her head before returning her attention to the screen. "This relationship is off to a wonderful start."

Rhodes worked for another ten minutes, presumably fishing through the NCIX file on Sasha Tovar or one of the other names on the list I'd given her. She showed something to York, who cocked a brow and shrugged, then she logged off the computer. When that was done she handed me a plastic card key.

"Your room is next door. We leave for Kirtland Air Force Base at six. Are you an early riser?"

I took the key without answering. A digital clock on the nightstand said 12:29 A.M.

York clapped me on the back. "Get a good night's sleep. Tomorrow we'll take a look at an antique. You're not going to believe the cockpit conditions in a 1970s-vintage Bear E bomber."

chapter 36

My room was identical to York's. I put my duffel on the bed, plugged my phone charger into the wall socket after a brief struggle with the adapter, sat in the upholstered chair, closed my eyes, and drifted into a meditative state somewhere between sleep and wakefulness. My mind seemed to work most freely when I did that.

Two hours later I dialed the number Rykov had given me, planning to turn him loose on Lorelei and Spotlight Studios. No answer, and the call didn't go to voice mail. I tried again. The number kept ringing for a long time, then stopped with a series of clicks as the line connected. Nobody said anything. All I heard was the sound of somebody breathing into the mouthpiece, a huff of air over the microphone, then, "Who is this?"

I didn't recognize the voice. I hit End and closed the phone, more disturbed than I should have been. After all, Rykov hadn't done anything to help me. But the idea that he had already been wiped off the board left me with a bad feeling.

I went to the bathroom and splashed water on my face. Regarded myself in the mirror, grimaced, retrieved my shaving kit from the duffel, showered and shaved.

As I pulled on my clothes I heard a muffled commotion coming from York's room. I pictured the scene as one of his minions made his report. The crazy Russian is awake, moving around. What should we do? York struck me as the kind of man who would hate being rousted at three in the morning. And one who would delegate any unpleasantness he had to deal with.

The phone in my room pealed. I picked up without saying anything.

"We're not leaving for another three hours," Rhodes said tiredly.

"Jet lag. What did you learn about Sasha Tovar?"

Long pause, probably while somebody whispered in her earpiece. "Fifteen minutes," she said, and hung up.

My door wasn't locked from the outside. No reason why it should be. I was a friendly, there by invitation, albeit one probably coerced or cajoled into the country by somebody in the American State Department who owed the General or Bassoff a favor. Still, I had half expected a lock.

At the end of the hallway I found an alcove with an ice maker, vending machines, and a man about my age standing next to a stool, a wire coiling from beneath his jacket collar to a white plastic earpiece. He'd been warned I was heading his way. That much was clear from his look of wide-eyed expectation. But he had no idea how to respond. I fanned a sheaf of small-denomination rubles in front of his face.

"Can I buy some change, friend? I didn't have a chance to exchange these for dollars on my way in."

Looking rattled, he patted his pockets and came up with a couple of crumpled dollar bills. I told him thanks, fed the machine, and hit the buttons for a bag of peanuts and a chocolate bar.

"Breakfast of champions," my new friend called out as I walked away, and I waved to him over my shoulder.

Rhodes was waiting outside my door, still in the same clothes, a charcoal pantsuit that eliminated any curves. She held a rolled tube of papers in her hand and waved it in my face like a baton.

"Provocation, that's all this is, Volk," she said, but she looked amused.

I offered her a handful of peanuts. "What does *breakfast of champions* mean?"

She pulled out a master card key and unlocked the door, kicking it open with a practiced movement. Inside she eyed the undisturbed bedspread and my packed duffel. Sat at the desk chair and crossed her legs.

"Sasha Tovar was born in Prague. Made her first documentary in 1998. *Nightfall in Lidice*, the story of the Germans' retaliation for the assassination of Heydrich in Prague. A few years later she produced and directed the film *Living in the Zone*. Have you seen it?"

I shook my head.

"It told the story of a family living in Pripyat when the Chernobyl reactor blew. The father was a member of the fire brigade that put out the flames around the building containing reactor number four. Two weeks after the meltdown, he and most of the others on his team were dead. None of them had been told the smoke and debris were radioactive. His wife and daughters stayed in Pripyat, and . . . Well, you should watch it sometime."

Hearing the story, I remembered seeing parts of the film. One shot that had become an iconic image from the disaster showed the tilted hulk of the Pripyat Ferris wheel as seen through the blown-out window of an abandoned apartment.

The door to my room opened, and York squeezed through. No tie, one loop missed by his belt, hair tousled.

"Since then," Rhodes said, "Sasha Tovar has been internationally recognized for her work. Most recently, she directed a film about organized crime's ties to the prostitution trade in Los Angeles."

"Crime," York said. "Now there's something you know a bit about, eh, Volk?" He hitched up his pants. "Guess we've decided to leave early."

"She's currently making a docudrama about McCarthyism and the Hollywood blacklists," Rhodes added.

York cut loose with something between a belch and a yawn. "That's been done to death. Hollywood loves the story line because they get to be the heroes. Nobody pays attention to the fact that most of the accusations were true. Damn near all of them *were* members of the American Communist Party, the most productive source of spies and agents provocateurs in the history of this country. McCarthy might have been a horse's ass, but his inquiry was right on."

Rhodes closed her eyes for a few seconds. When she opened them again she failed to hide her exasperation. By then I had decided that York's chatter was mostly show, trying to get a rise out of me or make me underestimate him.

"But here's the funny part," York said. "We had to go to Moscow and look at *your* files to find out about this stuff. Our government can't keep anything secret, but somehow it managed to hide evidence that implicated hundreds of Americans as Soviet spies. That only gets out when the most repressive regime in history opens *its* files."

When he turned to face Rhodes, he nearly knocked a lamp off the nightstand. Face flushed, breathing heavily, he waggled a thick finger. "I'll bet he knows more about that stuff than you do, Elizabeth. Tell her, Volk. How many spies were the KGB and GRU running in the States, beginning in the twenties and thirties? How many men did America lose in Korea because Stalin got the bomb ten years earlier than he should have? You think he would have cut Kim Il-Sung loose on the Korean peninsula if Russia was still years away from going nuclear? How many Americans were paid during the Cold War—hell, are *still* being paid—to send secret information to the Kremlin?"

"Twelve."

Rhodes did her best to hold back a laugh, stood and smoothed her skirt. "Relax, Scott. We're not here to fight the Cold War all over again."

"That's the problem. We stopped fighting it a long time ago, and they didn't. They just put on a different mask."

Rhodes grimaced at me. "All ancient history now, right, Colonel?" She had to brush past me to get to the door. Her eyes were a hand span below mine as she passed. Open and frank, brown irises with tiny red scribbles on the whites. "But it's still interesting, don't you think? All that history memorialized in those old Soviet cables." Her tone was airy, her lips curled in a friendly smile, almost as if she were about to wink, but something about her demeanor warned me that this wasn't idle chatter. "Have you ever read any of those? You know—the decrypted Venona cables?"

chapter 37

The three of us rode together in York's rented SUV, a white Ford Explorer. Rhodes took the backseat, leaving me in the front with York and his breakfast burrito. He bit off giant hunks and talked with his mouth full, ignoring the wet pieces that fell onto the wax paper spread out on his lap.

"According to published Communist dogma," he said, "the differences between our two countries could only be settled by violent confrontation. American Communists *agreed* with that policy. How is that anything but treason?"

Rhodes's face was reflected in the windshield as she worked in the flush of light from the screen of her laptop. I could see her stealing the occasional glance at me, worrying about my reaction to York's boorishness. Watching her reflection, I considered what I knew of Kirtland Air Force Base, not much more than what Valya had been able to glean from the Internet.

During World War II Kirtland served as a training base for the flight crews of B-17 and B-24 bombers, as well as the B-29 "Superfortress" of the type that dropped Fat Man and Little Boy on Hiroshima and Nagasaki. Situated on the eastern mesa above Albuquerque, the former private airfield eventually became the home of the Air Force Special Weapons Center, along with a unit of the Air Research and Development Command, ultimately making it one of the largest military installations in the U.S. Air Force.

They must have been thrilled the day my father's Bear E dropped out of the sky—after a stop in Greenland—and landed at Kirtland. The Bear and its surveillance equipment would have been an unexpected gift from the secretive Soviet regime. But the Americans' Soviet specialists must have wondered whether the prize was worth the risk. What was the story behind this pilot with the ferocious eyes? Was he a defector, one of those many disillusioned men, a former true believer now awakened to the error of his ways? Or was he a man on a mission, delivering a cargo of lies?

York grunted as a greasy chunk of sausage larger than the others oozed from the bottom of his burrito and plopped onto his pants leg, missing the paper. He tried to clean the mess while he drove, but succeeded only in smearing things even more.

As for Rhodes, her brooding persona was beginning to grow on me. I liked her fatalistic shrugs in response to York's more provocative comments, almost Russian in their acknowledgment that most such debates have no clear answers.

"Hollywood," York mumbled disgustedly, back to chewing again as we climbed toward the top of the mesa and the night surrendered to a widening band of pale blue on the horizon. "Politics as fashion statement. Stars who command ten million a picture claim they're being 'blacklisted' because they stopped by Caracas for a photo op with Chavez, a guy who would muzzle them and all the other intellectual apologists if they had the misfortune to live in Venezuela. Put it this way. How many great Cuban actors has Castro's government allowed to develop? Where are the towering Cuban intellectuals? I'll tell you where, they're all in America."

I thought about Cuba's high education rate and its competent health care system. I wondered how much America's policy toward Cuba has affected poverty there. But I didn't take the bait and answer York's questions.

York made a left turn. Rhodes tapped something on her keyboard, and the cone of light around her changed from blue to white.

"Hollywood's favorite script has been the same for the last sixty years," York rambled on. "The heroes—innocent writers, directors, actors. All of them harassed by the same villains, McCarthy and HUAC, until the golden age of cinema was destroyed. The fable has become the standard myth. Nobody asks anymore why Hollywood became so enamored with the most totalitarian expression of Communism, why it chose to ignore the armies of kulaks, intelligentsia, artists, dissidents, political enemies, and undesirables marched to slave labor and death in the Gulag. Nobody comes out and says the *truth*, that these American 'fellow countrymen' of Stalin were complicit in all those deaths, complicit in allowing that madman and his successors to trample Eastern Europe and threaten the rest of the world for decades."

Rhodes clapped her laptop shut and began packing it into its case. "Always the same, Scott. Using an ax when you should use a scalpel. What about *Freedom and You*? There's an example of Hollywood promoting the Department of Defense agenda. The list goes on."

I'd seen snippets of the film. A famous American actor who played a policeman on TV narrated a documentary about Russians training to look and sound like Americans as part of a plot to infiltrate the United States. The so-called documentary showed a "typical American town"—complete with a church, a town square, and a drugstore—supposedly built behind the Iron Curtain to help train teenage Communist agents to act like the boy or girl next door.

"So you're an apologist for McCarthy?" I said to York.

He took his eyes off the road to scowl at me. "You think this is a philosophical debate, don't you? Actually, you probably don't. You *know* why this is something we still need to worry about today."

The sun bloomed over the Sandia Mountains. I turned my face away from the sudden glare. "You bore me, York."

"I'll bet I do. You think we buy that fairy tale about you and your father? The tragic son looking for answers? Give me a break. You're GRU, one of Bassoff's men. Spent five years in Chechnya stirring the bloody stew. Assassinations, cover-ups, infiltrating the *teips* with the help of the Chechen woman—what's her name? Help me out here, Rhodes. Valya Novaskaya—that's it. We know all about you, man."

From the corner of my eye I saw Rhodes stiffen at the mention of Valya's name. "Take it easy, Scott," she said.

"Want to know my favorite GRU story?" York jerked the wheel to swerve around a slow-moving pickup truck. "A Russian scientist is ordered into the United States. Told to become a naturalized citizen and obtain technical information for the GRU. But I don't speak English, he says. Pretend to be a mute, they say. But what if I talk in my sleep, he wants to know? Don't worry, they tell him. We'll cut out your tongue before you leave."

"I once heard a KGB officer tell the same story about the CIA."

"There you go. The last bastion of someone arguing from an indefensible position—moral equivalency."

York wheeled the Explorer around another curve and we arrived at a checkpoint. He passed his credentials to a military policeman, who went into the guardhouse to consult a computer and make a phone call while two others watched our vehicle on either side, M16s slung over their shoulders. Another MP walked a snuffling German shepherd around the SUV.

"We had to get special clearance to come in the back way," Rhodes told me. "They're a bit more paranoid than usual."

Five minutes later the MP returned York's identification, hit a switch that caused the gate to roll away, and waved us through. We drove along a marked lane for several hundred meters and endured a second checkpoint. Another search, this one inside the vehicle as well, more documents to be filled out. Finally we were passed through and allowed to drive to a prefabricated metal building, where a sandy-haired man in a dark blue uniform stood outside, waiting for us. Solid build, ramrod-straight carriage. The gold insignia on the epaulettes of his dress jacket identified him as a major.

York got out of the SUV and talked to him for several minutes, occasionally glancing at me. The major handed him a folder. York studied whatever was inside, asked a question, then turned his body like a gun turret to regard me through the windshield. When he returned to the vehicle, still carrying the folder, the major followed him and leaned into my open window, one hand on the Explorer's roof. A warm breeze carried his musky scent into the cab. He gave me a cool, appraising look.

"Colonel," he said to me without inflection, his green eyes as flat as oxidized coins. "I'm Major Santori." He swung his gaze to Rhodes. "Hello, Elizabeth."

"Never routine with us, is it?"

"No."

York put the Explorer in gear, but Santori made no move to leave. He drummed his fingers on the metal rooftop, eyeballing me again.

"We lost three Superforts in Vladivostok late in the war. Our guys had engine trouble and were forced to land there. We never got them back." He paused as if to make sure I was listening. "Tupolev and his designers took them apart bolt by bolt to reverse-engineer them. They came out as Tu-4s with enough range to threaten us all the way over here." As he rolled his shoulders I could hear the starch pop in his tunic. "The old Bear inside the hangar incorporates more than a few Superfort design features. Guess what I'm trying to say is that your old man can thank Uncle Sam for giving him a better aircraft to fly."

He thumped the roof and strode to an electric cart, where two airmen were already waiting. They led the way across a wide expanse of grooved concrete, striped and numbered to direct pilots to runways, fuel depots, and hangars.

"The place we're going is a storage facility for the planes we captured or acquired from defectors," York said. "A hangar covering more than half a million square feet. With all these relics, they ought to turn the damn thing into a museum."

He kept talking, but I wasn't listening. My heart rate had kicked into high gear. My palms were damp. For the first time ever, I felt as if maybe I was close to filling that hole inside. Maybe I was closer to knowing my father.

chapter 38

Battleship-gray steel with three separate domes, the roof of the giant hangar loomed like approaching thunderclouds. We parked next to a set of double-sliding doors and got out of the SUV. The airmen opened a lock and pushed the doors back. York, Rhodes, and Santori stood to one side, watching me as though waiting for some sort of sign as I entered.

The vast emptiness inside was accentuated by a dozen or so airplanes scattered about. Two MiG-17 fighters, both with red stars painted on their silver wings, one of them missing its cowling, the engine stripped. Japan, Germany, Italy, Iran, Iraq, China, Korea—a veritable United Nations of planes was represented.

But only one of them captured my attention.

The colossal Tupolev Tu-95, code-named "Bear" by NATO, was the fastest propeller-driven aircraft ever flown, the product of unmatched aerodynamics and four powerful Kuznetsov turboprop engines. More than sixty tons of airplane with a range of 4,000 miles, it was the perfect platform for electronic warfare. Wings mounted high on the fuselage, swept back at thirty degrees. Belly painted midnight black to reduce

reflection during night missions. An ungainly condor of a plane surrounded by eagles, hawks, and shrikes, she grew larger and larger as we
approached, the rap of our heels on the polished concrete floor echoing off the high ceiling.

"Goddamn things first made an appearance in 1970," York said.
"Two of them flew Murmansk to Cuba. Radar installations from
Greenland to Key West—all along the entire eastern seaboard—went
crazy. You know what a ferret is, Volk?"

Ferrets are planes that skirt borders and feint attacks in enemy
territory to collect information about radar installations so that the
radar can be jammed, tricked, or destroyed in the event of war. A dangerous game played out over a global canvas. Silver scars marred the
fuselage of my father's Bear, marking where antennae had been removed.

"Well," York said when I didn't answer, "this was one hell of a big
ferret."

The airmen rolled a boarding ladder to the crew entry hatch above
the nose wheel bay. I pushed ahead to be the first inside, climbed, then
stopped at the top of the ladder when my head and shoulders were
through the hatch.

The cockpit was coated in dust. It smelled oily, musty, metallic.

Two seats up front, one each for the pilot and copilot. The forward compartment immediately behind the flight deck had room for
five crew members. When the plane was operational the compartment
held a communications operator, navigator, and defense systems operator stationed in the rearward-facing seats on the port side and a flight
engineer facing aft on the starboard side next to a spare seat for an ob-
server or a trainee. The bombardier's station was in the center of the
cabin. Only the brackets remained where a radar control unit, radar
transmitter control box, periscope sextants, and other hardware used
to be.

The major with the flat eyes was telling me these things from the
rungs of the ladder beneath me, but for the most part I tuned him out,
just as I had learned to do with York. My gaze was focused on the cockpit, on the cracked leather of the pilot's seat and the bewildering array
of dials, levers, gauges, and toggle switches in front, on both sides, and

overhead. Some of them were labeled in Cyrillic, and simple enough to read that I understood their purpose. Fire warning lights, altimeter, tachometers, course indicators, propeller pitch, wing flaps. Switches and levers for lights, autopilot, bomb bay doors. Others—radio compass repeater indicator, vacuum and manifold pressure gauges, and many more—had purposes I could only guess at.

The throttle controls were missing their knobs. I wondered if they had been pirated before my father strapped himself into the seat for the last time or if some enterprising American looking for souvenirs had taken them after he defected.

York, Rhodes, and Santori climbed into the plane behind me as I crouched next to the pilot's seat and ran my palm over the leather, darker in the saddle and lower back, touching the places my father would have touched, imagining that the indented contours sculpted into the seat had been shaped by the press and sweat of his body. After a moment I settled into it, wriggling into place. Placed my boots on the pedals and my hand on the throttles, and gazed out the windshield.

But I didn't see the steel I-beams and insulated walls of an airplane hangar in the high desert of the American Southwest. I saw mountain peaks powering up through the mist above Greenland and two F-4 Phantoms on my flanks, dangerous and unpredictable, escorting the lumbering Bear northwest along the curve of the Arctic Circle.

"Okay, Volk, you've seen it," York said. "Now Major Santori would like to have a word with you."

"How many crewmen were on board when he defected?"

All three exchanged looks, but it was Santori who answered. "Four to fly the plane. Your father, a copilot, navigator, and communications officer. Five more in the bay to work the surveillance equipment. A total of nine on this flight."

"What happened to the others?"

"Five of them decided to go back to Russia. You can imagine what happened to them there. The others were debriefed, vetted, debriefed some more, and eventually dispersed." Santori may as well have been talking about dandelion spores, not men whose lives had been forever changed. "Given new names, new beginnings. I know what you're thinking, Colonel. Forget it. We couldn't let you contact the ones still alive even if we wanted to. All the information about their new identities is buried."

"Did they all agree to defect in advance?"

Santori squeezed into the copilot's seat so that we were eye to eye. "The flight crew did. We don't know about the others. They claimed they'd been drugged and restrained."

He sounded doubtful, so I said, "What do you think happened?"

"I was still in diapers then. All I have now are old reports and interview summaries. How should I know?"

Rhodes shifted her weight. She had to lean forward against the back of my seat to keep her head below the clutter of switches overhead, so her face was close to mine. Even through the musty, oily smell of the cockpit I detected a trace of fragrance, citrus and spice.

"You know how it must have been," she said. "Whether they came willingly or not, they had to say they didn't defect voluntarily. Once they arrived here, things became more complicated. The debriefings lasted a long time, because truth was hard to come by. Was this a deception? Which one of these men was a spy? Was there something in the plane or its equipment designed to mislead us or to transmit information to the Kremlin? Nothing any member of the crew said would have been taken at face value."

"I want to talk to someone who was there. Someone who debriefed my father."

"Good luck," York said, but I was watching Santori when the corner of his left eye ticked ever so slightly.

"Their identities are protected," Santori said. "Besides, I'm sure they're all dead or retired by now." He looked away and waved his hand to take in the cockpit and the whole hangar. "Are we done here?"

chapter 39

The prefab building where we first met Major Santori turned out to house two rows of cubbyhole offices on either side of a narrow hallway. A doorway at the end of the hall led to a conference room with a round table, where we sat facing one another in a tight circle. Santori picked his teeth with a plastic toothpick. Rhodes opened her laptop on her crossed legs. York overflowed the chair next to me, pawing through the folder the major had given to him when we first arrived on the base. He slid a black-and-white photograph in front of me.

"Recognize him?"

It was the bullet-headed cop, Zubko, features slack, mouth hanging open. The intimidating expression he wore more effectively than a badge had been wiped away by death.

"When?" I asked.

"Neither him or his partner showed up for work yesterday. They found him in the stairwell of his apartment building." York handed me another photo, this one grainier. It showed a hollow steel trash bin lit by the flash of a camera. Inside, the parakeet-faced cop who had arrested me at Sheremetyevo nestled among paper wrappers, melon rinds, bottles, crumpled aluminum cans, and cardboard beer containers, a used condom stuck to his forehead. "This one turned up in a dumpster outside a bar where the cops like to hang out."

York removed another photo from the manila folder and skated it across the table. Rhodes clicked a key on her notebook and regarded me curiously over the top of the monitor. I suspected that her screen held the same image as the one in my hand.

Rykov. Easily identifiable by the birthmark on his left temple, a dark stain on his pale flesh. Only his head and shoulders were visible. Lips drawn back in a rictus, a grotesque parody of his thin-lipped smile. Eyes half closed, squinting as though he was trying to make sense of something just beyond his range of vision, but they were vacant, cloudy.

"Those were the guys who arrested you for Walker's murder, right?" York scratched himself in the crotch area. "Funny thing, all three ending up dead within hours of each other."

I kept looking at Rykov's birthmark and didn't respond.

"Rykov was one of those people your government spreads around like bacteria," York said. "He spent most of his career in foreign postings. So what was he doing working Walker's murder in Moscow?" He raised his eyebrows, then smiled. "Don't worry, that's a rhetorical question. Here's where we make the connection between Rykov and Walker."

York handed over a single-spaced document, everything crammed onto one page. Rykov's full name—which meant nothing to me—and his lineage going back three generations, including a grandfather suspected of being a Jew, which would have been a problem for Rykov during his GRU career. A list of dates marked the high points of his life—birth, school graduations, military service in Afghanistan, GRU enrollment and training, and foreign postings in Vancouver, Seattle, and San Francisco, along with a summary of his suspected activities at each location.

One line was highlighted in yellow. While living in Vancouver in 1995 Rykov had befriended American filmmaker Everett Walker during the filming of his documentary *Lost Innocence* by bribing local officials to obtain the necessary permits after the city authorities initially turned him down. The two became "close associates" with "frequent contact." All of this seemed consistent with the idea that Walker was a

Soviet and Russian asset, but I didn't trust either York or Santori to give me the truth.

I flipped the page, looking for something that identified the source of the information. "Where did this come from?"

York shifted his weight and exchanged a glance with Santori. "Don't worry about that."

"How do we know this is the real thing?"

"It's not a fake," Santori said. "We know Rykov the way a child knows a parent."

His face was bland. Scrubbed so clean his cheeks glistened. Flat, sleepy eyes, like a predator waking up from a nap.

"You're telling me that Rykov was a CIA asset?"

"Let's just say we sometimes exchanged information," Santori said. He twirled a pen in his fingers, watching it instead of me. "You talked to Rykov about how Walker died. Now you know that Rykov was one of ours and that he knew Walker from their days in Vancouver. Looking at it from that point of view, what does it tell you about why Walker was murdered in your warehouse?"

I recalled Rykov's tense demeanor at the Sheremetyevo terminal. The beating he allowed Zubko to administer, and the risk he took—in the form of reprisals by me or the General—by burying me for nearly a week in the depths of Lefortovo prison.

"I don't know why Walker got shot."

Santori leaned back, seemingly satisfied, but York pounded the table.

"You'd better give us more than that! Justify us letting you come over here and taking you on a guided tour."

When I didn't answer, York gritted his teeth. "Maybe you're next on the list, Volk. Whoever did this was good at their job. A true artist. Leaves a signature, a nice coup de grâce."

"Signature?"

"All four men ended up shot in the back, three times. Connect the dots you get a triangle, or a pyramid. The last round fired point blank, close enough to leave powder burns. Walker wasn't the first to die that way over there, either. You didn't know that? Don't your people tell you anything?"

"Same gun?"

"We don't know yet. Takes us a day or two to find out what the locals in Moscow know."

York hoisted himself out of his chair, and Santori followed suit. Santori seemed bored, now, as though a threat had been avoided. His manner suggested that I was just another clueless Russian not capable of doing any harm.

"Wait here, Volk," York said. "Somebody will bring in your father's CIA file shortly. Take your time with it. Then we're off to Santa Fe."

"Why Santa Fe?"

Rhodes was still staring at me. In fact, her gaze had intensified.

York leaned close enough so that I could smell the onions from his breakfast burrito. "Don't you want to meet your stepmother?"

chapter 40

According to the CIA, Stepan Volkovoy was a traitor. A pig. As I paged through the CIA's heavily redacted file, alone in the small room in the prefab building on the grounds of Kirtland Air Force Base, the proof appeared to be right in front of me. Dry, straightforward, spare—and damning.

Stepan had been recruited by the GRU in December 1967 to become part of an elite electronic reconnaissance air wing ostensibly attached to the Forty-Sixth Air Army. That was when the entries stopped being made in the file I saw at Isadora's dacha. As the General had suspected, that was when my father entered the shadowy world of spies.

And then, less then two months later, he became another kind of spy.

On January 30, 1968, he contacted a U.S. diplomat stationed in Leningrad. The so-called diplomat was a CIA station chief, as Stepan knew through some means not specified. I suppose that kind of information came easily to a man with the resources of the GRU at his disposal. Their first face-to-face meeting occurred on the banks of the Neva River during the long darkness of the northern winter.

Stepan was a station chief's dream—a walk-in who was willing to stay in place and keep providing information.

I knew enough about the craft of espionage to picture the seduction that followed. Clandestine meetings in cafés, train stations, and on the wide walkway of Nevsky Prospect. An afternoon at the Leningrad Zoo, an evening at the Kirov Theatre, a stroll around Palace Square in the shadow of the Hermitage. Did money change hands? In addition to being a pig, was my father a *chuzhoi*, a man who served as an agent against his country for money? I shuddered at the thought.

Stepan's descent into treason accelerated after his recruitment in Leningrad. He was passed along a chain of so-called diplomats and trade representatives as he rotated through postings in Leningrad and Murmansk, then east to Vladivostok and Sakhalin Island, and finally back to Murmansk. The details of the information he gave the Americans had been removed from the file. From what I could piece together, he initially provided locations of coastal and inland radar installations, which allowed the Americans to target their peripheral flights and penetrations of Soviet air space with far more precision.

Meanwhile, the scope of Stepan's duties within the GRU increased. He became the air force liaison to the laboratories developing the Soviets' most advanced Early Warning Radar stations, responsible for target acquisition and designation, and providing radar information to surface-to-air systems and air defense command posts. Using his high-level access, he helped our enemies locate bases, missile factories, biological and chemical research facilities, storage depots. He identified nuclear weapons facilities and test sites. With the help of my father and others like him, the Americans and Brits dominated Russia with their game of going "over the fence"—their slang for the Iron Curtain—to gather military intelligence. They won the "Wizard War," as Winston Churchill dubbed it.

I had learned the humiliating history of the Wizard War while studying at Moscow Military Academy. The ability of the Americans and British to prowl our coasts and overfly our sovereign territory—to eavesdrop and photograph almost at will—was a source of deep frustration to the Kremlin. And a cause for fear, because a plane that could penetrate Soviet air defenses to *photograph* Red Square could do the same thing to *bomb* Red Square.

I recalled a conversation with NSA agent Brock Matthews. "Imagine the nightly news in America filled with stories of Soviet bombers prowling your coasts, flying over Manhattan, Washington, and Boston," I told him. "Think of the public outcry, the diplomatic barrage, the calls for war." He had offered a wry grimace in response. "At least our news anchors would be free to report such things."

The names of the people who debriefed Stepan in the months and years following his arrival at Greenland's Thule Air Force Base had all been removed. But at least one high-level CIA officer suspected him of being a false defector.

So what? the officer had scrawled in the margin of a report from a Princeton University lab suggesting that the radar imaging cameras mounted on the Bear checked out as the most sophisticated devices of their kind at that point in 1974. *They knew we would have this in less than a year*, he wrote. *This is another Golitsyn.*

The last was a reference to the most famous Cold War defector, a man who tied the CIA's counterintelligence division into knots searching for a mole within its ranks and who many believed, then and now, was a KGB plant. Golitsyn fingered Philby, MacLean, Burgess, double-agent Kopatzky, and others, although his detractors claimed he offered those "gives" long after they mattered and only in order to position himself to do more harm to American interests. One of his harshest critics was FBI director J. Edgar Hoover, who was so convinced that Golitsyn was a plant that he curtailed counterintelligence cooperation between the FBI and CIA for the remainder of his tenure.

Like Golitsyn, my father spent years being debriefed, many of them as a prisoner held without charges or trial in conditions one agent described in a memorandum to his boss in Langley as "deplorable." When Stepan finally established his credentials after years of relentless questioning—or enough time had passed so that he was no longer considered a threat—he was given a new identity and a legend to back it up.

In 1981 he became Steven Morris, an immigrant from Poland. He was provided a green card and permitted a normal life—or one as close to normal as it could be, under the circumstances.

Because of his knowledge of Soviet radar, Stepan's first job was a four-year stint at a Los Alamos firm specializing in radar imaging software, a place where he could be "closely monitored," according to his principal CIA detractor. He worked with physicists, chemists, engineers, mathematicians, and scientists from a host of other disciplines, all under the constant watch of military advisors and security officers. He earned outstanding performance reviews and the trust of the chief security officer assigned to monitor him.

And all the while he fought the bureaucracy in Langley for citizenship.

Most immigrants at that time waited five years to become naturalized citizens. Soviet defectors who were Party members, like Stepan, often had to wait an additional five years. But an obscure section of the immigration code allowed persons who made an "extraordinary contribution" to "United States intelligence activities" to be given citizenship after one year. The Director of Central Intelligence could recommend five such persons each year. Stepan claimed that the CIA had promised citizenship in a year and then reneged. He lost the argument. Despite his pleas, Stepan didn't become a naturalized citizen until 1985, eleven years after his defection, and two years after he'd married a security officer from Santa Fe named Mary Montoya.

A year after obtaining citizenship, Stepan was hired by aerospace giant Lorelei. He divorced Montoya and moved to Burbank, California, to work in its research and development unit, modeled after Lockheed's infamous "Skunk Works." Reading between the lines of the report, I gathered that he was involved with their work on stealth technology, trying to make American planes completely or partly invisible to radar or other means of electronic detection. He worked at Lorelei for the rest of his life, until his murder on May 22, 2004.

During the whole time I studied the file in the room at the end of the hall I never changed expression or shifted in my seat. I don't know how much time passed, but I was sure that cameras were everywhere, recording my reaction to each bit of data in the file. So I gave them nothing. Sat there as if carved in stone, moving only when I needed to turn a page.

I knew that these documents told only the side of the story the CIA wanted me to know. Truth artfully mixed with lies. I had already been on a roller-coaster ride with Lachek, Isadora, and Rykov. Stepan was a defector, a pig; no, he was a *false* defector sent to confuse the Americans. Stepan was a false defector who had been turned by the Americans; no, he was a false defector who *pretended* to have been turned by the Americans. By now I knew the answer might never be clear.

I made a show of still reading long after I had finished, buying time to let things percolate. In the end I kept picturing Isadora's face, ravaged by the years, worn by worry and stress, her gaze never meeting mine fully. *Videmus omnia*, she had said as we watched the light fade in her quiet meadow. The Latin had meant nothing to me, but her translation made perfect sense. *We see all.*

Only now the phrase carried a more ominous meaning. Because *Videmus omnia* wasn't simply a curious Latin phrase. It was the motto of the elite air wing to which my father was assigned by the GRU in 1967.

Just like the CIA, Isadora had parceled her information selectively. And I didn't doubt that the parts both of them had left out were the most important.

chapter 41

"**We** need to kill Stepan's son." Bassoff's voice sounded loud through the earpiece buried like a weevil in Reese's ear. Reese adjusted the dial, his face twisted in disgust.

He felt trapped in his own study, an insect in amber, surrounded on three sides by dark wood and the gold and chocolate bindings of old books, the legacy of a passion for collecting that had stayed with him since his late teens. His chair was lodged behind his oversized desk, one wheel stuck on a cable that had managed to escape its mooring of tape. The cable was attached to a scrambler, a gray box studded with tiny lights that blinked so fast they appeared to be a moving line.

Bassoff made a difficult adversary in the best of circumstances. On the surface he and Reese exchanged information and cooperated the way a handler and his agent should. Bassoff asked questions and gave direction and Reese did as he was told, or explained why he couldn't. Beneath the surface, however, their suspicious natures and constant maneuvering kept everything churning furiously. Today Bassoff was at his insufferable worst, and the effect was intensified because Reese couldn't wheel himself away from the desk so that he could at least figuratively escape the man's voice. The sound of it was like wet gravel churning in a metal box.

"Stepan would have told you the same thing," Bassoff continued. "He was a killer from the sky, a man without conscience. He knew as well as anybody there is no room for sentiment in our business."

Reese struggled with Russian. His French and Italian were passable, but he could never seem to wrap his tongue around all the syllables and hard consonants that seemed so representative of the stark Russian landscape. Bassoff knew that, but he still spoke Russian most of the time when they talked, either because it was easier for him to speak obliquely in his native tongue or because he wanted to irritate Reese, Reese never knew which.

But not this time. Today Bassoff spoke English, and he was being as direct as he had ever been. In Reese's experience, a word like *kill* was bad any time, and it was particularly inappropriate during an overseas communication, even one that was scrambled.

"We shouldn't make any foolish moves," Reese said. "Volk might be useful to us."

"You said the same thing about Stepan. All those years you protected the man. I still wonder whether he did our cause more harm than good."

Reese couldn't swear to it, but he thought he heard a slight hesitation before the word *our*—a subtle way to imply suspicion. Bassoff had a nasty habit of slurping all the time, every sluicing intake delivered with perfect clarity through Reese's state-of-the-art earpiece, prickling his skin. Despite his concern, Reese answered within the same rhythmic beat of their conversation, careful not to rush in with words or allow a telltale pause.

"Only if you choose to ignore the reams of radar technology he provided for all those years."

Bassoff said nothing for a moment, breathing heavily and making a clicking sound with his mouth. Reese pictured him alone in some utilitarian office, mentally sorting through the possibilities like a rooting hog. Perhaps remembering—and wondering about—the furious days in the '80s when so much changed with such blinding speed. Information overload on both sides, everyone's lips locked around the nozzle of a gigantic hose blasting a never-ending stream of data—memos, reports, analyses, spreadsheets, transcriptions, diagrams, engineering prints, photographs, and case files—until all of them were choking on it.

Reese liked to remember those times. Those were the years when Stepan and all the others were most effective, when the fact checking and the double- and triple-sourcing for which Bassoff and his kind were so notorious failed to keep pace. Decades of work culminating in a payoff measured in short bursts, sometimes one line buried among thousands, waiting to be "discovered" by some rising star in the KGB or GRU.

But the part that he liked most was that the JANUS project had the potential to be a beautiful refrain, one last chance to repeat the successes of the past.

"Stepan's son," Bassoff said, returning to the topic. "His heart is in the right place. Blindly loyal to Mother Russia, the kind of man who would charge an enemy line with nothing more than a broken bottle. That's the problem. He's unpredictable."

Reese enjoyed the irony of the moment. Bassoff had stepped into the punch. He may have let the General make all the arrangements, but Bassoff was the person who had decided to send Volk to America. And he'd probably done it *because* Volk was unpredictable. He'd hoped Volk might turn over a rock and find something—or someone—rotten. Find the person behind all the things that had gone wrong. To find *me*, Reese thought.

But sending Volk to America was like tossing a bomb into a room full of airplane parts and hoping the explosion resulted in something that could fly. A true sign of desperation, one that Bassoff now wanted to erase as quickly as possible. Because by now, Reese was sure, Bassoff had gotten the mikrat. He would have seen the doctored Venona cable with the words *Beneš Czech delegation* and he would have connected the dots that led back to Reese. Bassoff didn't need Volk anymore.

"Let's give him a few days," Reese said, knowing Bassoff would do nothing of the sort. "See what he shakes loose over here."

Bassoff snorted. Sucked saliva. Hung up.

chapter 42

High mountains loomed to the south and east as we approached Santa Fe, glowing blood-red in the light from the afternoon sun.

"Sangre de Cristo," Rhodes identified the range from the back-seat. "The Blood of Christ."

"Superstitious nonsense," York said, peering past me through the passenger-side window to get a better view.

But I wasn't thinking about the scenery. I'd spent the trip north from Albuquerque trying to understand my father's motives and, now that we were close to her home, wondering about the woman York had called my stepmother. Mary Montoya. Stepan's wife for two years, divorced in 1985. Impersonally described in his file as 57 years old, 5'4", 125 pounds, black hair, brown eyes, one daughter by a prior marriage, one grandson who lived with her.

"Stop trying to analyze your father," Rhodes said. "He did what he thought was right. Who are you to judge?"

"Of course he did the right thing," York said. "He helped end the most murderous regime in history. Everything else is secondary."

I wanted to ask why they were taking me on a field trip like this, but didn't. I figured they were wondering the same thing I was about my father: Where was his loyalty for all those years, with America or Russia? They wanted to know one way or the other and, if their worst fears were confirmed, to assess the damage. The purpose of this trip, I thought, was to jar something loose from Mary Montoya about my father or about her work as a security official at the Los Alamos facility where they were both employed.

We crested a hill. Below us, Santa Fe looked like a cubist's dream. Subdued colors of the desert—pink, turquoise, and copper hues—painted on square and rectangular blocks of adobe and wood, all of it jumbled together in the purple shadows of the Sangre de Cristo range. York drove north into the city center, then east, heading toward the foothills of the mountains, which cooled to pale lavender as we approached. We drove into a neighborhood of clapboard houses separated by hip-high chain-link fences and driveways of dirt or aggregate. Peeling paint, low-pitched roofs, listing porches. Along the street a few unleashed dogs, a pack of kids riding bikes, and a pickup truck on blocks.

York stopped next to a dark blue Ford Taurus idled curbside in front of a house the color of ash. Three steps up to a tiny porch and a front door flanked by two open windows, white curtains billowing in the cooling breeze. One of the two men inside the Taurus nodded to York.

"Baker and Evans," he told Rhodes. "We have business in Los Alamos, so Volk's all yours for the evening." He slammed the door behind him and rested his elbows on the frame. "You can handle this, right? We'll reconnect in the morning."

Rhodes gnawed the inside of her lip as she watched him walk away. He motioned to the passenger of the Taurus to get in back, then wedged himself into the front seat. The car pulled away and disappeared around the corner.

"We just went off plan, didn't we?"

She glanced at me as she gathered her briefcase and purse. "Mary Montoya has been told to expect us. As you might imagine, this isn't something she's terribly happy to do." We both climbed out of the SUV. The sun was gone behind the mountains, the sky still light blue, the evening pleasantly cool. "She's not well, so cut her some slack, okay?"

A mastiff barked and bit at the links in the fence separating us from the backyard next door as we approached. Rhodes knocked and we waited on the porch, looking out at the mountains.

"My stepbrother lives north of here," Rhodes said. "He likes to paint. Now I see why. All those colors. It's like watching all the seasons pass in one afternoon."

I reached past her and knocked again. No answer.

The billowing curtains parted to reveal a wooden floor and the corner of a brightly colored rug. In front of the rug was a pair of mismatched chairs, one leaking its stuffing and a coil of a spring, the other a wooden rocker with a padded seat.

A boy raced up the street on his bike, skidded to a stop and hopped off all in one motion, then scurried past us and opened the door. Six or seven years old. Sturdily built, wearing a short-sleeved shirt, blue jeans patched at the knee, and a yellow rubber bracelet on his wrist. We followed him inside.

"Grandma's sick," he said, big-eyed and solemn. "She told me to let you in." He ran to a short hallway, shouted, "They're here!" then stood indecisively, fiddling with his bracelet.

"What's your name?" Rhodes said.

"Roberto Montoya." He puffed his chest when he said his name, rolling the first r and enunciating each syllable.

"You don't have to wait with us if you don't want to, Roberto."

"Okay, see you," he said, and dashed out the front door.

Rhodes sat on the edge of the upholstered chair. I walked over to a small fireplace. The mantel held framed pictures of Roberto atop a horse, posing with his classmates, and standing outside the entrance to Disneyland. Next to the pictures, an unlit candle, melted and listing. It smelled like cinnamon. The door to the kitchen had been left ajar. Dirty dishes piled in the sink, more on a metal dinette.

"You favor your father."

Mary Montoya was leaning on a walker in the hall door. Frail almost beyond belief, wearing a shapeless shift made of canary-yellow cotton and a blue shawl hung over her shoulders. Her skin hung in folds the color and texture of terra-cotta. Her eyes had sunk so far into her skull that she seemed to be peering from a cave. Slit tennis balls had been fitted over the front two feet of the walker, which she lifted carefully to take measured steps into the living room and settle painfully into the wooden rocker.

"You're with the FBI?" she said to Rhodes.

"Close enough," Rhodes said. "We're sorry to bother you, Ms. Montoya."

"Mary. I'm sure your colleagues have already told you that I won't talk about Stepan. I won't allow you to throw his memory to the wolves."

"That's not why we're here."

"Of course not." Mary smoothed the fabric on her lap, her gaze cast down until the job was done to her satisfaction. Then she peered up at me, studying me as if I were a model posing for a painting. After an uncomfortable period of silence, she eased back into the rocker. "So. You're his son." She gestured toward Rhodes. "I won't help them. But maybe I can help you, just a little."

"Thank you."

"*Tal padre, tal hijo.* You understand what this means?"

"I can guess."

"I'm sure you can. Like father, like son. He was good at *guessing* things, too. A fine talent to have." She pulled a handkerchief from the pocket of her shift and coughed into it.

"You're ill?"

"Pancreatic cancer. I'll be dead in months."

No hint of self-pity, just a simple fact. In my imagination I subtracted the effects of the cancer and erased two and a half decades of wear and tear, trying to see her as my father would have seen her. Twenty-five years ago she would have been lithe, raven-haired, smoldering. In some ways that vision of her reminded me of the way I pictured Isadora as a younger woman. Now, wasted to nearly nothing, Mary rocked gently in her chair, the colored mountains framed in the window behind her, still studying me with a curious intensity.

"What will happen to the boy?" I said after a quiet time.

"I've done my best for him, but nothing will be easy."

She continued rocking. Pulled her shawl tighter around her thin shoulders as though the room had grown colder. "You have a woman in Russia?"

Rhodes cocked her head, waiting for the answer.

"Yes."

"Just one? No lovers? No little dalliances with the girls in the clubs or the women in the hotels when you travel?"

"No."

Mary Montoya rested her head against the curved crest rail, sighed, and gave a barely perceptible nod to say that it was the answer she had expected.

"Tell me, *hijo pródigo*, now that you have met the American wife of your father. Did he love me? Was I the one who was always in his thoughts?"

I didn't answer.

"*Tal padre, tal hijo.* See how quickly you understand everything?" She closed her eyes and seemed to shrink even further into herself. "Find her. Find the one he loved in Los Angeles. She can give you answers."

"I don't get it," Rhodes said on the drive back into downtown Santa Fe. "Who are you supposed to find?"

I had guessed correctly that the purpose of this exercise from NCIX's point of view had been to use me to pry information out of Mary. They thought she would tell me more than she had been willing to tell them. And she had.

Or at least I thought I understood what Mary was trying to tell me. Stepan didn't love her. He loved another woman, and that woman could tell me more—more about why he did what he did, more about what kind of man he was. But I had already met that other woman. I had spent hours with her, and she hadn't told me any of those things.

Isadora had doled out her information selectively, hopscotching across sixty years of history, accusing my father of being a traitor, giving no hint that he was her lover. I had unfinished business with Isadora, but I certainly wasn't going to tell Rhodes or the CIA who she was.

"Who did Mary say you're supposed to find?" Rhodes repeated.

"The cancer is eating her brain."

"Don't patronize me, Colonel. I was there. Don't you patronize me."

chapter 43

Rhodes drove us to another Days Inn, this one made of stucco with faux wooden beams jutting from its facade.

"Tomorrow, Los Angeles," Rhodes said, clattering her roller bag across the tiled lobby to the reception desk.

"What about tonight?"

She cocked her head, waiting for an explanation.

"What's York doing in Los Alamos?"

"That's his business."

"Let's take a ride."

She glanced at the clock mounted on the wall behind the reception desk. Not yet nine o'clock. "I have someone . . . Look, there's nothing to see in Los Alamos at this time of night except empty buildings."

"My father worked there for two years."

"Back in the eighties. Everything has changed since then."

"What else are we going to do?"

"Babysitting you isn't my only job."

"I'll drive, you write your reports and send your e-mails."

"Let me count the things wrong with that. You have no license. You're an agent of a foreign government—"

I held up my passport and the ring with the key to the SUV. "I'm also a diplomat and an excellent pickpocket."

With an exasperated sigh she wheeled her bag around and clacked over the floor tile and out the door. "Take Highway 285. Follow the signs."

Around twenty miles later I took Exit 502 toward Los Alamos. We hadn't spoken a word. Rhodes had concentrated on her laptop—still upset, I think, by my refusal to say anything about what I thought of Mary Montoya—while I followed the yellow line west, not knowing what to expect when we got there. Probably nothing, just another sleepy desert town. A sign said we were still ten miles east of the city when blue and red flashes appeared in the rearview mirror.

Rhodes looked up from her computer. "How fast are you going?"

"Under the limit."

"Then why are they stopping us?"

Call it Russian paranoia. My insides were churning. The flashing lights meant something worse than a traffic violation, I was sure of it. "Do you have a gun?"

"Don't be ridiculous."

She retrieved a leather wallet from her purse and opened it on her lap with the badge exposed while I pulled to a stop at the side of the road. The strobing lights of the approaching car made her movements appear jerky and surreal. I watched in the rearview as it pulled up behind us. Its lights were mounted behind the grill.

"Big car, American brand, not marked."

"Relax."

Three men got out and walked to the SUV. One of them hung back while the other two split up to approach her window and mine separately. They both wore suits. The one nearest me was tall and thin, one hand flattening his tie to his chest in a seemingly unconscious gesture. I couldn't see his face, just the bottom of his chin.

When Rhodes rolled down her window, the man who peered

inside wore his gray hair and beard cropped short. Skin the color of creamy coffee, frown lines on his forehead, questioning eyes. A badge was clipped to the outside of his chest pocket. He didn't glance at her badge and ID.

"Roger Drake," he said. "Can I have a word, Ms. Rhodes?"

She joined him outside. The murmur of their voices carried, but not any of the words. A breeze fluttered the jacket and tie worn by the man standing beside my window. I still couldn't see his face. The butt of a 9 millimeter peeked from a shoulder holster under his left arm. He pressed his tie flat again. His shoes crunched gravel as he turned his back to the dust blown in the wind. A minute passed. Rhodes raised her voice, her tone argumentative—something about not returning to Santa Fe, immediately or otherwise. I couldn't hear Drake's reasons why he thought we shouldn't go to Los Alamos.

When I checked the side mirror, the third man had disappeared. I assumed he was on the passenger side, but then I saw him straighten near the rear wheel well on the driver's side, wiping his hands on his pants.

Rhodes got into the SUV and slammed the door behind her. "They want us to go back. I told them to go to hell."

I rolled up the windows, clicked on the blinker, and made a U-turn.

"What are you doing? You're going to reward those people for behaving like Nazis?"

"We're in trouble."

"You're crazy."

We topped a ridge, started down. The lights of the car disappeared behind us. I accelerated, looking for a side road.

"Slow down!"

"We were there too long if it was just a homing beacon," I said, thinking out loud.

She dug into her purse and came out with a subcompact Beretta. "Listen, Volk, I don't know what's gotten into you—"

She hadn't refastened her seatbelt. I skidded to a stop that threw her into the dashboard and then plucked the gun from her hand when she rebounded into the seat. I opened the door, jumped out, ran around the hood, jerked open the passenger door, and hauled Rhodes out by her arm. My face was so close to hers that our noses touched.

"Run! Now!"

And she did. She galloped ahead of me so quickly I labored to catch up after grabbing her purse from the floor of the SUV, following her down a short slope toward a rutted dirt road running parallel to a barbed-wire fence. My left leg burned, and by the time we reached the fence I was hobbling. I swung over it, using a wooden post for support. Rhodes followed with only a little help from me. Ten paces brought us to a gully. We crouched there, both of us panting.

"What the hell are you doing, Volk?" Rhodes hissed.

I slapped her purse into her hands. "Is your phone in here?"

"Why?"

"Call your stepbrother. The one who likes to paint. Tell him to pick us up at mile marker ninety-four. That's three miles east of here, so we need to get moving. It won't take long for your friends back there to figure out we weren't inside that thing when the bomb blew."

"What are you talking about?" she said, just as the SUV exploded.

chapter 44

"I've never met or heard of anyone named Roger Drake before to-night." Rhodes massaged the instep of her left foot, wincing. "He flashed CIA credentials and told me to take you back to Santa Fe."

We were crouched in the darkness near mile marker 94, both of us coated with dust from our dive into the gully and the long walk just completed. Initially she was frightened, then angry. I'd had to talk her out of going back to confront the man named Drake and his cohorts, telling her that they were long gone anyway. The wailing sirens of emer-gency vehicles carried from the direction of Los Alamos, the third set since the explosion.

"Then?"

"I told him we were going to Los Al anyway. He must have been surprised when you turned back."

"What reason did he give for refusing to let us go on?"

She checked the bottom of her injured foot. "He said York hadn't authorized you to leave Santa Fe."

"York's dirty."

She considered for a moment. "You don't know that."

"He's dirty. And he didn't care that you were going to fry with me."

"I've known York for ten years. He's not a murderer. He wouldn't kill me *or* a Russian agent. This is something your people would do."

"I'm not a Russian agent. I'm a man trying to find out what happened to his father."

"Right."

A Volkswagen Beetle slowed at the mile marker, its brake lights bouncing off the concrete ribbon of road like a red tail.

"That's my stepbrother," Rhodes said. "I'm already sorry I called him."

"Keep him in the dark. He doesn't need to know what happened back there."

We ran for the car. Rhodes opened the door and held the front seat forward so I could crawl into the back.

I hesitated for a moment, thinking that maybe Rhodes had it right. Maybe this *was* a Russian hit, not one ordered by the Americans. And if that was true, then Bassoff had to be behind it. Why was it suddenly so damned important to kill us? I wondered. What changed?

Rhodes and her stepbrother talked quietly in the front as we drove. As far as I could tell, he asked no questions about why his stepsister and a strange man needed to be picked up on the side of the road at midnight. The city of Santa Fe was a soft white glow on the horizon when I leaned between the front seats, interrupting their conversation.

"We need to go all the way to Albuquerque. Drop us near the airport, somewhere out of the way."

He looked to Rhodes for guidance, avoiding my gaze in the mirror. She chewed the inside of her lower lip. After a moment she told him to pull over at the next place we came to, and he did that a few minutes later, crunching over the gravel outside a brightly lit truck stop that was busy even this late. He stayed in the car while we got out and walked to the outside corner of the food market.

"I shouldn't have involved him," Rhodes said.

She brushed her hair back, her hand shaking. I took her hand in mine and held it, feeling the trembling and the coldness there.

"You didn't have a choice," I said.

"Yes, I did. I could have called my boss."

"I wouldn't have let you do that. Anyway, how do you know you can trust your boss?"

She wore an expression of fear and shock, her third stage of emotion since the explosion. This was not—could not be—happening, her face seemed to say. She shifted her weight to lean her shoulder into my chest, and I realized that her whole body was shaking.

"Seventeen years I've worked with her. That's how I know. Don't you trust the people who give you orders?"

"No."

"You're impossible."

I needed to change plans. My duffel was gone in the explosion, along with my cash, clothes, and cell phone. Rhodes wasn't going to help me get to Los Angeles, not unless she had approval from her boss or someone higher in the chain of command. An hour removed from a bomb that should have killed her and she was already back riding the same rails.

"Give me an hour, then call it in."

"No." She stepped away from me and reached for her phone.

I liked Rhodes. I thought she was honest and committed to the things she believed. But I couldn't trust the people she worked for. And I needed that hour.

"I have to do this my way," I said as gently as I could. "I need your phone and your gun."

She stared up at me, her face a pale oval, eyes wide. For a moment I thought she would refuse, but then she reached into her purse and handed me her cell phone and her subcompact Beretta. We walked back to the Beetle and she got in the front seat and I climbed in behind her and instructed her stepbrother to drive north, back the way we had come. I took his cell phone off the charger and put it in my pocket. Six miles later I told them to get out, and I slid behind the wheel. I held up the Beretta so that Rhodes could see it.

"Do you have an extra magazine for this?"

"Be serious. I fire it four times a year—on the range. Look, Colonel, you're making a mistake. You'll be caught before dawn. Stay with me, and let's sort this thing out together."

"I can't trust your people anymore."

"Trust *me*."

"I do trust you. But not anybody else, not in this country, at least."

I drove back to the truck stop, tossing both phones out the window halfway there. Parked the Beetle under a light so Rhodes and her stepbrother would be able to find it without looking too hard, and left the keys under the driver's seat. Waited until one of the truck drivers hopped into the cab of a rig hauling freshly cut logs, then climbed onto the trailer and lay flat in the space between the stacks as he headed south to Albuquerque and then, luckily enough, west on I-40 toward Flagstaff. The bark was still on the logs, and my cramped quarters were uncomfortable and sticky with resin as I stretched out and let the miles and the hours roll past. I figured I could hop one truck after another and make it all the way into Los Angeles with nobody the wiser.

PART V

It is essential to seek out enemy agents who have
come to conduct espionage against you and to
bribe them to serve you. Give them instructions
and care for them. Thus doubled agents are
recruited and used.

—Sun Tzu, *The Art of War*

chapter 45

"How could you possibly *miss* a hit you weren't even supposed to take?" Reese made a conscious effort to unclench his fists. Half-moon indentations lined the heels of both palms, livid under the light from his desk lamp.

"What's done is done," Bassoff said, his voice clear through the receiver screwed into Reese's ear. "Time now for damage control, not recriminations. Volk still needs to go away."

"No matter what happens to Volk, the hornet's nest you've riled up won't simply *go away*. Not this time."

Not after an NCIX agent was nearly blown apart by a car bomb in rural New Mexico. NCIX, CIA, FBI, and the NSA were all in an uproar. Agents were scouring the country, and Homeland Security—a name that always made Reese shudder at its Orwellian absurdity—had raised the National Threat Advisory from yellow to orange.

"You can manage them." Bassoff was all oily smoothness now. So far he hadn't slurped once during the call. "Just make sure Volk goes away," he said again.

"The repercussions from your little adventure will infect everything we do, including our latest project."

JANUS was important to Bassoff, Reese knew. In fact, if Reese had succeeded so far—and he felt sure he had—then Bassoff believed the project was more important to him than it was to Reese. Bassoff would already have spent countless hours toting the value of the military technology he expected Reese to provide. But in truth JANUS represented Reese's crowning achievement, and now the most important component of the project might have been scuttled by Bassoff's heavy-handedness. If too many people started investigating Reese and Lorelei, not even Matthews and his boss, the deputy director of the NSA, could stop them. The last delivery might not happen.

"Take Volk off the board," Bassoff said, using the same hectoring tone a schoolteacher might use on an unruly child. "Take him out now, not later."

"He's vanished. Like smoke. Who knows where he'll turn up next? You had him locked away in a Lefortovo hole. Why didn't you keep him there?"

Bassoff slurped, finally, a sharp sound that made Reese wince. "We all have our problems. Factions, isn't that what you call them there? Russia is no more monolithic than your country."

Reese bit his tongue when Bassoff used the word *factions*. Bassoff himself had made the decision to send Volk to America, Reese knew. The General merely facilitated. But Reese chose not to argue the point. Better to keep quiet about what he knew. Know everything, hold it close, reveal selectively—all practices that had served him well over the years. Now he needed to use them to buy time. *Just a few more days.*

"What did you say?"

"Nothing," Reese said. "I'll handle Volk. Stop interfering over here. Russia is your turf, America is mine."

He disconnected, then stared out the window at the Pacific. Gray and roiled this morning, clouds hanging low in the sky, fingers of sunlight poking between the gaps. He thought about Stepan's son loose in America. Where would he go? What would he do? If Volk was cut from the same cloth as his father, he would make his way to Los Angeles, the place where his father died.

Volk would take the fight to his enemy.

Reese drummed his fingers on the armrest of his wheelchair. Who epitomized Los Angeles during those years—Stepan's Los Angeles, at least—more than Katarina? Gone now from America for more than twenty years, but Katarina was not one to vanish without leaving her mark. If she was still alive, he could find her.

He switched on the computerized electronics that masked the source and location of his calls and altered his voice, then made a series of overseas connections, circling closer with each one. Finally he reached a man in the Kremlin who gave him the name Katarina had assumed nearly two decades before.

Isadora.

Reese rolled the name on his tongue, liking the feel of it, remembering her from the halcyon days of the eighties, lissome and graceful and oh so radiant. Not the qualities one would suspect in an officer from the KGB's First Chief Directorate.

Two hours later he had her on the phone.

Yes, she had seen Volk. Only a few days ago. "Like his father, but harder," she said. "Cruel, almost."

"I need your help."

"What's in it for me?" she said, and Reese smiled at the memories her question brought back.

chapter 46

I switched rides in Flagstaff. Cold and sore from the six-hour trip, I scavenged a meal when a delivery girl left her truck idling and trotted into an apartment complex with a stack of boxes in her arms, leaving several pizza boxes behind in blue insulated bags. Then I hopped onto the bed of a flatbed truck at a service station and wedged myself between two pallets loaded with plywood and shingles, the stacks covered by a canvas tarp. I could have hitched, but I didn't want to leave a trail, not knowing whether a bulletin had been issued for my arrest. Probably not, since the CIA and NCIX wouldn't want to start a panic over a rogue Russian agent—or whatever else they might have labeled me— but I couldn't be sure.

The flatbed took me all the way to the I-15 junction in Barstow. We hit a summer squall just as we entered California—rain sweeping in sheets illuminated by the lightning-laced sky—so I was soaked by the time the driver stopped to eat. A box truck with a faulty hasp, the inside loaded with alkaline barrels of dry-cleaning chemicals, took me to the coast.

My clothes were almost dry by the time I piled out. My stump ached, and the bruises from Zubko's truncheon throbbed with renewed intensity when I tried to stretch my stiffened limbs. Although I couldn't see water, I smelled the sea in the distance and saw the reptilian shapes of oil pump jacks when I passed between two storage depots. A sign for a trucking firm told me I was in or near the port of Long Beach. The air was misty and cool, but the glow behind the clouds suggested the sun was trying to burn its way through.

First thing, I needed money. I trudged along a row of industrial buildings that ran parallel to the rush of sound from a nearby expressway. Several warehouses, a storage yard, a distribution center. Trucks rumbled past, a few cars. I kept my head down and walked with a shambling gait. One car slowed, but nobody bothered me.

Four blocks away I turned into an alley, headed away from the ocean smell. The corrugated steel wall of a tall warehouse loomed on one side, a rusted chain-link fence guarding rows of containers and trailer vans on the other.

Ahead were two men, one old and the other young. They didn't see me coming. The old man was leaned back into the fence, his sleeve rolled up to reveal nut-brown skin stretched over bulging veins and thin cords of muscle, a tourniquet made from a length of rubber tubing cinched around his bicep. A silver spike glinted in his hand. The young man wore his hair cut short, low-slung jeans, and a white T-shirt. He held up his hand in a placating gesture when he heard the grate of asphalt under my boots.

"*No problema?*" he said, backing away, and I stepped close and crunched his jaw with an uppercut. He toppled straight back, all in one piece like a falling log. His head rattled the chain links musically, and then he slumped to the ground with his chin on his chest.

The old man started to run away, but I grabbed his collar. His feet bicycled in the air, and he thumped to the ground. I motioned for him to stay there, then squatted next to the dealer. His eyes were open, but empty. Bubbly pink drool slid down his chin. I removed a foil packet from his limp hand, gave it to the old man, and told him to go. He crawled for a while, then struggled to his feet and staggered off.

A fake Rolex clasped the dealer's wrist. His pockets contained a banded stack of cards with pictures of nude women and the number to call to arrange sex with them, a baggie of marijuana and a pipe, and nearly five hundred dollars—three hundreds, the rest in twenties, tens, and fives. I pocketed the money and went searching for clothes and a phone.

I found a used clothing store less than a mile up the road. Traded my soiled clothes and thirty dollars for a clean suit, lightweight and grayish-blue, something I thought would blend in. "Worn just once," the proprietor lied unnecessarily. I bought a cell phone at a convenience store along with a card that gave me thirty minutes of international talk time to Russia. Walked outside to the back of the store and spent another fifteen minutes figuring out how to use the phone and dialing numbers—first to get an access line to the carrier, then to punch in the code from the card, then to dial the actual number—before I finally made a connection. Moscow was eleven hours ahead of Los Angeles, so it would be 3 A.M. there.

Listening to the ring, I wished for Valya, but by now she would be in Georgia or South Ossetia, somewhere along the border, perhaps lying awake under a canopy of stars near one of the hundreds of villages there, watching the sun rise over the jagged peaks of the Caucasus.

On the third ring somebody picked up without saying anything.

"Vadim?"

"Alexei?" Vadim said.

"I need you to take a trip." I gave him directions to Isadora's dacha and told him her name. "Tell her I need the name of the detective in Los Angeles who tried to track her down, something to do with my father's murder. Do it now, then call me at this number," I said, and gave it to him.

"Got it."

I ended the call. Leaned against the rough texture of a stucco wall spray-painted red and green and black with graffiti. Two hours, that's how long it would take Vadim to reach Isadora. I dialed information, told the operator to connect me, then waited, one ring, two—

"Lorelei. How may I direct your call?" the receptionist said in a candied voice.

It was a good question. Holding the phone to my ear with my

shoulder, I took the blood-stained pen from my pocket and turned it in my hands. Who was Everett Walker trying to implicate with this pen?

"May I help you?" the saccharine voice said.

I hit the End button.

The sky was cut into thirds by twin contrails that had widened into puffy whorls turned red by the late afternoon sun. LORELEI. All I had was the name of a vast conglomerate. Somehow I needed to learn the identity of the person pulling the strings. Probably someone close to the top, I thought, someone with access to the company's deepest secrets. My target would have survived corporate downsizings, restructures, mergers, and management fads, skirted the career killers of bad quarterly reports and annual meetings and performance reviews. Maybe a scientist working in the throbbing heart of research and development, privy to all Lorelei did, covertly directing resources and new developments—a ghost in the corporate machine.

I went back inside the store and plucked a map from a display rack. Bought a cellophane-wrapped sandwich, two protein bars, and water, and scarfed it all down on the move, trudging along a street a few blocks off the water but still running parallel to it. Small eateries, a self-service laundry, a used bookstore, two coffee places, a muffler shop, then commercial buildings made of brick or stucco, the tallest only three stories. After twenty minutes of that I turned toward the sound of the waves at a place that sold surfing equipment and kept walking until I found a motel, its parking lot empty except for two cars. One of them, a Dodge Caravan, looked as if it had settled into the fractured blacktop and grown roots. The engine on a primer-gray Honda Accord pinged as it cooled.

Five minutes later I had a room, and in ten more I'd taken a shower and was waiting on the edge of the bed for Vadim to call. I flopped onto my back and stared at the popcorn-textured ceiling, stained in shapes like brown amoebas from upstairs water leaks. I put the phone next to my ear so I would be sure to hear it ring if I fell asleep.

Vadim would be at Isadora's dacha within an hour.

chapter 47

Reports flowed in to Reese's computer from all points on the map, routed to him through Lorelei's vast network and the servers made available to him by Brock Matthews and his boss. As a former Under Secretary of Defense, Reese already enjoyed a high security clearance, and his had been further augmented on the orders of the NSA's deputy director in Fort Meade. Linked to an array of foreign and domestic government agencies and civilian contractors, Reese was able to access real-time data from sources ranging from the LAPD to the CIA and the NSA. Now, parked at his desk in his home office, he scrolled through dispatches, bulletins, official statements, digests, memos, and directives, while Santori fidgeted in a dark leather chair on the other side of Reese's desk with an open file in his lap.

An agent from the FBI field office in Seattle claimed to have seen Volk buying fresh fish at Pike Place Market. Border Patrol reported a sighting at the crossing in Tijuana. A cop in Flagstaff took a call from a pizza delivery girl who described a man who matched Volk's description. The El Paso County Sheriff's office dispatched an officer to check out a call from an off-duty policewoman who claimed to have spotted him at a taco stand wearing a blue bandana and an eye patch.

Meanwhile, NSA and NCIX were in an uproar, their top officials demanding answers from the secretary of Homeland Security and one step away from requesting a congressional hearing. The CIA was in denial mode. No way had any of their agents stopped Rhodes and Volk near Los Alamos, to say nothing of planting an explosive, and everybody needed to stop making accusations and get on with the business of figuring out just what the hell really happened out there in the high desert.

Reese had learned over the years to confront unpleasant facts and take immediate action. One way to look at the events of the past two days would be to question whether the time had come to abort JANUS. Take the hit and move on—or move out, as the case may be.

But sifting through all the bad news, another way presented itself, possibly a better way. The original plan was to wait until Bassoff demanded all the latest data developed by JANUS, then deliver the information through normal means. A tamper-evident secure bag, a blind courier—someone who knew nothing about the cargo he carried or about the people watching him—and a private airplane. But maybe a different courier would do. One with unimpeachable credentials.

Santori cleared his throat. "Rhodes didn't get a clear look at two of the men who stopped them. But she talked to the third. Called himself Roger Drake. He was black, mid-fifties to early sixties, short gray hair and beard, just under six feet tall. She says that his ID and badge looked legit, but nobody has any clue who he is. He must have been good, because Rhodes is no dummy, and she didn't suspect anything until Volk hustled her out of the vehicle about thirty seconds before it exploded."

Reese pretended to study something on his computer monitor, but he was really eyeing Santori, and trying to recall one of Churchill's quotes, something to the effect that it was the clerks—the men who made sure the trains ran on time—who gave Hitler his power. Santori was worse than that. He was the most despicable kind of traitor—a man willing to sell out his country for a few dollars. Reese was sick of playing the game with him. Just having to *act* ignorant annoyed Reese, as did the thought that someone who didn't know better might not see any difference between the things Santori did and the things Reese did.

"This smells like one of the big wet ops contractors," Santori said. "Echo and Blackridge both have offices in Vegas. One of them could carry out the planning and logistics on a short time line. Acquire identification and explosives. Import talent from anywhere in the world." He ticked off each point on his fingers. "Pick a spot, lay the trap, plant the device. Boom!"

Santori wasn't telling him anything. Of course Reese would be suspicious of the black ops contractors, sophisticated outfits that had made billions fighting America's undeclared wars. A few had been smacked down for abuses in Iraq, but the Department of Defense continued to use them, and they were still one of the preferred ways for the intelligence agencies to conduct their covert operations. Many of the officers and owners of those companies were former CIA officers and station chiefs themselves. One of them had approached Lorelei in the months leading up to the "Shock and Awe" campaign in Iraq in '03, wanting capital to form a commercial division of mercenaries. Think of the profits to be made while the military is bogged down in the sandbox of Afghanistan and Iraq, he'd said, before Reese turned him down. But those weren't the people Reese was after right now.

"The first step is to find Volk," he said.

"And terminate him?"

"If you mean 'kill him,' Santori, then spit it out."

"Yes, sir. Do you want me to have him killed?"

Reese scowled as he adjusted his gloves. Not only were his damned hands weak and bereft of fine motor skills, they were always cold these days. But they offered a good excuse not to look at Santori. This was one of the hardest parts, to sit across his desk from this waste of carbon and pretend he didn't know that Santori had done Bassoff's bidding and hired the hit in Los Alamos personally.

It was odd, he reflected. Santori knew that Bassoff had already told Reese to kill Volk—in other words, Santori knew that Reese had no choice in the matter. But Reese still had to act as though he *did* have a choice, because otherwise Santori would realize that Reese had identified him as Bassoff's agent. And so they both went through their little charade, Reese acting like he was making a decision, and Santori acting like the decision was news to him.

"Yes," Reese said, adopting a tone of command, "Volk needs to die."

chapter 48

The ringing phone startled me awake.

"McIntyre is the name of the detective who investigated your father's murder," Vadim said. The sound of his raspy voice broke up somewhere between Moscow and Los Angeles. "Isadora couldn't remember his first name."

"Spell it."

"She didn't know how."

Using Everett Walker's bloody pen, I started writing on one of the bills I'd taken from the drug dealer, trying to think of the different ways that name might be spelled. *MacIntyre, McIntyre, MacEntyre, Macentire.*

"What else can I do, Alexei?" Vadim said.

"Nothing for now." I thought of Rykov, Zubko, and the parakeet-faced cop in the trash bin. "Watch yourself."

He gave me his dry, raspy laugh and hung up.

Information provided the number for LAPD's Robbery-Homicide Division at Parker Center.

"RHD." A man's voice, the gruff antithesis of the receptionist at Lorelei.

"Detective McIntyre."

"McIntyre's not on the job anymore. What can I do for you?"

"Do you have a way to reach him?"

"Who's this?"

I didn't want to raise questions. Not yet, at least. With all the people looking for me after the explosion in New Mexico, I *couldn't* raise questions. An official inquiry about my father would set off alarms from here to Washington.

The man on the other end of the line huffed in my ear. "You gonna give me a name?"

The stains in the ceiling appeared to expand and contract in the flickering light from the overhead bulb, the room turning dark, then lighter, then dark again. I tightened my grip on the phone and couldn't think of what to say next.

"Lots of luck to you. Fucking douche bag." He said the last part under his breath as he was hanging up, but it came through clearly enough. Holding the dead phone in my hand, I thought that I might as well have just had a conversation with Zubko. Some personality traits cross cultural lines, particularly among cops.

I dialed information again. The exasperated operator said too many people named McIntyre were listed for him to help me, especially if I didn't have a first name and couldn't pinpoint the city where that person lived. "I have several just in Long Beach," he said, just before hanging up.

There was no phone book in the room, so I went out to one of the busier streets and hitched a ride with a fiftyish man wearing a straw hat who chattered about how "people used to help each other before, now we're all castaways on our own private islands." He talked enough that I didn't have to, just said thanks when he dropped me next to a pay phone on Broadway near Redondo. One MacIntyre and three McIntyres lived in Long Beach. I called them all and asked for Officer McIntyre, saying the name the way Vadim said it. The responses ranged from a dull "Huh?" to "Don't call this number again."

On the sidewalk next to the pay phone a woman pushed a stroller and a pack of teenaged boys lounged beneath a streetlight, bare-chested, shirts hanging from their back pockets.

No good trying to do it this way. The L.A. basin was too vast, packed with too much humanity. I went inside a pizza shop two doors down from the phone and a waiter directed me to an Internet café located less than a mile north on Broadway. I walked there, bought time, searched *Steven Morris*, the name they gave my father in the States, along with the words *Los Angeles*, *homicide investigation*, and *murder*, and got fewer than a thousand hits. Several of them referred to the same article by Anna Wright in the *L.A. Times* Metro section that gave a brief report of a body found in a West Hollywood hotel room, tentatively identified as Steven Morris. That was all. No follow-up story that I could find.

I called the *Times* and asked for Anna Wright. While I was bounced around I learned that she was the person who covered the crime beat. The third person I talked to put me on hold for a long time. My computer monitor backed up to a wall-mounted corkboard covered with ads for handyman services, roommates, musicians and musical instruments, and two lost puppies. To my left, the proprietor busied himself behind a counter, where he served coffee and pastries. A college-aged kid chewed the end of a strand of hair while he studied the screen four computers away from me.

"Anna Wright," said a voice in my ear, clipped, impatient.

"I need information about a story in your paper."

"We don't provide information. We gather it. Sometimes print it. Go to the library, Mr.— what's your name?"

"Morris. John Morris. My father was Steven Morris. He was murdered on 22 May 2004. The police never caught who did it."

I thought I heard a hitch in her breath. I definitely heard the keys of a computer rattling.

"And you're conducting a private investigation?" The clicking continued. "Is that it, Mr. Morris?"

"Something like that. I'm looking for a way to make contact with the detective who conducted the investigation."

"Call LAPD." The way she said the words made it sound more like a question. *Have you done that yet? What did they say?* Something had piqued Anna Wright's interest.

"I can't do that."

"Why not?"

"Because I think they're the ones who killed him."

She didn't take the bait, but I could hear her breathing. The college kid got up to leave, shoving books into a backpack. Through the window beyond him a light rain spattered the glass.

"You have proof?" Wright said.

"No."

"Then you're wasting my time."

I didn't say anything, just waited, hoping her curiosity would make her give information in order to get more out of me.

"What kind of accent is that?"

"Russian."

"Why is a Russian interested in an old murder in Los Angeles?"

"I have about twenty seconds, then my phone dies," I lied.

"Find another phone and call me back on my cell. I'll tell you then." She rattled off a phone number.

"I won't be able to do that. Five seconds. You need to decide."

"Pat McIntyre lives in Culver City. He goes by Mac. Listen—"

I cut the call short. Dialed information. They didn't have a listing for anybody named Pat McIntyre in Culver City. I started to call back to go through the possible derivations of McIntyre's first and last names, then decided to call a cab to take me there. The driver dropped me near a pay phone on Washington Boulevard across the street from a Catholic church made of white stone with a bell tower capped by a cross. The phone book didn't list anybody named Pat McIntyre, nor any Patrick MacIntyre or any other similarly spelled name. A passing nun in a light blue habit stared at me like I was a crazy man when I started laughing to myself.

Anna Wright was no fool.

Dialing from memory, I called her cell phone. She answered on the first ring.

"We need to meet," I said.

chapter 49

Anna Wright tossed her bag to the end of the bench seat across from me and slid into the booth behind it. She had dark skin and glossy black hair that she fanned out with one hand.

"My maiden name's Garcia," she said by way of explanation. "Sixth-generation Spanish land-grant family. And your name is *not* John Morris."

When I'd called her from the pay phone across from the church she told me to meet her here, at a Denny's restaurant a short walk up the road from the white church. I'd been waiting for almost an hour.

"What makes you think that?"

"Steven Morris didn't have a son."

"Yes, he did. His son was born in Leningrad, Russia, shortly before he defected to the United States in a Bear E bomber that had been converted into a spy plane."

Her eyes were set far apart, and they widened as she probed my face for signs of deception. "That explains a few things." She dug into her bag and came out with a newspaper clipping of the same story I'd read earlier on the Internet.

"I've seen that."

"I wrote it right about the time I started working on a story about police corruption. That's why you won't find a follow-up. LAPD buried the case, and nobody raised a stink on behalf of the dead guy. Pat McIntyre was the first detective on the scene. He was also the focus of my investigation."

"Those two things are related?"

A waitress with her hair dyed with pink streaks and a rhinestone stud in her left nostril took our order for coffee.

"There were too many coincidences there," Wright said when the waitress left. "One of them was why McIntyre was at the scene in the first place."

"Why shouldn't he have been?"

"McIntyre was part of RHD's Vi-CAP Section. The guys called in to investigate high-profile murders—perps and victims from O.J. and Manson to Robert Kennedy. Why would he be investigating the murder of some no-name scientist? Guy ends up dead in a ratty hotel room, probably went to hook up with a prostitute and got thumped and dumped. Hell, he probably wasn't even supposed to die. Could be the hooker's boyfriend just swung a little too hard. Not your typical Vi-CAP case."

She took a sip of coffee, then her expression softened. "Sorry, I wasn't thinking."

"I never knew him."

"So fill in the blanks for me. Your father was a defector. That means he was given a new identity, right?"

I nodded. "After years of debriefings. No trial, no hearing, just one prison cell or safe house after another and endless interrogations."

"Then some twenty-odd years later he gets bashed in the skull, and you think it's connected?"

"That's what I want to talk to McIntyre about."

"I spoke to him a few minutes ago. He told me to fuck off. Quite a colorful character, Detective McIntyre."

An L.A. County cruiser pulled up outside the window. Wright followed my gaze, and together we watched another one join the first, then a Culver City police car.

She sipped her coffee, regarding me over the rim of her cup. "Sorry. I had to do it. This came in right before I left to meet you."

She slid a photograph out of her bag and pushed it across the table. A black-and-white shot of my face. Part of Rhodes's sleeve was visible on the left edge of the video still as she walked beside me through the terminal at the Albuquerque airport.

"You have to admit it's a good likeness." She started to say more, then gasped as I showed her the Beretta.

"Lead the way out the back."

"You're not going to use that."

Four sheriff's deputies and a policeman stood on the other side of the plate-glass window, less than ten feet from where we were sitting, but they couldn't see through the tinted glass. They were talking, not yet showing any sign of urgency. Most likely they were told to come pick me up without being briefed about the reason or who I was. I slid out of my side of the booth and into Wright's.

"What are you doing?"

Wright thought I was just another story for her paper. Part of a game that let her brush up against a dangerous world without feeling any of the fear. I looked around to make sure nobody was paying any attention to us. Drove my elbow into her right temple. Looked around again to make sure nobody had noticed, then arranged her with her face against the windowsill, aimed away from the side of the table where the waitress would stand. Slipped out of the booth and through the kitchen, where one of the Mexican cooks watched incuriously as I pushed through the panic bar and out the back door to an alley.

Moving at a fast walk, I made several blocks in minutes. Caught a westbound bus on Venice Boulevard and rode it to the beach, fuming the whole way because I was no closer to finding McIntyre than I had been before I found Anna Wright.

it. Mentally sifting through what I had been told by Bassoff and Isadora—neither of whom I trusted entirely—I knew that at least some of the information my father delivered back to Russia turned out to be wrong.

All of which might be moot now except that Bassoff still wanted to know whether my father turned traitor or whether another agent fed him bad information. If the latter were true, Bassoff had a mole in his network. So he sent me here to dig. Fine, I wanted to know those things, too, both on a personal and a professional level. That made investigating my father's murder—chasing leads like Anna Wright and McIntyre—a priority.

Next, the dead man in my warehouse.

Everett Walker lived most of his life as a GRU agent. The records Valya found in the archived records of the Communist International established that. Two weeks ago he had traveled to Moscow using false papers. He spent three days there looking for me, probably to tell me something about my father. The picture of him and my father on the grounds of the Getty Museum proved that they knew each other, and was probably meant to be his introduction to get me to talk to him. Among Walker's possessions was a concealed microphotograph of a World War II–era decrypted cable. The cable contained a handwritten note—*Beneš Czech delegation?*—pointing to the identity of a still-secret Soviet source. I believed that both Bassoff and NSA agent Brock Matthews thought the cable or the note written on the cable important enough to kill Walker. Walker also carried a pen inscribed with the name LORELEI INDUSTRIES. I felt sure the pen was meant to point a finger at someone inside that company.

All of which made investigating Walker and Lorelei another set of priorities.

Last, somebody wanted me dead badly enough to kill Rhodes in the process. Who? The Americans? I didn't think they would kill one of their own to get to me. Bassoff's mole? I doubted it. I wasn't close enough to anything to generate that kind of response. Bassoff? Maybe. If something had changed and now he no longer needed me, or if I was a loose end needing to be tied up like Rykov and the two cops, then Bassoff would order me killed and he wouldn't care if Rhodes was

Venice Beach was a circus, even at this hour of the evening. Wild colors graffitied on the walls and painted on trees. People of all ages, wearing everything from bikinis to business suits. A woman with an afro colored like a rainbow stepped out of the way of a girl on a unicycle circling a juggler. Bikers and skateboarders and bladers and children gliding by with wheels built into their shoes. Food everywhere. Pizza, burgers, hot dogs, corn dogs, snow cones, fry bread, cotton candy.

I sat on a concrete bench and stared at the ocean, contemplating the thumping, hissing waves and the lighted pier in the distance. Now that the authorities knew I was in Los Angeles the net would tighten. My margin for error, slim before, had almost disappeared. I needed to stop reacting and start planning, beginning with the things I knew or could reasonably infer.

Starting with my father.

Bassoff plotted my father's defection in 1974, then controlled his activities until his death in Los Angeles in 2004. I knew this because Bassoff had told me and because the label affixed in 1975 to the back of my father's photo in his service file with the name *O. Bassoff* confirmed caught in the crossfire. The only thing I could think of that might have changed was that sometime after I left Moscow Bassoff had gotten his hands on the Venona cable. And maybe the words *Beneš Czech delegation?* meant more to him than they did to anyone else.

Ants swarmed on an open bag of potato chips near my foot. A woman strolling hand-in-hand with her husband or boyfriend dropped a bill into the open guitar case of a musician, who sang out, "I sure do like the tips that don't make no sound." I turned my gaze back to the lighted pier.

So where to start? The McIntyre angle seemed stymied for now. I didn't know how to crack open a window into Lorelei; the company was too large, too complex. But I had a lead on Walker—his wife, Sasha Tovar. She might be able to tell me more. And, according to the interview I'd seen on the Internet, she lived somewhere in the Los Angeles area.

The phone rang. Caller ID showed a 310 area code.

I connected to the call without saying anything.

"McIntyre here," a voice said on the other end of the line, a deep rumble with a hint of brogue. "Understand you're looking for me."

I looked around the swirling Venice Beach crowd. Nobody paid any attention to me. "Who told you that?"

"Anna Wright told an L.A. County sheriff's deputy. She was a little worse for wear, but she managed to give him this phone number. He called me because I still carry some weight with guys on the job." The last part sounded as though he was trying to convince himself.

"You investigated the murder of Steven Morris?"

"No. I investigated the murder of Stepan Volkovoy." He waited a moment to let that sink in. "Last two hours I've gotten calls from the CIA, NCIX, and Wright, who's still trying to make a name for herself by dragging LAPD through the mud. Even if it means she has to skin my fat carcass to do it. I figured to go straight to the source of the problem. That'd be you, boyo."

The sea air was heavy with the smell of kelp, marijuana, and fried food. I couldn't stay here. If they had the number they could locate the phone. I needed to keep moving. But at least this call answered the question where to start. I'd have to track down Sasha Tovar later.

"There's a phone booth in Long Beach near the corner of Broadway and Redondo," I told him. "Go there and wait."

"This isn't a fucking treasure hunt, boyo."

I didn't respond. The fact that he had made the phone call told me he would do what I asked. Whatever McIntyre's motivation might be, he wanted the meeting.

"Half an hour," he said.

I memorized the number he'd called from. Turned off the phone. Found a kid on a bike. Deeply tanned, no shirt or shoes, pants so low on his hips they'd probably fall off if he stood up. I gave him two twenties to ride as far north along the boardwalk as he could go and throw the phone away.

"You in trouble, man?"

"Yes."

He looked at the phone and the money in his hand. "Two miles. I'll ride that far. More than that ain't worth my time."

Most people would have taken the money and tossed the phone into the nearest trash can as soon as I was gone. I nodded to show my respect.

"Deal."

chapter 51

I bought a new prepaid cell phone at a Venice beach convenience store. Then I hopped another bus, made one transfer to go south on the 405 to Broadway, then walked the rest of the way to Redondo. There I mingled with a small crowd outside the pizza shop where I'd gotten directions to the Internet café.

A man in blue slacks and a black windbreaker stood next to the phone booth, his head swiveling as he monitored the scene around him. Burly. Most of his weight around his middle. Skinny, old-man legs. A thatch of sandy-gray hair. He checked an alley near the phone, then came back seconds later and stood with his hands in his pockets.

I slid behind a concrete column and looked around for anything suspicious. A fair number of people were milling about, but none seemed interested in McIntyre or me. Nobody silhouetted inside cars when headlights swept over them.

I dialed the number McIntyre had called me from and watched him reach into his pocket for his cell phone.

"What now?" he said.

"Walk north on Broadway."

He hung up and lumbered toward me, looking wary, with one thumb hooked in his waistband. I backed into the niche behind the column and stood facing away from him as he went past the pizza place. Nobody followed. I waited, then crossed Broadway and walked parallel to him.

He didn't seem to like walking, or maybe the idea of being so exposed. He labored along, kept glancing over his shoulder, and nervously fiddled with what I was sure was a gun in his waistband. I walked faster, still looking for surveillance, but I saw nothing suspicious.

After I passed him I crossed back to his side of the street at a crosswalk, pretending to talk on my cell phone. He was focused on what was behind him, not ahead. When he drew even with me I shoved him against a brick wall and twisted his arm behind his back.

"Calm down," he said. "I called you, remember?"

I quick-frisked him. He carried an old-fashioned .38 revolver in a holster clipped to his belt and a clasp knife with a bone handle in his front pocket. I kept both. Grabbed his shoulder to pull him away from the wall and pushed him ahead, falling in beside him.

He blew out a heavy gust of air that smelled like scotch and cigarettes. "All this cloak-and-dagger crap is a waste of time. I need you as bad as you need me."

"Why?"

"Because I want to know who killed your pop as much as you do."

We passed a Taco Bell, the parking lot filled with shiny cars and teenagers of both sexes. One of them hollered something at us that I didn't catch. McIntyre was wheezing after only a few blocks.

"I don't spend night and day worrying about cold cases," he said. "Those days are long gone. But this one was different right from the start."

I shouldered him to the left down a residential street that led toward the ocean. "How so?"

"Because I was the guy they accused of killing him."

My hand was already in my pocket, gripping the butt of the Beretta. Now it tightened. "Did you?"

"No. But if I was going to, I'd have had to wait in line. Your pop made more enemies than friends."

"Who?"

"We gonna find a place to sit or what?"

"Keep moving. Keep talking."

"Here's what happened. Dead guy in a shitty hotel room, skull bashed in with a blunt object—a cop's nightstick. That was our first big clue that this case wasn't your normal homicide. The second was, the Feds took it away within two hours after I arrived at the site. Turned out the vic happened to be a protected federal source."

"Why were you a suspect?"

"Because the nightstick that crushed his skull was mine. My name and induction date were engraved on a metal plate on the goddamn handle. Fucking thing was a gift, not a piece of equipment."

"How did you know that the dead man was a protected federal source?"

He lowered his voice, although nobody was anywhere near us. "I told you, I still got pull. And I looked into this whole thing thoroughly. Believe me, I was motivated, big time."

I didn't believe him. He didn't kill my father. He was old, tired, and self-pitying. No match for the man I imagined my father used to be. But he was lying to me. I wanted to know why.

McIntyre glanced back the way we had come, rubbing his chin on his shoulder as if he were scratching it. I caught his arm and hustled him forward.

"What's the hurry?" he said.

I didn't answer. We were walking fast, almost jogging toward a traffic light marking a major street. Past that I saw ocean darkness and the scattered lights of boats on the water. We crossed at the traffic light. The street ended at a stretch of greenbelt and a small park dedicated to the Lone Sailor, the statue of a seaman overlooking the sand and water. McIntyre pulled up there.

"Wait a minute!" He put his hands on his knees, huffing. "Give me a second, will you?"

The light behind us changed. I watched the cars go through the intersection. One lagged behind. A beige sedan, battered and old, driver slouched low in the seat, a hat covering his eyes.

"I hadn't seen the damn nightstick in months," McIntyre was

saying. "Didn't even know it was missing. Somebody musta pinched it from my locker."

The driver of the sedan raised his head to look at us. Reached his arm out the window—

I dove headlong over a manicured hedge, heard the whistle of bullets pass over my head and the distant sound of shots, two bursts, then squealing tires. I jumped up and peered over the hedge. The sedan's taillights flared as the driver slowed to take a turn, then disappeared. McIntyre had dropped to the ground. He lifted his head just as I bounded over the shrubs and hauled him to his feet.

"Move!" I said, and ran him back the way I'd just come. He tripped and fell over the hedge, landing in the sand on the other side. Before he could recover I rammed the barrel of the Beretta into his back and propelled him down the slope, marching him over forty meters of sand directly into the water.

"What the fuck are you doing?"

When the waves reached our knees I shoved him into the surf. He came up spluttering. I grabbed a handful of hair and pushed his face into the water, all my weight on his back as he bucked and thrashed. When the waves receded I made sure his face stayed buried in the sand. Thirty seconds I waited. Then I pulled his hair to lift his face.

He heaved a huge gasp of air. Coughed, puked seawater and mucus, coughed some more. Another wave washed over us and McIntyre bucked again until I twisted his face out of the water and hissed at him.

"Who just shot at me?"

"Santori!"

The major with the green eyes as flat as oxidized coins, the one I had met in Albuquerque when they showed me my father's Bear. Major Santori.

"Why?"

"I don't know!"

I held his face under the water again, studying the dark beach behind me while he thrashed and flailed. It looked empty, but it wouldn't stay that way. I jerked McIntyre's head up. He coughed and puked more seawater, weakly this time.

"Where does Santori work?"

"Century City. Company called Lorelei."

"How do you contact him?"

"I don't. He calls me."

I jammed his face back into the water and sand, and searched his pocket for his cell phone. Wet, but the display lit up when I opened it. This time I didn't hold McIntyre under for nearly as long, but he gasped and retched even more than before.

"How did you get my number?"

"From Anna Wright." He had trouble getting the words out between choking coughs. "That was the truth. But Santori told me what to do and say."

I'd gotten McIntyre's name from Vadim, who got it from Isadora. That meant that Isadora was connected to Santori, and that Isadora was just as tainted as him.

I clouted McIntyre with the barrel of the Beretta. Did it again to be sure he would stay out. Threw his gun and knife into the sea, dragged him onto dry sand, then took off, jogging into the darkness along the edge of the water.

chapter 52

I jogged along the beach for nearly a kilometer before I opened McIntyre's phone and thumbed through the call history. Based on the times and eliminating the calls made to and from my phones, two numbers looked like they might work. I called them both. The first rang several times then connected to voice mail. A woman's voice. The second rang without anybody answering, not even a voice mail.

I left the beach and took backstreets to the Internet café on Broadway and bought time on another computer, one that couldn't be seen through the window on the street.

From Anna Wright to McIntyre to Santori, I'd made progress. I would wager almost anything that Santori was the man who crushed my father's skull. But I didn't have a way to follow up on Santori right now. So I would go down the other path, and take a harder look at Walker through his wife, Sasha Tovar.

Sasha Tovar didn't have a listed number, but she did have a Web site dedicated to herself and her work. The wife of the late Everett Walker was a statuesque twenty-six-year-old when they married in 1991. He was seventy-one. The gossip about why she had married him, she was quoted as saying in *The Hollywood Reporter*, made her "love him all the more." She had been born in Prague and discovered there by Walker during the filming of *Sign of the Times*, his epic about the Russian Revolution told through the eyes of the idealistic young son of a nobleman émigré.

An artistic photo of Sasha Tovar dominated the home page of her Web site. The timeless portrait could have been made when she was still a young model in Prague or two weeks ago in a Los Angeles studio. Bone-white features that looked as though carved from darkness. Tilted eyes and dramatic cheekbones beneath blond hair swept back and arranged in sleek curves. An ageless, implacable beauty.

Once she was in Los Angeles with her new husband, Sasha modeled, acted in small movie roles, and appeared in two minor plays to lukewarm reviews. According to an article in a trade publication, she found her "true calling" on the other side of the camera while visiting her family in the Czech Republic in 1998. She "discovered a story waiting to be told," she said, and Walker agreed to back it financially. That first documentary told the story of the Nazis' reprisals for the assassination of Heydrich, Hitler's lieutenant and one of the architects of "the Final Solution." The film, called *Nightfall in Lidice*, won an Academy Award for best documentary feature. Clicking through several screens on the computer, I watched several YouTube clips from the film, some of which I'd seen before while researching Walker from the computer in my loft.

I navigated away from her site and Google-searched state and county records for Sasha Tovar and Everett Walker. A deed with both their signatures had been scanned into the county database, showing them as the owners of a home in Hollywood Hills. A more recent "map of the stars" Web page seemed to confirm she still lived there. I memorized the address and directions.

I logged off the computer and paid the clerk. Bought a screwdriver and a palm-sized hammer at an auto parts store and used them to hot-wire a Suzuki motorcycle. Rode it north to Hollywood. Wound higher in the hills among houses so large any Russian oligarch would have been proud to own one. A few probably did. I stopped on the edge of a bluff that overlooked a secluded enclave of mansions and sat astride the bike, studying the layout.

Sasha Tovar lived at the end of a cul-de-sac in a split-level house shaped like a horseshoe open to the hills. White stucco, red tile roof, decorative wrought-iron fixtures. Several lights were on, but only one of them in the upper floor, a muted glow from a long row of windows on a wraparound balcony above the ravine behind the house. At least one unit had the place under surveillance. A van with the logo of a carpet cleaning company painted on its side.

Two hours later, near midnight, I left the motorcycle parked between two cars on the street and scaled the brick wall on the side of a home perched on the bluff overlooking Sasha Tovar's. The back was a U-shaped courtyard dominated by a pool. The pool lights gave off enough illumination to navigate to the rear of the property, where a perimeter of crushed white shells bordered another wall, this one topped with decorative iron spikes.

I landed on the other side in gravel and scrub brush and picked my way along a ravine, crouching beneath a low canopy of trees. Careful to stay in the darkest places, I worked my way higher around a spur of rock to approach Sasha's house from the rear. When I could see the back of the house clearly, I huddled between two boulders beneath an enormous water tower.

The second-floor balcony stretched all the way across the back. Covered patio furniture encircled a stone fire pit, visible in the diffuse light passing through the drawn shades. Nothing changed for more than an hour. Cold wicked through the fabric of my light jacket where it touched stone. A police cruiser made a turn through the cul-de-sac out front, crawling along the street. It remained out of sight for several minutes before its headlights swept away, so I assumed its occupants had stopped to talk to someone in the van.

Another hour came and went. Lights blinked out in the valley below my hideout, but Sasha's house remained the same. Just as I was beginning to wonder whether she was there, a shadow passed in front of the light behind the drapes in the master suite.

I stood and stretched, mentally debating one last time whether to risk going down the mountain. But I didn't really have a choice. This was my one link to Walker and the cable he carried at such a price. How many had paid a similar price? Lives dedicated to gathering the information and lives devoted to protecting it and, once the secrets were out, to break the code and assess the damage. Then what? More of the same. Nearly fifty years of a Cold War that flared in hot spots all over the globe.

The cable opened a door to all those things. But at bottom, there among the stories of all those lives and times, resided a murder. Whoever ordered Walker killed in my warehouse had a reason. If I could find the motive I could learn the answers to all the other questions. But to do that I needed to delve into Walker's past and figure out why he went to Moscow in the first place. And Sasha Tovar represented the one link I had to Walker.

That alone justified the risk I was about to take.

It was 1:31 A.M. when I started down the mountain and crossed the ravine.

chapter 53

Sasha Tovar's house was surrounded by the same kind of brick wall with spiked wrought iron as the one behind her neighbor's. I climbed over it into a backyard half the size of a soccer field, warily alert for a dog while I skirted the pool and a cabana to flatten my back against the rear wall of the house. No lights or sirens triggered by motion sensors. No dogs.

I placed a lawn chair beneath the upstairs balcony and stood on it to reach the base of the balcony deck between two concrete balusters. Chinned up and grabbed one of the balusters about halfway up, and from there it was a simple matter to pull myself higher, swing my good leg over the top of the rail, and land silently on the other side, crouching on all fours.

The light in the bedroom was off now. The darkness accentuated the noises of the night. The rattle and scrape of stones tumbling into the ravine behind me. A high-pitched chuckling that sounded like crying babies—the yammering of coyotes, I realized. A hollow voice from the radio in the unmarked car parked near the carriage house. The muted drone from the Hollywood Freeway.

The exterior wall on the balcony was mostly glass, one panel of it a sliding door that locked from the inside. Still in a crouch, I crab-walked across the tile and pressed my ear against the pane. It vibrated, a thrumming sensation with a regular pulse. Music, I realized. Sasha Tovar was listening to music.

Careful to make as little noise as possible, I wedged the flat head of the screwdriver into the gap where the edge of the door met the jamb and worked it up and down until the latch released. The door slid open with a whisper. Some people place a long rod in the tracks of a sliding door to prevent someone like me from doing what I'd just done, but not Tovar. Still no wailing alarm or growling dog.

I closed the door behind me. Let my eyes adjust to the lack of moonlight inside. A digital clock and a strip of light from a CD player provided the only illumination. The female voice on the CD was sultry and deep. One of the artists Valya likes, but I didn't know her name. To my left, a king-sized bed flanked by matching nightstands. The bed was empty, its covers undisturbed. To one side of it a low dresser with a matching mirror on top and a small seating area—a love seat and two plush chairs facing a coffee table. To my right, under the window, a writing table with papers spread on top of it.

I crept along the wall until I was behind the love seat. The room had three interior doors, all closed. The largest one—double doors, I saw as my eyes adjusted further—appeared to lead to the rest of the house. Another probably led to a closet. A slit of light leaked beneath the third door. In the quiet between songs on the CD came the faint hiss of a shower running. Feeling safe enough to look around, I checked the drawers in the night-stand, found a loaded .38 Smith & Wesson revolver, silver with a black grip, double action. I emptied the cartridges and tossed them under the bed, then returned the gun to the drawer.

The shower stopped. I moved to the side of the bathroom door, where I would be behind it when it opened. Steam seeped through the cracks around the door frame. It carried the smell of soap and lotion. I pictured the former model methodically moisturizing her skin, maybe inspecting herself in the mirror, dispassionately measuring the toll of age.

The door opened, and she swept past me in a cloud of steam, wearing a sleek dressing gown, her hair wrapped in a towel. I put my hand over her mouth and rode her facedown onto the bed.

chapter 54

"I am *not* here to hurt you," I told Sasha Tovar, whispering into the wet pile of hair behind her ear. "I just want to talk. Nod to tell me you understand."

She nodded. Her body felt like iron under the silky material, all rigid muscle in the stress of the moment, but she hadn't reacted with the terrified fury I had expected from a woman attacked in her own bedroom.

I removed my hand from her mouth, but hovered over her in case she tried to run or activate a hidden alarm. Her eyes gleamed in the light from the bathroom. Wide open darting around the room, looking for an escape, but not panicked. As I slowly pulled back she scooted away from me and sat up, taking quick, shallow breaths.

"I only want to talk," I said again.

The towel on her head had come loose, revealing long blond hair. Her robe was red with the name *Armani* embroidered above her left breast. The moist skin of her neck glimmered with her fluttering pulse when she looked at me for the first time.

"He sent you from Moscow," she said. Deep voice, a hint of an accent, still shaky but far more controlled than I would have guessed it would be. Easily recognizable as the narrator of her films.

"Who?"

"You think I have a *name*?"

I didn't like her unnatural calm, or the feeling that she expected me to know more than I did. Her demeanor worried me far more than the presence of the police outside.

"Did you kill Everett?" she said.

"Yes," I lied.

"And now I suppose you want that?" She pointed to the loose papers on her writing table.

I had no idea what *that* was, but I nodded anyway, and she approached the table slowly, her eyes on me as she pawed the pages together, squared the edges, and placed the sheaf in my hands. It was a script. Titled *Betrayed—America's Lost Innocence*, written by Sasha Tovar and Everett Walker.

She opened the drawer under the table, pulled out a pack of cigarettes, and shook one loose. Removed it with her full lips and lit it with an engraved silver lighter. Her hands trembled slightly, but that was the only sign of fear or weakness I could see. She dragged deep in a way that reminded me of Rykov.

"Read it," she said on the exhale. "You'll see it's what you want. Not that it will do you any good. You're a week too late."

She moved to the love seat while I sat in the upholstered chair between her and the door and riffled the pages. Seventy-nine of them, broken into three acts, spattered with red-penciled notes, revisions, and arrows looping lines of narration from one place to another. I started at the beginning, skimming at first, then reading more carefully as Sasha opened one of the blinds, tucked her feet under her long legs, and chain-smoked while she gazed into the blackness of the ravine and the moonlit hills behind her house.

The script was a confessional of sorts. Everett Walker admitting to his past as a Soviet agent. He had joined the Communist Party U.S.A. in 1939 during the period of Socialist Realism, when Communist society was depicted in heroic and romantic ways. Once he got started, he never looked back.

Some of what he did was inconsequential, including many of the things Valya had already noted from her systematic review of his films. Sympathetic portrayals of Stalin and his successors. Idealistic treatment of Soviet Communism, glossing over its failures as an economic system and ignoring the stain of evil that sent millions to their deaths in the vast archipelago of gulags. Biographical depictions of Julius and Ethel Rosenberg that contributed to the mythology that they were both innocent of the charge of espionage. Pro-Soviet propaganda planted in the media.

Other activities were more serious. As an award-winning cinematographer and, later, director, Walker's stature increased. His first commercial film was a runaway hit, spawning sequels made by others, earning him millions. He became a consultant to one of the multinationals that gobbled up a studio in its quest to dip a finger into every possible revenue pot. That position enabled him to control content through subtle manipulation during production and by wielding an authoritative hand in the cutting room.

More important, it allowed him access to the people working on the latest in camera and film technology being developed by the military contracting side of the business. Nobody thought much of his interest in that part of the company. Here was a board member, a famous cinematographer who loved to see the latest gadgets. Where was the harm showing him a few nonclassified prototypes? Walker did not have the access or knowledge to gather information directly, but he used his contacts, his reputation, and his influence to recruit others who did. And everything he got he passed on to his master in Soviet and Russian intelligence, unnamed but identified as a man who pulled strings from Moscow using an international network of *rezidenturas*.

Bassoff, I thought, hearing the General's voice in my ear. *Bassoff has been running agents all over the world for years.*

The whole thing took less than an hour to read while Sasha smoked and stared moodily into the dark hills behind her house, still strangely serene. When she saw me turn the last page, she arched her brows.

"Well?"

I held her gaze, trying to think through the consequences of a script such as this. Then I paged back and reread sections of it. Early in the film, shortly after the introduction, the script described the origins of America's spy program in the Office of Strategic Services and fingered many of the Soviet spies who started their career as double agents there. One of whom, name unknown, was allegedly close to both Roosevelt and Churchill. Written in cramped cursive with a red pencil, somebody—Everett, I assumed—had added the words *Beneš Czech delegation?* The writing was similar to the writing on the Venona cable.

I held the script so that Sasha could see the words. "Who wrote this note?"

"Everett," she said after glancing at the page. "He wrote reminders like that all the time to make sure he followed up on something that interested him." She lit another cigarette.

Twenty pages later an oblique reference to a Soviet defector appeared during a discussion of Russian sources who had provided intelligence information to the CIA and FBI. According to the script, this person defected in a spy plane and became a leading source of Russian disinformation, then turned his focus to gathering intelligence after he obtained American citizenship. My father wasn't mentioned by name, but the reference was clear enough.

The single most explosive accusation in the script appeared on page 70. Walker claimed that his network and others were run by a senior military or Defense Department official. Called "Saturn" in the script—a reference to the rings around the planet, like rings of spies—this person had supposedly been operating for decades, supplying information to the Soviets and, Walker suspected, other foreign governments. The list of the stolen classified information Saturn supplied to the Russians included details about sophisticated imaging equipment, special photographic lenses, and a cloaking material that was "thirty times blacker than the material currently used on our spy planes, constructed at an atomic level to absorb light."

I looked up. Sasha's eyes were closed, her head leaned back, a trail of smoke curling in the air from the cigarette she held between two fingers.

"Why did Walker write this? Why the sudden change of heart?"

"It wasn't so sudden. After the Wall fell nobody knew what was next. Chaos followed by economic transformation, then gradual erosion until Russia no longer seemed to stand for anything anymore, except making money and brutalizing Chechnya. Then the journalists began to die. Sixteen at my last count. Thrown out of buildings. Shot. Beaten with a hammer. Killed in strange *accidents*. Everett lost hope."

"Why did he go to Moscow?" I said.

She ground the butt of her cigarette into a crystal ashtray. "I've asked myself the same question. He wanted to meet somebody there. He said he made a promise to a friend to do it before he died."

Maybe it was wishful thinking, but sitting in that room staring at the darkness in the hills, I wanted to believe that the promise Walker had made was to my father, and that the message was intended for me.

"He expected to die?"

She tilted her head toward the script. "After that was released? Yes. He was right."

"This is old news."

"Don't pretend to be a fool. Things like this don't end. Think of how much money is at stake. Not just the money to be made selling information, but the money to be saved by governments from Russia to China to Iran if they don't have to *innovate*. Stealing saves them billions, gives them a window into our capabilities, helps them know in advance how we'll respond to any crisis, from terrorism to the question of missiles in Poland."

I held the script open to page 43. "What can you tell me about this defector?"

"He's dead. Murdered right here in L.A. five years ago."

"Did you know him?"

"Only what I learned during our research. He piloted an ultra-secret spy plane to this country, and some foolish CIA agent bought his story and gave him a new identity and a new life smack in the middle of our defense industry. A man like that would have been like a wolf in a caged flock of sheep."

Isadora had said something similar.

"What name did they give him?"

"Steven Morris. Nobody anybody's ever heard of. The worst ones bury themselves in the woodwork." She rolled her head as though her neck was tight. "Look at what Everett has unleashed. God knows what's happening in Moscow. I mean besides turning someone like you loose—violent, unpredictable, probably sociopathic. Does that sound about right?"

"Close enough."

She opened her brown eyes wide and set her jaw. "You can murder me, but the script is already in circulation. Dozens of people have it. You can't put that genie back into the bottle."

"Who is the person you call Saturn?"

"Figure that out, you win the prize. Can you imagine how many people are looking for him? And he's probably right under their nose, another Philby sent to hunt for himself. Whittaker Chambers was right. The people of this country don't know the meaning of deception. So naïve, so hopeful, so sure that everyone shares their views. He called America's refusal to believe the spy scandal of the '30s and '40s 'invincible ignorance' that was 'rooted' in the character of America, 'so incapable of conspiracy itself that it refused to believe others practiced it as an art form.'"

This confirmed what I had suspected about why NCIX and the CIA had let me into the country. They were looking for a mole, somebody feeding the reinvigorated Russian bear massive amounts of sensitive information. Because that person might have been close to my father, they had concluded I might uncover clues they had missed.

"Who financed your film?"

She lit another cigarette, drew, and exhaled, almost as if she had to think about the answer to the question. She waved away the smoke between us.

"We were going to have to do that ourselves. We knew nobody

would touch this project, not with Lorelei featured so prominently. Everett's old studio actively tried to make us shelve it."

"Spotlight Studios."

"That's right. A copy of the script leaked into their hands three weeks ago, and all hell broke loose."

chapter 55

Sasha Tovar described Spotlight as a studio that took root in the golden age of Hollywood, which lasted from the end of the silent film era in the late 1920s to the 1950s. Spotlight grew to employ more than three thousand people during its heyday in the early '90s.

"Then it was purchased by a huge conglomerate," she said. "One with many defense industry ties. The perfect place for Everett to ply his dual trades."

"Lorelei."

"That's right."

"Who is your contact there?"

She got up from the love seat and returned to the bed, near the nightstand. I was still sitting between her and the door.

"I deal with the creative people at the studio," she said. "I have nothing to do with the business side, certainly not with any of the other divisions of Lorelei outside of Spotlight."

She sat on the bed and stretched one leg toward me and drew her other leg up so that the lower part of her robe slipped open to reveal the inside of her calf and thigh.

"Did you see my film *Nightfall in Lidice?*" she said.

"Parts of it, yes."

"And? Did it move you?"

Did it? Powerful images of the razed village, of broken bodies, of uniformed men with their hands clasped behind their backs, regarding the carnage they had wrought as though they were farmers looking at their fields. Goya's disturbing imagery shuffled among photos of people bundled into trucks and carted off to the camps or stood up against a barn wall lined with mattresses and shot ten at a time.

"How could it not?"

"Then it served its purpose."

"Why Lidice? Why not Katyn, more than twenty thousand Poles shot? Or the grain storage barn at Gardelegen, where a thousand were burned alive? What about Grischino, Jósefów, Kovno, Babi Yar?"

"Quite a list off the top of your head. No doubt both of us could point to more massacre sites all over the world." Her angular features became sharper when she was angry. "Why do you think a Czech would pick Lidice?"

"I saw enough of the film to know. You shot it and you narrated it with a feeling that was more than just nationalism."

"How perceptive of you," she said, but I was listening with half an ear. She was talking to buy time, and that was fine with me, because I was mulling over what I had learned, sensing progress, trying to figure out my next step.

"My grandmother was one of the Lidice villagers sent to Ravensbruck concentration camp," Sasha said. "She was barely sixteen." She adjusted the hem of her robe, but it didn't stay in place. It fell away again, revealing even more leg than before. "One thing that came of it was that she stayed in Germany after the war. My father is half German."

She reclined against the headboard and rested her hand casually on the top of the nightstand. She seemed to be thinking about something, then she stiffened and widened her eyes as if she had remembered an important clue.

"I have more for you. A list of sources, photographs—I keep them here."

She opened the drawer of the nightstand and reached inside. Whipped out the revolver. Wasting no time, she aimed for my heart and pulled the trigger.

chapter 56

The hammer clicked on an empty chamber. Sasha pulled the trigger again, with the same result, her eyes wide and incredulous. I twisted the gun out of her hand, ignoring her shocked expression.

"You don't need to do that. I'm not here to hurt you."

"Then why *are* you here?"

A good question with several answers. As always, the General's orders had been ambiguous. Learn what you can about this stupid American who was killed in your warehouse—who killed him, why, and what they would give to keep their business private. The kind of orders that left no tracks, kept open the definition of success and failure, gave me plenty of room to maneuver and hang myself.

The kind of orders that required me to adapt on the fly.

But behind the General—behind everything, in one way or another—stood Bassoff and his network of spies. And now my vague mission had jelled into something tangible. I was here to assess the damage done to Saturn's network, to protect a Russian source. Or, if Bassoff's fear that the network had been compromised appeared to be well founded, I was here to determine whether the Americans had fooled us, whether they had learned the lessons of conspiracy better than we thought; in that case, my job was to stop the bleeding.

Dawn was breaking. Light the color of pewter cast the contours of Sasha's aristocratic features into the same shadowy look as the photo on her Web site. The years hadn't erased the fashion-model cheekbones or the sultry pout of her lips. If anything, her face revealed an underlying aspect of melancholy that would have been impossible in the young woman who stalked the runways of Prague.

"What if Everett had it wrong?" I said. "What if some of the information he and the others like him were providing was really *disinformation* sent to hurt Russia?"

"Not a chance."

According to the bio on her Web site, Sasha had been in America for less than two decades, but in this respect, at least, she had adopted a very American way of looking at the world—without nuance. The Soviets produced Golitsyn, Nosenko, and many others who may or may not have been false defectors sent to mislead Western intelligence. Was it so inconceivable that the West had achieved equally successful counterintelligence coups of its own?

The doorbell rang.

Sasha stretched her arms above her head, releasing some tension, her expression a mixture of fear and curiosity. "What now, my new Russian friend?"

I peeked through the curtains. The valleys between the hills still lay in purple shadow. Above the hills, muted shades of gray laced with pink splashes, as though painted by a watercolorist with half his palette missing. I needed at least an hour to get away.

I prodded Sasha to the intercom, letting her feel the hardness of the Beretta digging into her back. The person at the front door identified himself as a police officer. "Checking in," he said. "Is everything all right?"

I pushed the MUTE button. "How long have they been doing that?"

"They've had a car out front since yesterday."

Probably within a few hours after I left Rhodes outside of Santa Fe, I figured. "How often do they check in?"

"Yesterday it was every three hours or so."

I told her to tell him she was fine, and she did that.

When the conversation ended I ripped long strips from the satin bedsheets, bound her wrists and ankles, and bundled her into the walk-in closet. She shouldn't have to stay that way for too long. If she didn't answer the next time they buzzed her, somebody would come inside. She didn't say anything until just before I left.

"One thing about Everett." She was lying on her side, forced to twist her head around to look me in the eye. "He was wrong about many things, but he had talent—a gift for stirring emotions. Looking through the viewfinder, he was a god."

I got out of Sasha's house while the hills were still in deep shadow. Kept to the low ground, picking my way carefully up to the neighboring yard. No lights on in that house. I jumped the fence to the street and crawled to the edge of the bluff where I once again overlooked the cul-de-sac. Two black-and-whites were on the street, parked side by side, facing in opposite directions, lights off.

I backed out to the Suzuki and rode away down the winding roads. I abandoned the motorcycle less than an hour later, close enough to walk the rest of the way along Olympic Boulevard to the Lorelei building in Century City.

Time to find Santori.

chapter 57

The Lorelei building gleamed in the rising sun. The lights in the stone and steel monument sign glowed crimson, listing more than a dozen company names in all. A low stone wall ran the length of one city block in the front. At the end of the block the wall gave way to wide concrete steps leading down to a plaza, an apron made of concrete inlaid with a broad pathway of gray bricks. I pushed through a throng of smokers to glass doors that opened onto the first-floor lobby.

People walking to the elevators swiped a key to go through the turnstiles. Those without a key had to check in at a guard station. A directory in the middle of the lobby listed the same companies as those on the sign outside. Several rows of individual names were listed beneath the company names, but not Santori.

I took the stairs down into the cavernous parking garage, one floor after another, all of them the same except for different colors painted on the pillars. I searched for an area that looked as if it might be reserved for executives, but couldn't find one area that distinguished itself from another.

I went out, crossed the street, found a fast-food restaurant, bought breakfast, and settled onto a high stool where I had an angled view of the building.

Several of the conversations around me were in Spanish. Two uniformed police officers shoveled hash browns and eggs at a table behind mine. They ignored me, just as I paid little attention to them.

Six hours later I was no closer to finding my quarry. I'd eaten, walked around the block, read the newspaper on a bench—no mention of me or reporter Anna Wright—all the while keeping an eye on the comings and goings in the Lorelei building. Early in the afternoon I grabbed another meal, this one at the counter in a noodle shop, where I could see the street and watch the main entrance in the reflection in the front window.

Ten minutes into my meal Elizabeth Rhodes pushed open the door and stepped inside.

She wore a brown suit with a boxy skirt that ended just past her knees. Hair pulled back in a severe bun. She hugged a shoulder bag in front of her body, one hand buried in it as she approached. I didn't know how they found me, but I wasn't surprised that they had. I pushed out a stool with my foot, and she sat facing me.

"I didn't think it was possible for someone to stay off the grid for so long. Do you know how good our real-time facial recognition software has gotten?"

"Am I under arrest?"

"You shouldn't have run away in New Mexico."

The lunch crowd thronged the sidewalk outside, breaking around a man and a woman casually talking to each other next to a lamppost. The woman glanced at us through the window. A man in a suit stationed himself at a table on the other side of Rhodes and watched us over his menu.

"Have you figured out who Drake is yet?" I said, referring to the man who had pulled us over near Los Alamos.

"No. We've searched all the databases for pictures. Present and former CIA, FBI, military, diplomats, foreign nationals. I'm still dizzy from looking at so many photos."

"What about Major Santori?"

She cocked her head to one side, assessing me. "What about him?"

"He works for Lorelei."

"Not exactly. He's a military liaison between the air force and Lorelei's aerospace group." She fingered a brown hole in the Formica countertop, but I could tell her curiosity had been aroused. She appeared to have her own reasons for wondering about Santori. "Why are you interested in him?"

"Because he took a shot at me last night near Long Beach."

She looked disappointed. "Major Santori might be involved in many things. But he's not a drive-by shooter."

"Let's find him and ask him."

"That's not possible."

"Why not?"

"Because Santori went to Washington yesterday to meet with my boss, who still has lots of questions about what happened in New Mexico. He's there now."

Had McIntyre lied to me about Santori? Torture and truth often don't go together, I knew that, but I hadn't given him time to think before dunking him in the Pacific. He hadn't had time to concoct a story.

"What time did Santori's flight leave?"

"Sometime in the afternoon."

I hadn't gotten a clear look at the man in the beige sedan. Slouched, hat pulled low, and when he did look up all I remember seeing was the weapon in his hand. I had only McIntyre's word that it had been Santori. But I simply couldn't get the idea out of my mind that McIntyre had been telling the truth.

The phone in Rhodes's bag started buzzing. She answered it and listened for a moment. The blood drained from her face, and she raised her stunned gaze to meet mine, then slowly withdrew a Beretta from her bag, just like the one I had taken from her outside Los Alamos. She ended the call and motioned to the man in the suit. He approached us, blocking the view of the other patrons, his hand beneath his coat.

"Why would you do that?" Rhodes said, gazing at me in wonder. "I had you read all wrong. I—I didn't think . . ."

"What are you talking about?"

"This is my fault," she said. "I should have detained you in Los

Alamos." Anger slowly replaced the shock in her eyes. "You need to answer me, Volk. Why did you kill Sasha Tovar?"

I stared at her, thinking that Sasha couldn't be dead, that she was safe in the closet of her bedroom. Then I looked away to gaze out the window. Beautiful Sasha, with her sensuous mouth and elegant eyes and all her artistic genius, left bound and helpless, like a sacrifice. I had missed all the warning signs telling me that she was in danger just as surely as Rhodes had me confused with her killer.

chapter 58

To access the vault in his home office, Reese first entered eleven digits on a keypad mounted on the wall low enough for him to reach easily from his wheelchair. When a row of three red lights blinked, he keyed in a second series of seven digits. The last number was a 3. If he hit any other number, alarms would blare throughout the house, at Lorelei, and at the Western Division of the San Diego Police Department. The vault would go into lockdown mode for 24 hours, impossible to override and impenetrable by any safecracker. He punched the number 3, and one by one the red lights turned green, and then the wall slid away to reveal a stainless steel door.

He rolled forward to a massive dial mounted in the middle of the door and spun it one way and the other, five turns in all. Metallic clanking noises indicated that the locks were disengaging before the huge door swung open on hydraulic hinges. He wheeled himself inside, pressed a metal disk that electronically closed the door behind him, and went to a wall-mounted safe, where he spun another dial.

Stacked inside were paper files that dated back to the late 1940s. Next to them was a portable hard drive that held scanned documents covering the last ten years. The paper files were individually labeled, his laborious handwriting progressively shakier, like the readout from a seismograph recording his fading dexterity. Twelve files, one for each of the dozen handlers he'd been assigned before Bassoff, who insisted on maintaining only computer records. Reese couldn't even name them all anymore.

The beautiful blonde in the bookstore that rainy day in Rome was his first. Hannah, she had introduced herself over steaming cups of *caffé corretto* later that afternoon. She seduced him. Bound him to her with a lethal combination of lust and puppy love, later fueled to almost unbearable highs during their time together in 1950s Vienna, known as the "turntable of espionage," an enchanting city left physically intact but socially fragmented by war. During those years Vienna's dazed citizens questioned their wartime role and their fate. Were they Nazi collaborators or Nazi victims? Were the Soviet and Allied soldiers who prowled their streets liberators or occupiers? Postwar Vienna was a crossroads between East and West, a place crawling with purveyors and purchasers of information. Everything anybody might want to know, and some of it true.

Reese never knew what happened to Hannah. One morning he left for work at the embassy, leaving her warm and asleep in his bed. When he returned to the apartment that night she was gone. No trace she had ever existed. Within a week he was contacted by the man who would become his second Soviet handler.

He stared into the safe and sighed. The external drive held ten years of information covering the whole span of his relationship with Bassoff. It would be the first thing NCIX investigators wanted to see. A Rosetta Stone for deciphering his deception, at least from their point of view. Matthews and a few others in the top ranks of the NSA would know better, of course, but Reese no longer cared either way.

To him the hard drive wasn't the most important item stashed here. He pushed it aside and piled five decades of files on top of one another to clear a path to the back of the safe. There he found what he was looking for—a leather-bound document folder secured with an elastic band. He took it from the safe, set it on his lap, and adjusted his glasses before carefully opening it. The documents inside had turned yellow with age.

Does a son bear the sins of his father? Over the years Reese had wasted much time worrying about the theology behind the question. But as time passed, determining the answer became a practical exercise. How much would he have to do to erase the stain of his father's treason? May 29, 1943: a date burned into Reese's memory. One that refused to fade as the past receded, because it was forever out there, in books and on the Web—on the NSA's Web site, for God's sake!—an ever-present record of his father's betrayal, hiding in plain sight, always in danger of exposure.

If Major General Gordon Reese had been just anybody, his legacy might not have been so important. But Gordon had been a prodigy, graduating from West Point in 1904 and joining the Aeronautical Division of the U.S. Signal Corps when it was formed in 1907. This precursor to the modern air force was charged with "all matters pertaining to military ballooning, air machines, and all kindred subjects." By the end of World War I, Gordon was a full colonel and a roving ambassador for the U.S. Army Air Service.

After a series of promotions to major general, Gordon spent the years leading up to World War II stationed in Berlin. Then came November 9, 1938, and *Kristallnacht*, the Night of Broken Glass, a coordinated attack on Jews throughout the German Reich. Three days later, SS leader Reinhard Heydrich reported 7,500 businesses destroyed, 267 synagogues burned, and 91 Jews killed. Along with all the other members of the U.S. diplomatic delegation there, Major General Reese was recalled from Germany. His orders took him to London, where he became a liaison to the Czech government in exile of Eduard Beneš.

Sometime during those years the man known in the history books as one of the "founding fathers of the United States Air Force" became a Soviet source. The yellowing documents in Reese's hands—listing contacts, codes, and drop points from Berlin to Prague to London— provided graphic evidence of a decade of treason.

How does one become a spy? Reese could only speculate about the person or thing that initially led his father to betray his country. Perhaps his father justified giving information to Stalin on the grounds that the Soviets were allies, intent on ending the German threat and willing to pay the ultimate price in blood and treasure. He had witnessed the evils of Nazism firsthand, and he may have believed the Western powers weren't doing enough to stop its spread. Or he might have been seduced by the idealistic language of Communism: the struggle of the proletariat, the masses fighting exploitation, seeking ownership of the means of production.

Reese would never know. Source 19, as Reese had come to think of his father, bitterly, was killed by a V-1 flying bomb near London's Battersea Park in the summer of 1944.

Reese never had the opportunity to confront him. When he found the leather document folder after his father's death—and after the first wave of shock and horror of reading it had receded to a dull roar of pain—Reese entertained the idea that he had been a double agent. But those fantasies had long since evaporated. The question of whether to open a second front in Europe was one of the most urgent issues of the day. The fact that Stalin had the answer as soon as Roosevelt and Churchill made their decision was an unimpeachable indictment of Major General Gordon Reese.

A sin that Reese had lived the rest of his life to atone, although he hadn't intended it that way. In the beginning he'd been charged with moral clarity, unsure of his path but certain it had an end. He hadn't yet realized that some roads have no exit.

His father's disloyalty had long since ceased to preoccupy him. Reese had nearly six decades of his own conduct to ruminate over during any sleepless hours. His own decisions, right or wrong, churned in his gut. Allen Haynes, shot full of fentanyl in his hospital bed in the V.A., was the latest in a long line of dead men and women that included Stepan Volkovoy, Everett Walker, and many others.

Reese slipped the yellowing documents back into the leather folder and removed a packet of letters bound with a frayed red ribbon tied in a bow. He gently tugged one end of the ribbon so that the satin knot slipped loose almost of its own accord. He often liked to work his way back in time, so that he ended with clearer memories of happier days, and he did that now. When he finished reading the last letter he gently ran the pad of his thumb over her signature, written with graceful, flowing letters that served as an appropriate metaphor for how he most liked to remember Hannah, his first handler and first real love.

A few minutes later he slid the letters back into the folder and set it on his lap so he would be sure to take it with him when he left the vault. The rest of the files didn't matter anymore, but he didn't want anybody to see the contents of the folder.

That done, Reese opened another packet of documents. There on top, a copy of a report ostensibly from Everett Walker to someone on Bassoff's staff, written all the way back in 1992.

But Everett Walker hadn't written the report. The man was a cinematic genius, so talented that his films always moved people. Even the most simplistic agitprop seemed artistically rendered under his discerning eye. But Walker didn't understand the details of the sophisticated cameras developed by Lorelei's military R&D teams, and though he recruited several sources he never rose to the level of a source himself.

The author of Everett Walker's most important reports, both the parts that were true and those that were not, was Reese. The most damaging information—the false leads, the test results that turned out to be wrong, the missteps that were a natural part of the espionage business—those things that hurt the Soviet and Russian cause always appeared to come from someone like Walker or Stepan Volkovoy or one of Katarina's many sources.

The damaging information always came from a source that could be sacrificed.

Never from Reese.

Reese kept *his* reports in a separate file. Reese had given the GRU sixty years of gold, starting with his reports to Hannah. Now he was counting on the power of his currency in Moscow to make JANUS his crowning achievement.

chapter 59

They cinched my hands behind my back with flex-cuffs, drove me to nearby Parker Center for processing, and then put me in a wooden chair in a room with a tile floor and a window made of one-way glass. Two detectives interrogated me for several hours. They didn't ask anything about how I got into the country or my previous trips to the States, nor did they question my ties to Russia, the Kremlin, or the General. They may as well have been interrogating a local drifter, albeit one accused of breaking into a Hollywood Hills mansion and murdering the famous director who lived there.

I figured someone high up in the food chain had instructed the detectives to lay off the international aspects of the case. Focus on the crime, they must have been told, and if you can prove he did it we'll decide on the next step. If you can't, the Feds will take over.

Their examination was professional in every way. Direct and oblique, cajoling and confrontational. Promises and threats. As difficult as it can be without brass knuckles or a sap, but all done with an air of practiced competence.

I admitted I had been in Sasha Tovar's bedroom the night before. This confirmed what they knew or would know soon enough. Prints, fibers, hairs—something was going to connect me to the master suite. I didn't have the receipt from my meal at the breakfast place, so they sent people to check whether and when people remembered seeing me there, trying to nail down the time line.

The younger of the two detectives, a short, Hispanic man with thick wrists and fingernails gnawed to the quick, showed me a hand-drawn diagram of the murder scene. Sasha's bound body had been found in the master closet by the housekeeper. Facedown, shot in the back three times. I couldn't tell from the crude marks on the diagram whether the entry wounds were in the shape of a triangle, but I suspected they were. That didn't mean the shooter was the same person who had killed Walker, Rykov, and the two cops in Moscow, but it did mean the same person was likely behind all the murders. The detectives didn't say as much, but from their tone I knew ballistics hadn't matched the Beretta they'd taken off me at the noodle shop.

The older detective asked about Sasha's current "projects," regarding me steadily as I told him I didn't know anything about them. After another hour of questions, he used the ball of his thumb to smooth the edges of his report.

"Very slick," he said. "You told us all the things we already knew, and not much we didn't." He fiddled with the papers some more. Motioned for his partner to follow him, then left.

I didn't have to wait long. The next person came in within a minute, tall and tan, his paunch barely visible beneath his suit jacket. He sat on the edge of the wooden table.

"I'm Commander Swanson," he said, and he slid a crime scene photo across the tabletop toward me.

A man sprawled on beige carpet. Black pants, white shirt rucked up, the back of his head a gory stew of bloody hair and brains. The lower right corner of the photo was date-stamped May 22, 2004.

"We thought he was Steven Morris," Swanson said. "A high-level employee in Lorelei's special projects section. Turned out we were wrong. Couple hours after we found the body, the Feds stepped in and showed us how smart they are. He was Stepan Volkovoy, former defector. Dear old Dad, to you. And word got around that he was giving away our secrets to your government."

I couldn't see my father's face. All I could see was black hair, broad shoulders, right hand clenched into a fist, probably one last muscle contraction before he died. I flipped the photo over and pushed it away.

Swanson scraped crud off the tabletop with his thumbnail and regarded the dirt stuck there sourly. "Some fat prick named York delivered that big news, a day or two after your father bought it. I understand you've had the pleasure of meeting him. You know what I told him, way back then? I said, 'If you guys are so fucking smart, why did you turn the son of a bitch loose in the first place?' You know we've got a federal program to *help* guys like your dad? Pay them money, set them up with the American dream. How fucked up is that?"

He swung his foot like a tail. The movement caused his entire body to rock.

"I guess you guys have your turf wars in Moscow, too, don't you?" He gnawed his thumbnail and spat the pieces onto the tile. "Yeah, that's gotta be a universal problem. The part that gets me, though, is now those same geniuses want us to release *you* into their custody. How's that for rewarding incompetence? How long before *you're* back to doing your damnedest to fuck us over?"

His disgusted gaze met mine and held it. Somebody banged the door outside, but he still didn't look away. "Tell me about you and Mac McIntyre," he said.

I did, taking him through the first phone call on Venice Beach to when I left McIntyre on the shoreline. I didn't say anything about Santori, shots fired, or dunking McIntyre in the surf.

Swanson didn't say anything for a while after that, just picked at something on the table some more.

"McIntyre's dropped out of sight," he said finally.

I didn't respond.

"You didn't help him find his way to the bottom of the Pacific, did you?"

"No."

Swanson chewed on his lower lip and cut his eyes at me. "Those people won't show me your file." He gestured vaguely toward the one-way glass. "But I know your type. I spent time in the jungle and did a tour in Saigon, too. I know your type," he repeated.

He stood and adjusted his jacket.

More banging outside the door, louder this time.

Swanson grimaced. "You're federal property now, Volk. I can't do anything about that. But once this is cleared up, I want you out of my city. You understand? This isn't Moscow, and it's damn sure not Chechnya. You get where I'm coming from?"

When I didn't answer, he shrugged and left the room.

chapter 60

The hills behind Sasha Tovar's house were bathed in the violets and reds of early evening as an LAPD officer, so young and well scrubbed he almost squeaked, drove Rhodes and me into the cul-de-sac. Her hair was down now, hanging to her shoulders, but she didn't appear more relaxed. She kept both hands on her lap, the ridges of muscle on her forearms revealing the tension she felt.

I had insisted on returning, if only to form my own impressions about what happened to Sasha, and Rhodes had reluctantly agreed. But I think her reluctance was feigned. She would take me wherever I wanted to go, I believed, because her temporary job description seemed to be to watch the crazy Russian, see what he does next, figure out what he's up to.

I massaged my wrists. The flex-cuffs were gone, but my skin still bore the marks where they had bitten the deepest. My head and back still hurt from the beating Zubko had administered. And my leg ached, as always.

I paid no attention to the cops who hauled me out of the car and hustled me inside and up the curved staircase. Rhodes followed a few paces behind, I think, but I couldn't see who else was in the group. The double doors of the master suite were winged open. It looked different in the blare of lights, the walls painted sea-foam green, the ceiling a neutral cream with white crown molding. But the soothing effect was lost in the buzz of technicians milling around the entrance to the closet.

The sliding glass door was open a crack. I hadn't left it that way. The towel was still crumpled on the bed where Sasha had tossed it. The chair in front of her writing desk lay on its back. The top of the desk was empty except for a lamp and a leather desk mat. No papers cluttered its surface.

The script I had read last night was gone.

My escorts herded me past the bright lights and technicians and into the walk-in closet, made small by the presence of an M.E. and her assistant. Floodlights threw a harsh glare on the scene. Sasha lay on her side, just as I had left her, but now she was curled into a fetal position, looking small and abandoned. I had an eerie sense of déjà vu from early that morning and, strangely, I superimposed what I was seeing now onto my mental image of the police sketch, as if that drawing was acquiring depth and color and smell.

The main difference was that now I could see for certain that the wounds in her back formed a triangle.

"York thinks you're guilty as hell," Rhodes said quietly. She stood at my shoulder, hair tucked behind her ear, expression bleak. "How many people besides you knew the M.O. of the person who hit Rykov and the others in Moscow?"

"York doesn't have two brain cells to rub together. You knew. *He* knew."

"But we weren't here with her last night."

"If you really thought I was guilty, we wouldn't be having this conversation."

"You're holding something back. I don't know what, but you know something more about what happened here."

The techs were coming and going, exchanging notes, their heads together in hushed conversation. None of them paid any attention to what we were saying. I decided that Rhodes had earned the right to answers. Not all of them, but some.

"Whoever killed her took a script."

"Why?"

"I don't know. She said it's already been widely distributed, and—"

All at once I realized why somebody might have taken that particular script. Everett's cramped red note: *Beneš Czech delegation?* Identical to the words written on the Venona cable Walker brought to Moscow.

"Walker's edits and notes were scrawled all over the pages in red pencil," I said. "Something in them—perhaps something only he knew—had to be what they were after."

"So?"

"Think about it. How many people could have had access to her handwritten changes?"

"I don't know."

"It's a definable number. Whether it's two or two hundred, we can make a list of suspects based on the assumption that one of them didn't like what Walker had written."

"You're making a very big leap in logic," Rhodes said. She had no way of knowing about the handwritten note on the Venona decrypt and the apparent connection it had to Walker's note on the script. Despite the question in her voice, I made no effort to enlighten her. She knew I was holding back, and she was either going to do things my way or she wasn't. Simple as that.

Rhodes looked doubtful. "If we had anything else to go on, I'd say you're grasping at straws. As it is, well . . ."

She led me out of the master closet and through the double doors into the hallway. She dialed a number on her cell and talked for a few minutes, her hand cupped over the mouthpiece. When she finished she turned to me.

"My office is making inquiries about who might have had access to the script. Meanwhile, what now?"

"Let's find McIntyre. I want to know if he was really lying about Santori."

"LAPD and the FBI are combing the city for him."

"Where did he live?"

"Why?"

"Maybe you and I will see something the others missed."

chapter 61

According to Rhodes, twice-divorced McIntyre lived in the Fairfax district. His second-floor unit occupied the top corner of a dirty brick apartment complex.

Our LAPD escort led us along the precast concrete balcony past the numbered doors. One was propped open to reveal a woman in a sleeveless white T-shirt lounging on a couch, television blaring, her diapered toddler sprawled on the mud-brown carpet at her feet. A few doors down, the cop peeled away yellow crime-scene tape and unlocked the door to McIntyre's abode.

A matching green couch and easy chair faced a dusty TV. Metal-and-glass dinette surrounded by four chairs made of tubular metal, cushions worn all the way through in places to show the foam stuffing. Lamps with stained shades that used to be white. Rotten bananas on the kitchen counter, shrunken and black. Dirty dishes in the sink. A pungent odor pervaded the place. Cat urine, maybe.

The single bedroom contained an unmade bed with disheveled sheets. A book by Joseph Wambaugh rested on the nightstand, open and facedown. The drawer to the nightstand held a gay-porn magazine.

The chest of drawers contained socks, underwear, polo shirts, and an empty ankle holster for a small-caliber pistol, probably a .32 revolver. Mirrored bifold doors opened to reveal a limp brown suit and two dress shirts hanging in the closet. On the floor beneath the shirts was a hamper filled with dirty clothes. Underwear, a white shirt with pale blue pinstripes, and blue slacks like the ones McIntyre was wearing when I met him the day before. Wrinkled and covered with sand.

I stood in place and made a slow turn, panning the bedroom, then walked into the living area and did the same. Rhodes stood behind me and to my left, mimicking my movements. The fresh-faced cop waited in the doorway, watching us, his head and shoulders framed by the black dress of a starved blond model on a giant billboard across the street.

Rhodes shifted her weight. "If this was a simple missing persons case, I might start looking in West Hollywood for pickups. But I don't think his sexuality has anything to do with this."

The police had already rifled through everything in the apartment. The chances of us finding anything here were slim to none. Still . . .

I went to the kitchen. It was so small I could have put one hand on the stovetop and the other on the counter opposite the stove and done a set of dips. Except for several pieces of cheap silverware and a pad with nothing written on it, the drawers were empty. The refrigerator held only a yellow bottle of mustard, a half-eaten sub wrapped in plastic, and a carton of milk that sloshed strangely when I shook it, as if it were filled with marbles and water. I emptied it into the sink. Lumpy curds and a thin trickle of sour milk poured out.

Warm curds and milk, I realized. The carton was warm.

I motioned at the cop. "Tell him to leave us alone," I told Rhodes, and after a brief hesitation she did, shutting the door on his curious gaze.

I rocked the refrigerator back and forth to pull it from its corner beside the countertop. Asked Rhodes for a dime and used it to unscrew the back cover from the coils. Sandwiched under the metal panel I found an envelope, the flap crinkled as if it had been opened and closed several times. Inside were two sheaves of hundred dollar bills banded with brown paper strips marked as holding five thousand dollars. One of the bands was loose, about half the bills missing.

Rhodes took a bill and held it up to the skylight, snapped it between her hands. "Looks real. What do you suppose it was for?"

To kill Sasha Tovar? I didn't think so. More likely he was paid to lead me to the park in Long Beach.

"I think it's a payoff," I said.

She narrowed her eyes, considering that. "Maybe. What now?"

"Let's pay a visit to Spotlight Studios."

chapter 62

We hit Santa Monica Boulevard after nightfall. Rhodes worked her ever-present laptop in the front, sitting next to the babyfaced cop. I sat in back and considered everything I had learned in the last few days. I was convinced that all the loose threads would lead to one person. My job was to keep pulling on them, hoping that one wouldn't break and I could follow it to the end.

The Lorelei building powered up into the night sky like a lit sword. Pedestrians, buses, cabs, cars, and trucks swirled around it in a steady flow. We joined a line of cars at one of the pull-ins on the side, and the cop parked in a tow-away zone. Rhodes told him to wait in the car.

"One of my people called ahead to make sure someone would still be here to meet us," she said, her heels clicking over the marble tile on the way to the guard desk inside.

The main offices of Spotlight Studios were located on the seventh floor. Rhodes's fear that people would have gone home for the night was unfounded. The lobby still bustled. Marble floor, walls made of glass with brushed-metal trim, music piped into the elevator and the lobby. The receptionist wore a headset. She finished her conversation, directed a call somewhere, and asked if she could help us. I couldn't tell if hers was the candied voice that had answered my phone call yesterday. Rhodes flashed her badge and asked to see the person in charge, then we drifted to one of the corner windows facing Fox Plaza and the MGM building, and waited, staring out at the lights.

A few minutes later a man approached with his hand extended. Late thirties, hair slicked back, tanned and brisk.

"Jason Moore, public relations." He studied her identification and the business card she gave him. He handed back her ID wallet and led us to a conference room that offered the same view as the one in the lobby. "Water? Coffee?"

"No, thank you," she said.

We settled into high-backed leather chairs. Moore steepled his fingers under his chin.

"What can I do for you, Ms. Rhodes?"

"It's about Sasha Tovar."

"We heard." He nodded sympathetically. "We've already been contacted by the police. Several members of the entertainment press have called as well, wanting a statement. It's a terrible thing."

Rhodes pulled a spiral pad and pen from her bag and poised the tip of the pen over the lined paper. "Your company financed her documentary *Nightfall in Lidice*."

"Yes, we were one of three studios that co-financed the project, along with two distribution partners. Why is this important to"—he glanced at her card—"the Office of the National Counterintelligence Executive?"

"Who were the people at Spotlight involved in the project?"

Moore stiffened. "Should I be talking to our lawyers?"

"Bring them in. We'll talk to them separately. Meanwhile, start pulling the names of anyone from Spotlight who was involved with any of Sasha Tovar's films, including the one she was working on most recently, *Betrayed*. From the janitor to the head of the studio, I want every name."

"Do you have a warrant?"

"You choose, Mr. Moore. Cooperate now, or in three hours federal agents will pull into the loading dock in a panel truck and start loading boxes of documents." Rhodes had a way about her that I admired—menacing and logical at the same time.

Moore spluttered, more to preserve his pride than to win the argument, I think, then he left the room in search of someone with authority. I pointed to the phone in the middle of the table, black with four speakers orbiting it, and shook my head to tell Rhodes not to talk. She nodded and went into the lobby, where I could see her standing with her back to the window, her phone pressed to her ear.

While she was gone I rooted in her bag for the Beretta she'd acquired to replace the one I'd taken before. Made sure the magazine was full and slipped it into my pocket. I was more likely to need it than she was.

chapter 63

Cameras in Spotlight Studios' main conference room at the Lorelei building beamed real-time images to the monitor in Reese's office thirty stories higher. He zoomed closer on Volk's face, noting the similarities to Stepan. And the differences. Just as Katarina—or Isadora, as she now called herself—had told him, this man had a harder edge than his father.

Reese chuckled when he saw Volk steal the pistol, not surprised that the son had inherited his father's instinct for survival. He leaned back in his chair and put his bare hands within inches of the glowing orange coils of a space heater, as close as he could get without roasting his palms. He'd had the protective screen removed long before. His fingers were gnarled, bent by time and rheumatoid arthritis, his knuckles swollen, his veins a purplish-red in the places where they ridged his mottled skin. Old-man hands.

Look what's become of me.

He dialed Santori on a cell phone. No answer. Santori should have left Dulles several hours ago, on his way back to L.A. on one of Lorelei's company jets. The same jet he'd taken last night after his missed shot at Volk. Reese didn't know who killed Sasha Tovar, but he guessed that Santori had arranged it. Bassoff must have decided that her script cut too close to him, that it couldn't ever see the light.

Reese dialed Santori again. Still no answer. Another mistake by Santori. Now was the time to *over*communicate, if only to keep abreast of what Reese was doing. Santori had made several tactical errors in the past two weeks. Not getting Haynes on the first try was a fuck-up, pure and simple, but he had also made other, telling blunders. A note left in the Bell helicopter. A phone number in the call history of his cell phone. They would have cost him if Reese hadn't already known the truth.

But none of that mattered now.

Reese had his own moles, one of them working on the ninth floor of Bassoff's precious *Steklyashka*. As a result, Reese saw many of the same reports Bassoff did, including the one from less than a day ago analyzing the contents of the Venona cable Bassoff had finally gotten from the General.

Bassoff's analyst had connected the dots. The note on the cable pointed directly to Major General Gordon Reese, the father of retired Under Secretary of Defense and current chairman of the board of Lorelei Alfred Reese. Oh, how Bassoff must have chortled when he read *that*. All these years Bassoff had been searching for a way to leverage him—short of giving him up and losing his most valuable agent— and now this tidbit has fallen into his lap. Bassoff might wonder how much Reese cared about his father's reputation, but he would definitely try to use this information, and when he did, Reese would make him believe that Reese would do anything to protect his father.

Reese watched the monitor as two men wearing suits and ties walked into the Spotlight Studios conference room and Rhodes—who had returned to the room a few minutes before—stood to meet them. He could let the lawyers handle it for now, let them delay things indefinitely. But why bother? One call and the heat would be off for at least a week. That was enough. Within hours or days everything would be over, one way or the other, and Reese would be done. That was a good thing. He was sick of living all the lies.

chapter 64

The executives and lawyers at Spotlight Studios refused to provide any information about Sasha Tovar's film *Betrayed*. I watched in silence as they stonewalled every question Rhodes asked, including one for a list of people the edited script had been distributed to. When Rhodes aggressively pushed for answers, one of them left the room, saying he needed to make a call to Washington.

Her cell phone rang less than twenty minutes later.

She bent her head to listen, holding the phone so tightly her knuckles turned white. When the call ended she stowed away her notepad and motioned for me to leave with her. The studio hack, Moore, gave us a greasy smile as we walked out of the conference room.

A security guard rode the elevator down with us and marched us off the premises. He kept his hand on the butt of his pistol the whole time. We watched him walk away as the cars and trucks rumbled past us on Century Park East. Our police escort was nowhere to be seen.

"Sorry, Volk," Rhodes said.

"What happened?"

"That was my boss on the phone. Her boss got a call ten minutes ago from the majority counsel for the Senate's Select Committee on Intelligence, telling NCIX to, quote, 'Back the fuck off Lorelei,' unquote."

"How many people have that kind of pull?"

A breeze fluttered her hair over her eyes. "What?" She pulled out her phone and began typing with her thumb. "I don't know, a few hundred think they can try, maybe."

"Cross-reference those people with everybody who has ties to Spotlight Studios and saw Sasha's script, and we'll have our list. Our man will be there. Then it's just a matter of elimination."

She kept thumbing her phone. The crimson lights on the monument sign glowed over her head. My gaze was drawn to the huge letters on the top of the sign.

"Who's in charge of Lorelei?"

"It's publicly held, owned by every Tom, Dick, and Harry in their 401(k) plan or as part of an index fund tied to the S&P or the Dow."

"Who runs it?"

"A board of directors."

"Who's in charge of the board?"

"They vote on anything important." She still wasn't looking at me. "Listen, Volk, the Spotlight Studios thing is a dead end. Let's check in and see what they've found on McIntyre. Then let's go pound through files the old-fashioned way."

I put my hand over hers to stop her from playing with her phone. Startled by my touch, she lifted her gaze to meet mine. I read confusion, hurt, anger—she didn't like being told to back off any more than I did. I tried to be gentle.

"You can't help me now. I get it. All I need from you is a list." I gestured over my shoulder toward the Lorelei edifice. "Give me the names of the people at the head of that monster—the real power, not the ones who meet shareholders and appear on the financial news programs. Tell me who's in control, and I'll find our man."

She pulled her hand away from mine. "I can't do that. Look, Volk, my job is to stop people like you from getting that kind of information."

"We both want something, Rhodes. I want to know what happened to my father. You want to find a mole. Let's help each other."

"Who said I was looking for a mole?"

"Everett Walker said it, in his script."

"Right," she said, dragging out the word. "The missing script. Do you know how many crackpot conspiracy theorists we deal with every day?"

"Somebody has been scattering corpses from Moscow to L.A.," I said. "He has a reason for killing these people. You need to decide who you're going to help. Me or whoever's up there pulling strings."

She glanced at the towering Lorelei building, gnawing the inside of her lip. For an instant I thought I had her. Then her expression hardened.

"That's just it, Volk." She edged closer until our noses almost touched. "You *don't* get it. *You're* the bad guy. *You're* the goddamn foreign agent I'm paid to worry about."

chapter 65

Rhodes walked away from me to call for a car. She stood with one hand covering her ear and her head bowed. The call lasted for a long time.

"About an hour," she said when it finally ended, and we walked across the street to a coffee shop. I told her I didn't want anything, and grabbed a table next to the window while Rhodes stood in line. The two people in front of her were talking on their cell phones. The party of three at the table next to me gossiped about the latest movie star in rehab. The other patrons, all of them singles, sent text messages, talked on cell phones, and worked on their computers, wirelessly tethered to some form of work or entertainment. Everyone disengaged from the physical world, lost in places or lives far away from where they were at the moment.

Rhodes set her coffee and Danish on the table and sat in the chair across from me. When she pried off the lid, steam rose from her cup, carrying the scent of roasted coffee and vanilla.

"Tell me about Moscow," she said, sucking the foam from the wooden stirring stick. "You told Mary Montoya you have a woman there?"

"An adoring wife, two children, a wonderful apartment, and a dacha surrounded by acres of woodland for when I want to get away."

"Spare me the sarcasm. And don't pretend to be a pauper. We have a list of bank accounts you probably don't remember owning."

"Then why did you ask?"

"Nothing comes easy with you, does it? You're always on the attack. *Nastupatelnost.*"

I nodded, not surprised that she was familiar with the word that symbolized the policy of Russian intelligence—raw aggression.

She bit her pastry and talked while she chewed. "We know how your agencies work. They still teach about the Trust at Langley, and we're well aware it wasn't an isolated phenomenon."

The Trust was the name of a group of supposed anti-Bolsheviks created by the Chekists in the 1920s. Its purpose was to disseminate false information from Russia and, by pretending to be on the same side as the anti-Bolsheviks, expose émigré leaders in places like Estonia, Berlin, and Paris so that they could be assassinated. For six years it was enormously successful, crippling the émigrés' dissident movement and convincing many in the West not to push for change inside Russia because of the false rumor that the Bolsheviks were teetering on the brink of failure anyway. The Trust ended only when the Soviets sacrificed it for *another* subterfuge they thought would be even more effective.

Rhodes took another bite of her Danish. "Or how about Pavlovsky's Trap? Quintessentially Russian."

There were many variations of the trap used to identify potential defectors. Fences, markers, or installations were placed to appear like border outposts or safe houses. Somebody pretending to be an ally or friend would lure a suspected subversive to this "border," where he would be greeted by uniformed police and debriefing agents from the "host" country. Most of the defectors would name friends or others who were similarly inclined, unwittingly betraying the people they cared about the most. After the debriefing concluded, the would-be defector would be refused admission to the bordering country because of a diplomatic problem or some other plausible reason. Then he would be returned to Soviet custody—which he had never left, of course—and he and all those he had named would be taken to prison. Many of those trapped this way never knew they had been in Soviet hands the whole time.

I shifted my weight, trying to ease the tension in my neck, tired of sparring with Rhodes. "Those things are only concepts to you," I said. "Your leaders don't understand deception at a strategic level. It's the difference between a chess grand master and an amateur. One sees twenty moves ahead, the other sees two."

Rhodes wiped her mouth with a paper napkin. "You don't think much of us, do you, Volk?" She glanced out the window, where a blue Taurus was pulling into the parking lot. I started to rise, but she put her hand on mine to stop me. "We're not *that* stupid. We don't think you abandoned the strategy of *nastupatelnost* after the fall of Communism, and we try to know our enemy as well as he knows us."

Reflected light painted the windshield of the Taurus with green neon cut by slashes of red from the taillights of an idling panel truck. I had to angle my head to see inside. At first I could make out only the shape of the driver, a dark form that rose almost to the roof. Then the lights from the panel truck disappeared as it pulled away, and the man inside the Taurus became visible.

NSA agent Brock Matthews eyed me through the glass with his usual fixed intensity. He held a cell phone against his ear, lips moving. As soon as he saw me notice him he got out of the car and stood next to the open door, visually sweeping the area with his predatory gaze. He finished the call, slammed the car door closed, and straightened his cuffs before marching into the coffee shop. Tall, put together in hard planes and angles, Matthews strode toward me with his brow furrowed. He kicked a chair away from the table and sat heavily.

"We have a problem, Volk."

"Nice to see you, too, Matthews."

"I just got off the phone with a pissed-off cop named Swanson. They found McIntyre buried under some loose dirt at a construction site in Torrance. The back of his skull looked like a bowl of tomato soup."

"Volk has been with me ever since he was released from police custody," Rhodes said.

Matthews glanced at her. "That's no good, Elizabeth. McIntyre bought it last night or this morning while our friend here was on the loose with no supervision. Right around the same time Sasha Tovar took three bullets."

Both of them looked at me.

"Well," Rhodes said finally.

"Makes sense," I said. "McIntyre was accused of bludgeoning my father to death, so I gave him the same treatment."

Rhodes shook her head. "You didn't, though. Did you?"

I stared at Matthews. I'd known him for six years, off and on. He had popped into my life at odd times ever since our first meeting in Washington during the joint intelligence meeting where he had waxed on about how "you fucking guys never give up." Seeing him meant something bad was about to happen, I thought. He had been all over Walker's death from the beginning—before it even happened, when he came to see me in Vadim's Café, and afterward, when Valya saw him outside GRU headquarters while I had my chat with Bassoff.

"You're everywhere, Matthews. Why did you come to Vadim's Café the day Walker was hit? 'Touching base,' I think you said, but that was bullshit, wasn't it?"

"Yeah, right. *I'm* the one running around killing people. Listen, we need to get moving. LAPD issued an APB, and we have to get to a place where we can control the situation. You understand? You're a whole lot better off with us than in their gentle hands."

He stood, towering over the table, and motioned for us to follow. As he led the way out of the coffee shop to the Taurus another thought occurred to me. If anybody could plant a leak to make it appear as if it had come from Sixth Bureau, Matthews could. And what better way to make sure I was out of Moscow while Walker was murdered and planted in my warehouse than to leak the whereabouts of Lachek?

chapter 66

We piled into the Taurus, Rhodes driving with me next to her and Matthews in back. I felt a chill in my spine, imagining the muzzle of a gun pressed against the back of my seat. Rhodes accelerated out of the lot, pushing me deeper into the seat.

"Where to?" she said.

"Take the four-oh-five south," Matthews said. "We have a safe house near the airport. I'll guide you when we get close."

I rotated my body so I could see him. No gun. Instead he was texting or e-mailing someone from his phone.

"A witness put you and a fat man named Bassoff at my warehouse right at the time somebody was blowing holes in Everett Walker," I said. "Another one saw you at GRU headquarters a week or so later."

He flipped his phone closed and looked at Rhodes. "How much does he know?"

"Only what he's been able to guess about our, ah . . . our situation. He read about a mole in Everett Walker's script."

When a car rounded a turn ahead of us, its headlights briefly illuminated Rhodes's face. She squinted in the glare, her features squeezed into their now familiar worried expression, brows drawn together as if to shield her eyes from something more than the stab of light. Then the car swept past us, and she dissolved into a dark silhouette.

"All right, Volk." Matthews sounded tired. "We've got a problem. A GRU officer named Bassoff has been running agents in the U.S. for a long time. Nothing new about that, we do the same thing over there. Most of the time things stay kosher on both sides."

He paused and held up a finger while he read something on his phone. "Swanson," he said to Rhodes. "Think he has a way to track this vehicle?"

She looked at him in the mirror. "I don't know."

Matthews tapped another message, then closed his phone, looking concerned. "So back to our problem, Volk. One of Bassoff's agents—a man we've labeled *Saturn*—has been operating for decades. We know this, but the trail disappears whenever we get close. We think Everett Walker might have known his identity, and that Walker went to Moscow to find out how much his silence was worth."

I remembered Rykov saying something similar, but I didn't believe it then and I didn't now. From reading the script and hearing Sasha Tovar talk about her husband, Walker struck me more as a man who would go to greater lengths to honor a commitment to his friend than to sell his silence about the identity of a Soviet mole. But I played along to keep Matthews talking.

"So you think Saturn ordered the hit on Walker?"

"Yes, and we suspect he's behind Tovar's murder, too. He's trying to cover up something, but we don't know what."

I had always thought of Matthews as a man who was wound too tight, often on edge. I figured that was part of the persona he adopted in a foreign country while on assignment. But seeing him here on his home turf, I realized that the man never relaxed.

"Why would I want to help you find a Russian agent?"

He leaned forward against my seat back, studying me. "Because Saturn is the person who ordered your father's murder."

He said it as though it would trigger an emotional reaction, so I gave him one. I hardened my features and dropped my gaze as if I were trying to hide my anger.

"Why?"

"He found out your father was working for us."

I had heard from all sides now. Isadora and Matthews, both claiming my father had worked for the Americans. Everett Walker, writing in his script that my father was a major source of disinformation to the Americans and one of the Russians' most valuable officers. And Bassoff, who said he didn't know.

We were on the 405, Rhodes weaving the Taurus through traffic. My left leg throbbed. Moving it triggered a spiking jolt of phantom pain, like electrified wires shoved into the nerves in my thighs. Sometimes my foot feels as if it is still attached, twisted at the same impossible angle as when the tibia and fibula splintered under the pressure of a homemade vise built by Chechen rebels in the high mountains. I haven't been whole for a long time now, and all of that happened in a place far different from this sprawling cradle of humanity. But sometimes I have to remind myself to forget the past.

Rhodes noticed the strobing colored lights first, in the rearview mirror, then both Matthews and I swung around at the same time to see two black-and-whites, their flashers tinting the rear window blue and red.

"What do you think?" Rhodes said.

Matthews turned to face me, his expression grave, almost apologetic. "We don't have a choice. We have to deal with these yahoos. Pull over."

chapter 67

Rhodes took the next ramp off the 405. To our right an asphalt shoulder and a chain-link fence ran parallel to the road. To our left, a dirt berm carpeted with green plants like thick-bladed grass, then the ground fell away on the other side to the freeway below. I couldn't see how far the embankment dropped, but up ahead the freeway appeared to be a long way below our level.

"Relax, Volk," Matthews said. "We can handle this."

One of the police cars veered around us and slowed abruptly, forcing Rhodes to brake hard as she pulled onto the shoulder. The other car thumped our rear bumper when it skidded to a stop.

A pair of cops piled out of each car. Matthews jumped out to meet them, but his protests were lost in a jabber of raised voices and shouted orders. One of them drew his weapon and circled the Taurus in a crouch, arms extended. He yelled for me to keep my hands in sight.

"Do what they say," Rhodes warned.

The cop closed in. The muzzle of his gun, a Glock with a black rubber grip, quivered inches from my face beyond the side window. He released one hand and snatched my door open, then backed away, still shouting.

I stepped out, hands shoulder high, palms out. Another police car screeched to a stop, lights flashing. Swanson leaped from the passenger side while the car was still rocking. He stabbed a finger at me.

"Cuff him. *Now!*"

He strode toward Matthews, who had already wheeled to face him, both of them jabbing fingers, shouting about jurisdiction and just whose "goddamned property" I was. Rhodes joined the argument, as did a man in a business suit who had arrived with Swanson. The cops surrounding me continued to shout excited instructions at each other.

The fresh-faced young cop who had guarded the door to McIntyre's flat approached me from behind, flex-cuffs in his hands, careful to stay out of the line of fire of his partner, who had circled the Taurus and now stood to one side, aiming his gun at my head.

But it was the first cop, the one with the Glock, who lost his composure. Seeing that I was covered, he rushed up to me, put his mouth close to my ear, said, "This is for Mac," and clubbed the butt of his Glock into the back of my skull. I spun with the blow but still caught enough of it to see a blinding flash that dropped me to my knees.

"That was fucking stupid, man," somebody said, and somebody else grabbed my left wrist and wrenched my arm behind my back. I went with the momentum of the turn and jacked the heel of my right hand into his chin. It was the fresh-faced cop. His teeth crunched together as his jawbone cracked.

And I kept moving.

I swept my leg in an arc that caught one of them behind the heel and sent him flying backward. The top of his head smacked the fender of the Taurus on the way down. I planted a boot on his chest and leaped over him, catapulting myself across the hood to the other side of the car, gathering steam, ignoring the shouted curses and commands to halt. Something whistled over my head, followed immediately by the staccato drumbeat of gunshots.

I reached the berm on the edge of the ramp, pounded through the carpeting of grassy plants, and launched myself in a dive that seemed to last forever. The ground rushed toward me. I tucked and tried to roll, landed with a sickening whump, rolled some more and tried to regain my feet, but couldn't, so I tumbled until I slammed into a concrete trough.

Vehicles rushed past on the 405 above me. More shouts, and then a searchlight blared down, stuttering over scrub bushes and grass toward me. I bolted away. Pulled out the Beretta and fired several rounds in the air, hoping the sound of shots would slow down the pursuit. Twenty meters, thirty, the cold light dancing crazily along with me. At the far end of the gutter I came to a dark mouth in the concrete. I skidded, twisted, dived into a corrugated steel culvert, and plunged ahead, burrowing like an animal on my hands and knees.

chapter 68

The other end of the culvert opened onto another concrete gutter on the opposite side of the 405. I emerged muddy after the long crawl, scraped and bruised from the tumble down the embankment. Blood trickled down my neck from the hammering I had taken from the Glock. But I was mobile, and still free.

I raced up a slope to run parallel to a chain-link fence with a curved overhang and clad in opaque plastic sheathing. Found a spot where somebody had scooped out a crawlspace in the dirt beneath it. Wriggled through it, crossed a mucky drainage basin, splashing through standing water, and jumped another fence into the sprawling parking lot of a giant retail store.

Colored lights still flared on the other side of the freeway. The searchlight darted along the embankment in sharp, frantic jabs. Shouted instructions floated over the fence across the gutter, meaning that several of my pursuers had come through the culvert. No helicopter yet.

I jogged along the edge of the parking lot until I found an ancient Datsun pickup. Waited a few seconds to make sure no one was around. Shattered the window with my elbow, unlocked the door, and climbed inside. Turned on my back and popped an access cover under the steering wheel. Found two red wires, stripped the ends with the knife from my prosthesis, and twisted them together, the process taking longer than it should have because my hands were shaking. Located the ignition wire—brown in this case—stripped it, touched the end to the connected red wires, then revved the engine with my free hand on the pedal when the ignition sparked.

I drove out of the lot slowly, signaling each turn, staying a hair under the speed limit. Stopped at the parking garage at LAX and retrieved the Venona cable from the glove compartment of the rented Prius using the key I'd stashed in the wheel well. Mentally debated exchanging the pickup for the Prius, but decided I would keep the Prius in reserve, my last untraceable mode of transportation.

I drove out of the garage, abandoned the Datsun in a mall parking lot, then walked two miles to an economy motel beneath the flight path into LAX. Two stories, tarpaper roof, lap-metal siding, the steel rail on the second-floor balcony listing dangerously. I paid cash for three days. The clerk took my money indifferently and handed me a key attached to a triangular piece of plastic with the number *221* flaking off both sides. Once inside the room I locked the door and propped a chair under the knob.

The wall adjoining the room next door rang hollow when I tapped the butt of my knife against it. I worked the tip of the knife into the brittle wallboard and rotated the blade to make a hole big enough to get my fingers inside and pull. The board crumbled into chalky pieces held together by glued paper, which I ripped away and tossed into the bathroom until I had an opening a meter and a half tall between two metal studs. Once I removed the pink insulation, only a thin sheet of wallboard separated me from the room next door. I could kick my way through it and be gone in seconds.

That done, I smoothed the Venona cable flat on the bed. Positioned the remaining chair so that it faced the door, perched myself on the edge of the chair, and tried to focus on the papers.

I was trapped, nearly out of time.

I had to *think*.

PART VI

Who is the third who walks always beside you?
When I count, there are only you and I together
But when I look ahead up the white road
There is always another one walking beside you
Gliding wrapt in a brown mantle, hooded
I do not know whether a man or a woman
—But who is that on the other side of you?

—T. S. Eliot, *The Waste Land*

chapter 69

Reese thumbs through the pages of a NCIX subpoena served on Lorelei less than an hour ago, delivered to his Century City office by a gray-haired corporate lawyer in a thousand-dollar suit, who now squirms in the club chair across from Reese's desk. To the left of the lawyer, Santori, freshly returned from D.C., occupies a matching chair in the corner with his legs crossed and his arms folded.

Reese studies Santori while pretending to read the paperwork. He doesn't look like a sociopath, but how many do? In the six years Reese has known him, Santori has killed more than a dozen people, most recently McIntyre during a very busy night before he jumped on the plane to the East Coast. He always looked happiest after nights like that, but today seems to be an exception.

Reese drops his gaze to the six-page subpoena in his hand demanding that Lorelei produce records—lots of them—despite the pressure brought to bear by the politicians in Lorelei's pocket. Meaning that NCIX is deadly serious, and that they believe they're closing in. Good. He turns the page, scanning the details of what they want. Financial information about the Tovar documentaries, including a list of the Spotlight executives who worked on her films. The names of board members and officers at Lorelei and each of its subsidiaries. Source documents for Lorelei's tax payments and financial reporting.

None of that troubles Reese. Most of it is publicly available, particularly regarding Lorelei subsidiaries that routinely bid and perform government contracts. The Pentagon requires reams of information about the firms that design and build its missiles, radar, imaging, and guidance systems.

What gives him pause now is the demand that Lorelei provide a detailed list of all the research and development projects in the pipeline that have military applications, not just those using government funding. *That* cut too close to JANUS for comfort. The team working the JANUS program had already grown to three hundred, scattered from Menlo Park to Princeton. The program couldn't be left out of any response to an inquiry like this, but neither could its findings—or even the current direction of its research—be revealed in any way except for the way that Reese had been planning for years.

JANUS changed the rules of the game, skipped a generation in the push for stealth technology. Bending every wavelength of light to render small objects invisible was the *first* step in the new technology. Lorelei's scientists had figured out how to do the same thing with larger, irregularly shaped objects, and to render such objects invisible to radar as well as the naked eye. Imagine the devastation to be wrought by one bomber or a single tank that can't be seen or detected.

"We can delay this for hours, but probably not days," the meticulously coifed lawyer says. He keeps crossing and recrossing his legs, looking out the window at a summer squall building in the west.

He had achieved the rank of colonel working in the Judge Advocate General corps for twenty years. Now, Reese knows, he makes more in a week working for Lorelei than he used to make in a year.

"It's overly broad," the lawyer says. "It will take a long time to compile, they already have most of this information in one form or another, that sort of thing. But it won't take them long to invoke *national security* and get a judge who'll go along with it. And we'll look like unpatriotic assholes if we're perceived as putting company above country. Not to mention what it does to our eligibility to bid future projects."

JANUS is the only project that concerns Reese. The others matter not at all. They're background noise, nothing more, marginal improvements to existing technologies.

But JANUS will buy ten years. Longer than the United States kept the secrets of the bomb, for Christ's sake! Long enough to change history in the quiet way that the most important things usually do. No medals, no magazine covers, no credit at the Kennedy School of Government, just quietly effective. The way Reese likes best.

He glances at Santori picking lint from his slacks. The subpoena and the fact that Volk is still on the loose are major blows to Santori, Reese knows. Bassoff will be asking pointed questions, dangerous questions for Santori. Worse, the Feds are close. If Santori can't get things squared away they'll be pounding on his door any day now, cuffs ready for the perp walk.

Reese decides to let Matthews and the other geniuses at the NSA worry about the details. They're the ones who'll have to keep the subterfuge going after he's gone. He's done his part, played his role to perfection. All that's left for him is the final act.

He flings the subpoena so that it skids in a half circle on the slick top of his desk in front of the lawyer. "Don't delay." He addresses the lawyer, but he watches Santori's head jerk up, his eyes wide. "Give them what they want as quickly as it can be done."

The lawyer notes something on his pad, holding it between his body and Reese like a paper bulwark. Santori starts to protest, but Reese quiets him with a raised palm.

"Of course we'll cooperate." Reese leans back in his wheelchair and folds his hands over his belly, satisfied with his decision and Santori's reaction. "This is a matter of national security," he says in his best public relations voice, the one he used to employ so effectively at press conferences, back when he did such things.

Santori's cell phone chirps while the lawyer is still packing his briefcase. He listens for less than ten seconds, ends the call, then waits impatiently for the lawyer to leave.

"Found the fucker," Santori announces when they're alone. "Holed up in a motel near LAX." He checks his watch as he heads for the door that leads to Reese's private elevator. "In thirty minutes he's a dead man."

chapter 70

I push aside the Venona cable and settle back into the creaking hardness of the motel chair, no closer to answers now than I was an hour ago. I cup my face in my hands and drag them downward, stretching sandpapery skin, pulling my eyes wide open. I listen to the noises of the night— a passing plane, rumbling thunder, hissing rain. The striped pattern of light on the floor and the corner of the bed ripples with the motion of the blinds in the air from the vent.

A figure darkens the window.

My hand drops to the butt of the Beretta.

Another shadow joins the first one. They merge for a moment as one of them pushes the other out of the frame, then they both disappear.

Using my left hand, I gather and refold the papers on the bed and stuff them into the pocket of my jacket. Glide over to the hole I punched in the wall and press my ear against the last layer of wallboard. No sound. Maybe the family next door went out for food.

I step back and punch my foot through the board. It makes a dull crunching noise, and chalky dust puffs up, but nobody screams on the other side. One more kick before I thrust my head through the gap. Two roller suitcases, dirty clothes on the bed next to an empty baby bottle, but no people. I kick away more of the wallboard until I have a hole big enough to crawl through, then hunker down and wait.

Nothing happens.

Maybe I panicked. How could they have found me so soon? But as soon as I think that, I dismiss the thought. An unseen helicopter, a camera triggered on a street corner on my way here—as Rhodes said, it's tough to stay off the grid. However they did it, the people now on the balcony outside the room are there for me, I'm sure of it.

Four rounds left in the Berretta. Stay put or attack?

Waiting works best in most cases, because the person in hiding has the advantage of position and can shoot anything that moves. But I can't fire until I know their intentions. If I kill a legitimate American agent or police officer I'll wind up in a secret prison or on a rendition flight to a foreign country not as squeamish about using the *zhgut* and the *dubinka*, the club and the truncheon. "Beat, beat," Stalin once wrote next to the name of a man on a death list, a fat "album" complete with photos and biographies of the poor souls marked for death. I don't want to endure the American version of Stalin's punishment.

I unwedge the chair from the doorknob but leave the door locked and the security chain in place. Squeeze through the hole in the wall into the room next door. Creep to the window and peek through the blinds. Two men stand on the balcony, both wearing business suits. I recognize CIA agent York by the shape of his silhouette, large and round. The other man looks familiar, but I'm not sure who he is until he turns sidewise.

Santori.

York and Santori, together here in this unlikely place. Here without any other support, plotting like hitmen. Which means neither one of them is legitimate in any sense of the word.

I flatten myself against the wall where I still have an oblique view of the men through the blinds. They'll move soon enough, and when they do I'll be ready.

chapter 71

Reese calls NSA agent Brock Matthews from his Bell helicopter as it tilts through a long curve over downtown L.A., heading south for San Diego. Home. Home for the last time, if all goes according to plan.

"You're off?" Matthews says, his voice amplified by the headset.

"I'll be home in less than an hour. Santori got the word, and he's on his way." Reese levers his seat closer to the windshield. "Who's going to win that fight?"

"Volk."

"Santori might surprise you."

"Santori's toast. He just doesn't know it yet."

The lighted derricks and cranes and container ships of the Port of Long Beach pass below, always a pleasant sight to Reese, who likes the idea of industry, of people and products moving all over the world. Huntington Beach appears through the front canopy, with the sprawl of Newport and Laguna Niguel beyond it, a breathtakingly beautiful stretch of coastline, even at night in the rain. Coils and splashes and fans of light along the edge of the blackened sea. None of the desperation of day-to-day life evident from here.

"Then what?" Reese says.

"Then we see how long it takes Volk to put the pieces together. His woman in Moscow has Rykov's file. She'll get it to him. And if not I'll figure out a way to have Rhodes nudge him closer if we need to. Things will move quickly after that."

Dead air fills Reese's earphones for a moment.

Matthews says, "We weren't supposed to lose Rykov."

Reese doesn't care about Rykov. He already spends too much time reliving what happened to all the people on his own long list. Matthews says something more that Reese fails to catch. Something about Katarina, although Matthews calls her Isadora.

"What about her?" Reese asks.

"I said, did you phone her?"

"Why?"

"That was a mistake. Bassoff is cleaning up his messes."

Reese remembers the way Katarina sold out Stepan, throwing him to the wolves in America and Russia. Stepan's heart was always in the right place. At least he *thought* he was working for his country, even if he had been duped. Katarina had sold herself so many times she should have strapped a mattress to her back.

"I would do the same thing in Bassoff's place. I'm surprised he let her live this long."

Matthews says nothing for a moment, and Reese contents himself with the view of the dark Pacific rolling away to the west in a never-ending black dome sprinkled with a few lonely lights.

Matthews clears his throat. "I need to say thank you, sir, personally and on behalf of our country."

Reese chuckles. Matthews is the latest in a long list of control officers. Better than most. He knows how, when, and to whom he needs to ping-pong bits of information and disinformation to achieve his aims. And at six years he has been the second-longest American control officer in Reese's career. But Reese can't even remember all their names anymore. They come and they go. Everybody does. "Skip the horse-shit, son," he says, and cuts him off.

He hits a button to open a line to the pilot, thinking that the San Diego harbor is always well lit at night. "Make a pass over the Midway before we land."

"Yes, sir," the pilot says.

Reese settles in for the remainder of the flight. He used to wonder how the end would feel, but now that the time has come he finds himself impatient just to be done with the damn thing.

chapter 72

I watch York and Santori talk on the balcony for several minutes. Then the manager joins them in a circle of electric yellow light cast by a bulb mounted over one of the doors. He's dark-skinned, soft but not fat, shiny black hair like a pelt. Money changes hands, but he still looks uncertain. Santori grabs his sleeve and leads him toward the room I rented, past my post in the window in the room next door, York trailing them. By the time they reach the door I've lost sight of them.

Somebody knocks, three tentative raps, probably the manager.

Nothing.

Now somebody pounds the door.

"Police, Volk!" Santori yells. "Open up!"

The manager must have been turning the key in the lock at the same time, because I hear the door open and thud to a stop as it hits the end of the chain. That sound is followed by a loud crash as either Santori or York kicks in the door, shattering wood and snapping the chain.

I slip out of the room next door. Nobody is left on the balcony. If they played it the way I think they did, Santori and York sent the manager through ahead of them so that he would take the first bullet.

I crab along the balcony, holding the Beretta beneath my chin in two hands like a man at prayer, ignoring the shocked face of a guest staring at me two doors down. Edge into the room to find all three of them gawking at the hole in the wall. York starts to turn, but I club the back of his head with the Beretta before he can.

Santori whirls, his gun hand rising, the muzzle blossoming orange flame as I bull into York's dead weight, pulling the trigger. Both of our shots go wild, and I plow into Santori. We knock the manager to the floor and tumble onto him.

Santori fights with controlled fury. He clamps my right wrist at the same time that I grab his and launches his head at my face, grazing my cheekbone as I recoil and then thrust my head forward. The crown of my skull connects solidly with his nose, splattering blood, but my momentum gives him enough leverage to roll off the hapless manager, and somehow in the brawl he's able to grab my thumb and torque it backward and I lose the Beretta.

Twisting, rolling, we both grab his gun, and our struggle becomes a battle of strength and will, our faces inches apart, me on top. His face flames red, veins popping, sweat and blood lathered in his eyes, and he slowly caves under the strain as I wrench his hand back at an impossible angle. The gun kicks, blasting a stray bullet. Trembling with the effort, I increase the pressure until I feel something pop in his wrist. He gives in gradually, grunting with every inch lost, the muzzle of his automatic jittering down toward his belly.

He rips his left hand loose, bucks wildly, and claws at my eyes, but I clamp my knees and ride him, forcing the muzzle into his heaving gut, absorbing his blows with my shoulders and the top of my head, crushing his hand as I work my finger into the trigger guard.

The gun jerks between us.

This time the sound is muffled but still loud, and Santori stiffens beneath me, eyes goggling and inflamed with burst blood vessels. The air leaks out of him in a prolonged "Uhmmm." It smells like coffee.

He's still gurgling when I push myself off of him, his gun in my hand, gasping for breath. The motel manager is dead, crumpled face-down, the side of his face a goulash of blood and brain matter. He must have caught the stray bullet. York moans. A bloody, egg-sized lump is already swelling from the back of his head, but he'll probably live. He carries a full-size Beretta in a shoulder holster, which I take because it has a full magazine.

Then I stand in place, chest heaving, feeling jittery and light.

I think if Santori had landed on top of me instead of the other way around, I would be dead. He was at least as strong as me. Weight and leverage were all that saved me.

As tired as I am, I have to move. One or more of the frightened guests must have called the police by now. Voices on the balcony carry inside, everybody too afraid to peer into the room, but that won't last for long.

Santori shudders and belches blood. His flat eyes appear to be tracking me, but I don't think anything's registering. The crimson circle pooling around him tells me the bullet passed right through him. The exit wound will be the size of my fist.

I go into the bathroom, moving unsteadily, slightly dizzy. Use York's gun to knock out the opaque windowpane and scrape away the remaining shards of glass. No foothold outside, just a four-meter drop onto a strip of cracked asphalt between the motel and a chain-link fence. I slide the Beretta under my waistband, stand on the porcelain tank, back out the window feet-first, hang for an instant, and let go. Land hard, most of my weight on my right leg but enough on my left to send a shot of fresh pain up my thigh. I climb the fence and drop into a patch of chest-high weeds. Crouch there in the rainy darkness, listening.

Raised voices, the whoosh of cars on the 405, sirens in the distance.

Staying low, I lope toward a busy street less than a quarter of a mile away. Moving fast, I reach the parking garage at LAX in twenty minutes. Stop at a bathroom on the ground floor to clean up the best I can, washing the blood off my jacket in the sink when I'm alone. The rectangular plastic key still rests on the metal lip inside the left front wheel well of the Prius. The driver's license is in the glove box.

I drive out of the garage and head south—wet, shaking as I daub the blood on the back of my head with a damp paper towel, but free for the moment.

chapter 73

I park the Prius on a side street near the Internet café on Broadway and walk the rest of the way through a misty drizzle. The proprietor takes in my cuts and bruises, but accepts my money without question. I go to a computer in the back, far away from the only other customer, set up a free Gmail account in minutes, and compose an e-mail to Valya's main account.

We already searched the names of the Czech delegates to the Trident conference. Nothing matched. But now the idea has taken root that this might be an exclusively American problem.

Two lists, I type. *Americans who traveled with the Czech delegates to the Trident conference. Officers and directors of Lorelei Industries, USA.*

Click on Send. Wait. Most of the time Valya's e-mails are routed to her cell phone, so this one should reach her soon.

I don't bother with Spotlight Studios or any other Lorelei subsidiary, because I've decided to stick with Everett Walker's lead. He started down this path long before I did, and he carried the hidden cable and picture of my father for a reason—he wanted to communicate with me. He must have carried the pen with the name *Lorelei* on it for the same reason. Walker aimed the gun. I just need to pull the trigger.

An e-mail pops into the inbox. Valya. *Can you call me?*

No.

One hour, she writes. *I'll find out. And I have to scan something to send to you.*

It is almost ten in the morning in Moscow, the same in Tbilisi or Grozny, but wherever she is Valya is there for me when I need her, as always.

While waiting for her next message I search for news about Sasha's murder, learning nothing I don't know. Reports of McIntyre's death have hit the Web, but only a one-paragraph piece that contains his name, age, and status as a retired LAPD detective.

Three spam messages appear. I delete them.

I think about Walker's script and his photographically reduced cable with the handwritten note *Beneš Czech delegation?* and the pen in his pocket that said Lorelei. For the hundredth time I try to draw a connection.

A message hits the inbox. *These Americans accompanied Churchill and Beneš on the Queen Elizabeth*, followed by a list of names, none of which means anything to me.

Another new message arrives. Following the name *Lorelei* is a list of its directors and a roster of more than a dozen company names, many of which I recognize from the crimson sign outside the Lorelei building. Beneath each company are the names of its officers. None of them matches any of the people who were part of the Czech delegation to the Trident conference.

I type the words *No help* and hit Send. Just as I do so another message appears.

Rykov is dead.

I know.

He left a note for you about a box of documents sent to him by Lachek's lawyer in Macao. And this memo.

A document attached to the e-mail opens with Adobe Reader. A memo from Rykov to me, six single-spaced paragraphs summarizing the parts he believed I would find interesting in "the Bassoff dossier," as he labeled it. The dossier was one of many he found in Lachek's box of files.

I read the memo quickly. Most of it is old news by now.

Bassoff was the architect behind Stepan's defection in 1974. It was his first major triumph, launching his career according to what Rykov had learned from Lachek's files.

The radar imaging equipment in Stepan's plane was technology the Americans would have had within a year or two anyway. That was the "give." Stepan's real cargo was a Byzantine snarl of half-truths and lies about the officers, agents, and structure of the GRU in America. He fingered Russian officers and agents who had lost their usefulness, protected the identity of moles, and accused loyal American officers of treachery. Doled out over the course of several years of debriefings, calibrated to do the most damage, Stepan's accounts set the American counterintelligence apparatus back by years.

Even better, after the Americans thought they had drained him of all useful information, they gave him a new life in Los Alamos and Los Angeles. Once he settled in, Stepan mined a rich vein of information, delivering reams of technological data to Bassoff.

But Stepan finished second in the pantheon of Bassoff's triumphs. Foremost was an agent-in-place in America, a man who had started his career in the U.S. Army, then the Department of Defense, and, later, one of the largest defense contractors in America. Still active, that agent had become the GRU's longest-running and most important asset in America. No name was given, but I had to assume this referred to the person Matthews and Rhodes called Saturn.

Valya e-mails again. *Did that help?*

Not sure, I write back.

Do you think 19 is the same man as Bassoff's agent?

Doubtful. 19 would be too old by now to be active.

I think about Lachek and the files he apparently kept on his friends and enemies. "There is a man, there is a problem. No man, no problem," Stalin once said. But Stalin would be wrong in this case. Lachek's death triggered his attorney to send the box of files, and problems are about to cascade everywhere among all the people in Lachek's world. Intelligence officers like Bassoff, political and military officials like the General—I probably only know a fraction of the damage that can be done by those files. And who benefits? Possibly the same man who arranged for me to get a whiff of Lachek's scent in Macao, knowing I would deal with him Stalin's way. NSA agent Brock Matthews. Matthews's fingerprints seem to be everywhere, and it is the Americans who will gain the most from all the havoc released.

The only other customer in the place gathers his things and goes to the front counter to pay his account.

Miss me? Valya writes.

No.

Ya right. R U safe?

I think about that one for a moment, decide I am as safe as could be expected. Every part of my body hurts, but I seem to have escaped pursuit, at least temporarily. *Yes. How did you get this document?*

Someone delivered it to the loft after Rykov was murdered. I don't know who.

Probably the mousy-haired woman with the angry eyes, I think. She looked the type to do Rykov's bidding after he died. *You're still in Moscow?* I type.

Yes, I decided I'm not wasted here.

I have to press the heel of my hand against my jawbone to stop the welling emotion brought by that comment. It makes me think of Mary Montoya, my father's short-lived wife in Santa Fe. Sitting in her rocker waiting to die, stacking time and stacking pain. *Find the one he loved*, she told me. *She can give you answers.* Isadora, the KGB's main illegal officer in L.A. during Stepan's years here. Isadora was Stepan's Valya, but I fear she may have consumed him the same way a black widow consumes its mate.

A new message arrives.

Remember what I told you? You are not Stepan. Whether he was good or evil has no bearing on you. Who was it who said that the relationship between father and son always brings pain?

I read the message twice. The first time I think of my father. The second time I think of 19, too old to still be an active agent, but what would his children think if they knew? If they were faced with evidence of their father's guilt? Traitor or patriot, they would probably wonder. Would they put their thumb on the scale the same as me?

I scroll back to Valya's first e-mail. Start at the very top, the chairman of Lorelei. *Under Secretary of Defense (Policy) Alfred Reese (Ret.).* I Google him. Compare his biography to what I've learned about Saturn. U.S. Army, Department of Defense, private industry.

Maybe.

I keep digging. His address is there in black and white, listed on the Web pages of half a dozen philanthropic organizations, surprising for a man of his wealth and prestige, unheard of for an intelligence officer. In addition to Lorelei he serves on the boards of eight other conglomerates. He received the Congressional Medal of Honor.

Maybe not.

A message appears. *You ok?*

Checking something.

I research six more Lorelei board members during the next hour. Nothing jumps out at me, not the way Reese did initially.

I navigate back to the first search pages about Reese. Click on every link without finding anything for twelve pages. On the thirteenth page I find a link to a feature in *Newsweek* magazine and click through it, mostly skimming. I stop on a picture showing two men in uniform standing on the banks of the Thames, Big Ben in the background. Second Lieutenant Alfred Reese and his father, dated 1943.

Reese is part of an American military dynasty—the grandson of a navy commodore and the son of Major General Gordon Reese, who was one of the "founding fathers of the United States Air Force." I Google *Gordon Reese*, find his Wikipedia bio, and learn that he was stationed in Berlin before the war, then—my fingers pause over the keyboard, my heart begins racing—then Gordon Reese moved to London as a liaison to the Czech government in exile there.

After a pause, I resume searching. More links, more stories, more air force history. No word on whether Gordon Reese attended the Trident conference. But there wouldn't be, would there? Not if he was a man who did most of his fighting in the shadows.

I surf back and find Reese's address. Right there in the open, almost as though he wants to be found. MapQuest tells me the drive to San Diego will take one hour and fifty-four minutes.

Maybe Reese is my man, maybe not. But I like the idea of starting at the top. Why not find the big dog and make him howl?

Another message comes in from Valya.

When r we going 2 swim under the full moon?

Soon, I type back. *Very soon now.*

chapter 74

Nighttime in San Diego, lightning lacing the sky outside Reese's home office, Bassoff's voice crackling over the line. "I need it, Reese. This is not negotiable. You *will* get it to me, no matter what the risk to yourself."

Reese settles back into his wheelchair, his heart thudding. "It's too much, too fast," he replies, keeping his tone level and steady. "I can't do it."

"Oh, my. Such defiance. A side of Under Secretary Reese we've never seen before."

"Let me give it to you in pieces. Too suddenly, everything comes back to me. I can't risk that. I've earned the right to take things slowly, Captain. Sixty years . . . I've earned it."

Bassoff slurps, snorts, and hacks, every wet, tubercular note amplified in Reese's headset. It takes Reese several seconds to recognize the sound as laughter.

"If you don't do it my way, I'll expose you for sure," Bassoff says. "You might as well take the chance."

"Exposure hurts you as badly as it does me. Your greatest strength is that nobody knows how much you really have."

"Hmm. I always knew you had a limit, Reese. I used to wonder when we would reach it."

"Now you know."

More hacking laughter carries over the line. "Maybe not."

Reese forces himself to keep breathing steadily, taking care not to reveal his excitement. JANUS will be infinitely more successful if Bassoff believes he wasn't meant to have the information.

"Meaning what?" Reese says.

"Meaning there is something you fear more than exposure."

Reese closes his eyes. They have finally reached the endgame. Bassoff has worked so hard to get this information that now he trusts it completely.

"You can't threaten me," Reese says. "There's not a soul on this earth who means anything to me."

"No, not on this earth, but I think there's a soul burning in hell that matters to you. I know your secret, Reese. Such a burden to live with all these years, protecting his memory, hmm?"

"I don't know what you're talking about."

"I think you do." Bassoff is almost purring, like a cat lapping milk. "But don't worry. I'm willing to let the secret of Source 19 die with you."

Bassoff pauses, but Reese says nothing.

"You can't ask for more than that," Bassoff says. "One last batch of information can't hurt too much, can it? Something you've done a thousand times before. Once a *chuzhoi*, always a *chuzhoi*, I like to say."

"You're scum, Bassoff." Reese says, putting a quiver in his voice to send the message to Bassoff that his victory is complete. "You're not even a life-form."

Bassoff chortles. "Yes, yes, of course. I'm scum." Still laughing, he disconnects.

Reese strips off the headset. Checks his e-mail and finds a message from Matthews. Volk is moving, expected to arrive at Reese's home in less than thirty minutes.

Reese's heart leaps. He feels alive, electrified, all his senses heightened. Two days ago he'd eaten a roast beef sandwich at his desk, and now he smells cooked meat. A loose sheet of paper rustles in a puff of air from the vent, thunderously loud in the unnatural silence of the rest of the house. All the people who normally turn his home into a beehive of activity—the house staff, rotating security teams, secretaries, gardeners, technicians, handymen—had been ordered away an hour ago.

He swivels his chair to face a monitor on the credenza. This computer controls everything in the house. Lights, temperature—from here he can warm the travertine floors in any one of the eight bathrooms—the sound system, televisions, appliances, intercoms, hidden microphones, and security cameras. He navigates through several screens devoted to security, making sure the grounds and house are empty of people, all the alarms disabled, the links to the San Diego Police Department closed. Then he shuts down the cameras. Anybody who checks later will see only a freeze frame of whatever they were recording at the moment he hit the key.

Once he finishes with that, he powers his chair onto the balcony. Folds his gloved hands over his belly and stares at the dark waters of the Pacific. A lonely light hovers far out to sea, little more than an amber smudge blinking in and out of existence through the rain. A fellow traveler in the darkness, Reese muses. Gliding along, wrapped in a brown mantle, hooded by the night.

chapter 75

The drive to San Diego takes two and a half hours. By the time I arrive, the rain is coming down harder, striking the windshield and the road like bullets. The closer I get to the address, the darker the streets become, until finally only occasional lights are visible from the road.

At the top of a hill are two columns made of stone slabs. The crested wrought-iron gate set between them stands open. I drive through and follow the path of a winding driveway to a courtyard dominated by a circular fountain. Left is an oversized garage with a carriage house on top. The soaring main house looms on the right, smoothly flowing walls and tall windows, lit up as if for a party. Manicured lawns, sculpted beds of red and white flowers, stone walls, a long deep terrace leading to a double front door built for elephants.

No guards or any other kind of security in sight.

I roll out of the Prius. Draw the Beretta. Charge toward the entrance pointing the gun with both hands, turning to sweep the area, walking backward up marble steps. Security cameras mounted above the door glow with red indicator lights, but they don't track my progress as expected. They remain pointed over my head, lifeless and blind.

An intercom set into the wall to my right crackles. A disembodied voice tells me "Push" just as a harsh buzzing indicates the lock has disengaged.

Inside is an entrance hall that seems big enough to land a jet, illuminated only with a diffuse light emanating from somewhere across the room, beyond an enormous landing. Two marble staircases set twenty meters apart loop their carved wooden banisters upward to meet at the mezzanine. Still no sign of anybody, but I have the sense of being watched as I take the stairs two at a time and hurry toward the light.

A gleaming marble-clad hallway leads me to a set of open double doors and the source of the light. Staying low, I cross the threshold and sweep the room with the Beretta. A low electrical hum startles me, and I throw myself away from the sound, roll onto a knee, one leg extended, and take aim at a man in a wheelchair.

Thick but not fat, gloved hands resting lightly on the arms of his chair, a woolen blanket covering his lap. Large head, heavy jowls that make his face appear to flow into his shoulders like a scoop of ice cream into a cone. His legs below the blanket look like spindly posts beneath the sharply creased fabric of his pants.

Reese holds himself perfectly still. The man before him is a distorted reflection of the man he used to know—Stepan thirty-five years ago when he stepped off the ladder in his flight suit beneath the immense fuselage of the Bear. But Volk's face is thinner than his father's, etched with harder lines. What had Katarina said? *Cruel, almost.* And right now his finger is tightening on the trigger.

"What took you so long?" Reese says as calmly as he can.

"Reese?"

"We have an hour, then some of the staff will return. You'll have to be gone by then." The vault is behind him. Careful to make no sudden moves, he spins his chair around, keeping his eyes on Volk. "No need for the gun, you know."

Volk's gaze is steady, penetrating. This is not a man to spend too much time with, Reese decides. A man like this will learn too much too quickly, and if he doesn't get the answers he wants he won't hesitate to force them out. Fine, Reese thinks. No need to wait all the way through the night. Finish with business, then end it quickly. The idea appeals to him. He likes doing the unexpected.

He pushes the knob on the arm of his chair and rolls ahead. "Follow me."

I watch Reese trundle away from me, then survey my surroundings. We're in an office. A huge desk dominates one side. Dark shelves and leather-bound books cover the walls on both sides of the desk. The wall behind the desk is made entirely of glass, open on hinges to a balcony facing the ocean. The air is thick with the smell of salt water and seaweed and wet rock.

Reese glides over marble between couches and chairs that form a U-shaped seating area. Presumably the open side is where he presides over meetings in his wheelchair. As he rolls, he thumbs a remote-control device in his lap, and a small panel in the wall slides away to reveal a keypad.

I make another circle, taking in the entire room, including a series of framed photographs—all of them scenes of war. Le Mort Homme at Verdun, a line of French troops in a bunker awaiting the inevitable German attack. The battleship *Arizona* dying beneath smoke and flames at Pearl Harbor. Omaha Beach on D-Day, the view from inside a landing craft as troops wade ashore. An aerial shot of a British fighter wing over the English Channel, probably during the Battle of Britain. American infantrymen huddled in a bunker at Chosin Reservoir, coated in white frost and misery. Balls of napalm fire, bright orange against the green jungles of Vietnam.

Many others.

"I like to remind myself why we fight our covert wars, Volk." Reese has reached the wall and turned his chair to face me. "So we don't have the big ones. Our job is to keep the balance of power equal, eh? Make sure neither side thinks it has an advantage."

He rotates back around and keys a series of digits into the keypad as I approach. A row of red lights begins flashing. Gloved fingers moving quickly, he punches in more numbers, and the red lights turn green one at a time. Then the entire wall, bookcases and all, slides away to reveal a stainless steel door.

Reese whirs forward to a dial mounted in the middle of the door and spins it back and forth. When he completes the last turn, servomotors whine, and the door sucks away from its housing.

"Come along," he says, and I step through the opening into a room ten meters square stacked with metal filing cabinets in front of concrete walls.

He trundles to a wall-mounted safe, opens it, and hands me a file.

"Your father's," he says. "I thought you'd want to see it first."

"You killed him?"

"Why would I do that? No, he was killed by the CIA. A man named Santori."

"Santori worked for your company."

"The CIA posted him as a military liaison. He keeps watch on me and Lorelei."

I don't know whether to believe Reese about Santori. I heft the file, feeling the weight of the thing—all the accumulated documents, photos, and whatever else, the sum of a lifetime in hiding.

"My father. He was a patriot?"

Reese nods. "Sometimes you play so many sides that you forget which one you started on, but Stepan never did."

"And you? Have you forgotten?"

His gaze sharpens. "You haven't figured out who I am?"

"I want to hear it from you."

"I've been working for your side since before you were born."

"So *you* are a traitor."

The skin around his eyes contracts, and his face colors. It seems as if the man buried inside the flesh is about to erupt. Then he visibly relaxes.

"I've always been true to the things I believe. Can you say the same, Colonel? Every time you pulled a trigger in Grozny or launched a missile in the mountains above Tindi, were you sure your cause was just?"

A man like me is not supposed to have doubts. How many times have I told myself that, and how many times have I wondered just the same? I wave the Beretta toward his legs. "What happened?"

"Guillain-Barré syndrome. An autoimmune disease, triggered in my case by an infection. Paralysis started in my feet and worked its way up. Properly treated, most people regain full function. I wasn't one of the lucky ones. My goddamn legs never stop aching. They tell me it's probably psychosomatic." He nudges his chin toward my left foot. "Like your leg, I imagine."

I toss my father's file onto the floor next to his chair. "You keep it. Burn it, for all I care."

"All business, is that it? Okay, we can do that."

He reaches into the small safe and withdraws a metal canister. Clumsily, the gloves making things difficult for him, he opens it, removes a spool of tape, and holds it in the air between us.

"Looks like the old super-eight-millimeter film, doesn't it? Trust me, it's not. It's altogether different, virtually indestructible, and we can cram enough data on it to fill ten encyclopedias. The thing I like, it's not what people expect. It travels easily, you see."

"I won't be able to get that out of the country."

"You won't need the can or the spool. The film will survive almost anything."

I still don't understand. Too many shots to the head, not enough sleep, maybe. He looks disappointed.

"Wrap the film around that thing," he says, pointing at my leg. "Beneath your boot. Even if they scan it, the titanium will hide the signature of the tape."

"I don't think that will work."

"Then think of something else."

He tosses the spool into the air, and I catch it instinctively as he motors past me, putting his chair between me and the door, and slaps his palm on a metal disc built into the wall. The door begins to hiss closed behind me.

I growl and leap across his body to punch the disc, but the door keeps moving, sucking closed. Reese maneuvers away from me, watching as I try to figure out how to open it.

"Calm down," he says. "Neither of us can do anything now. We're in lockdown. Nothing in the world will open that door for the next twenty-four hours."

"Why?"

"Because I don't want you loose out there anymore. The authorities will find everything in this room. They'll draw their own conclusions. You'll be searched, but they'll have to let you go, eventually. You're a legal agent of your government, here with CIA and NCIX permission. Everything you did, you did in self-defense."

"What about you?"

He reaches into the wall safe again. Pulls out a gun—a .45 Colt automatic. I don't feel threatened in the slightest. I can't pinpoint how or why, but his intentions are clear. "Wait! I have questions"—

"I think I'm finished here," he says, and he lifts his chin and places the muzzle beneath it and squeezes the trigger.

chapter 76

Twenty-four hours trapped in a metal box with the blood and the stench of a man nearly decapitated by the force of the bullet—the only way to get through it is to disengage. Go through the motions. Detach my prosthesis and remove the boot and the synthetic rubber form made to look like a real calf and wind the film around the titanium, then put everything back. Review all the files in the wall safe. Then retreat inside my mind and erase the image of Reese and the peacock tail of blood and gore decorating the wall behind him.

Twelve hours later, having considered everything I know from all different angles, I detach my prosthesis again and unwind the tape. I need to find a better hiding place.

The next day the servomotors hum, the big door sucks away from its housing, and I step through the portal into a circle of men in assault gear, poised for attack. Standing behind them are Rhodes, arms folded under her breasts, and Matthews, hands on his hips.

"Dead guy in here!" one of the men sings out behind me.

"You've got a lot of questions to answer, Volk," Matthews says.

I spend the next two weeks in isolation, somewhere inside an inland facility that took several hours to reach while I was shackled in the back of a windowless van. They strip-searched me as soon as we arrived. Gave me orange cotton overalls to wear. Took my prosthesis for several hours, minutely inspecting it, I'm sure, then they returned it, but without the knife.

Matthews led the questioning, but more than a dozen others took part, together and separately. Reese had killed himself, that much was clear from the forensics, apparently. A shovel found in the trunk of Santori's vehicle had bits of skin and hair from McIntyre's head. They didn't know who killed Sasha, but I wasn't guilty of murder, they agree. My crime, according to each one in a long series of interrogators, was espionage. Skeptical, sarcastic, friendly, abusive—nothing changes my answers, but nothing seems to convince them I'm not a spy, either.

One of the guards tosses my clothes into the room. "Change," he says, then locks the door behind him.

A few minutes later I'm led along an antiseptic hallway and through a doorway into an underground garage. Hands cuffed in front and attached to a leather belt cinched around my waist, legs shackled, I'm loaded into another van. After two hours of driving we get out in a different concrete garage. Jet engines roar all around us, the airport sounds inescapable. My guards take me to a room with a conference table and chairs. They remove the restraints and leave. A minute later Matthews enters.

He settles into a chair across from me, regarding me silently for a moment.

"One last time, Volk," he says. "Did Reese give you anything?"

"No."

He nods, and leans back into the chair. "Sorry to do this to you, but . . . You understand."

Two men enter the room. They're dressed in scrubs, surgical masks, and gloves.

"This makes five times. Where am I supposed to have hidden something?"

I remove my prosthesis and shrug out of my clothes. Stand balanced with one hand on the wall while they wand my clothes and my body. Matthews turns around when one of the men asks me to bend over the table and probes my anus with a gloved and lubed finger. Another man wheels in a portable X-ray machine. While we wait for the X-rays to develop, they dismantle my prosthesis and inspect the parts one at a time.

They know what to expect. One of the techs expertly works the mechanism where my knife would normally be, then fiddles with the other components, stripping it to the smooth rod of titanium. He finds nothing.

"What will happen to all of Reese's money?" I say.

Matthews looks surprised. "I don't know. I'm sure he had a will. God knows how much we're talking about."

"Enough to help a boy named Roberto Montoya in Santa Fe?"

"It's not my money."

I don't say anything, just watch him while he thinks it over. He shrugs.

"Maybe."

"And some for the families of Rykov and the two cops in Moscow. Not a fair trade for them, but better than nothing, don't you think?"

Matthews shoots his cuffs. Gives me an appraising look. "We might be able to help out there, too."

Neither of us says anything for a few minutes. Matthews crosses his arms and studies the carpeting, then snaps his fingers.

"Ah, yes, I almost forgot." He pulls my knife out of his pocket. "I'm going to give this back to you. Maybe I shouldn't, but hell, you're back to being a friendly now." He waves the blade in the air to draw the attention of the technician. "Take a look at this again, will you?"

The tech takes the knife from him and inspects it. He fingers the blade, ticking the ball of his thumb on the tip, making a metallic thrumming sound, turning the whole thing this way and that.

I pretend to watch while he does these things, but I'm really focused on Matthews. Looking for a sign. A tic, a sheen of sweat. Tight lips, shaking hands. But he calmly watches along with me, his features serene. Either he feels no fear or he has nothing to hide.

The tech strokes the grip, the handle wrapped in sharkskin worn smooth by use. He tests the butt, the bolster, and the spine, looking for loose joints. Unscrews the cap, empties the contents of the hollow grip into his palm, and sifts through them with his finger. Matches, thread, a coil of wire, a hook, and a short length of fishing line. He returns them to the handle, screws the cap back on, then twirls the blade like a drumstick and sets it next to the pile of my clothes.

"It's clean."

Another technician enters the room carrying the developed X-rays. He shakes his head no in answer to Matthews's raised brow.

"Get dressed, Volk," Matthews says. "We're sending you home." He grins in his familiar way, hard planes and angles, without mirth. "After all you've been through we'll put you on the plane ourselves. No need to bother with the security lines."

chapter 77

A flight attendant cruises down the aisle, lightly touching the back of each seat for balance. Her hip jostles the man in the aisle seat, his shoulder bumps the woman in the middle, her elbow brushes my arm, and the surface of the water in my plastic cup trembles almost imperceptibly. One small touch telegraphed across people and time. Ripples lapping ashore, some of which can never be traced back to their source.

I chug the rest of the water, crush the cup and stow it in the storage pouch, then rest my head in my arms on the fold-down tray. Close my eyes and concentrate, trying to see past the distorted mirrors of deception and time and make the connections between what I know and what I can infer. Try to find the relationships. Solve the puzzle.

This time I start at a different beginning—not on a foggy night in Macao but rather a spring night in Washington, D.C., in 1943 and a phone call to Iskhak Akhmerov in Manhattan to report on the day's events at the Trident conference. A call that led to a cable, New York to Moscow. A cable that was deciphered by the code breakers at Arlington Hall, one of whom speculated about the identity of Zamestitel, whom some thought was Vice President Wallace. *More likely to be Harry Hopkins??* he wrote.

But neither he nor any other analyst wrote the words *Beneš Czech delegation?* next to the footnote addressing the identity of "19." That was added later.

Everett Walker was the messenger. The Venona cable was his message.

Not the actual decrypted cable available to everyone on the NSA Web site. That one—the real cable—lacked the all-important clue. Reese buried his message in the particular cable Walker brought with him to Moscow. The one specifically prepared with the handwritten note about the Czech delegation. How he put the cable into Walker's hands and manipulated Walker into making the trip to Moscow, I don't know. But the note supposedly written by some anonymous Venona code breaker was made for one pair of eyes.

Bassoff's eyes.

Reese used Walker the same way he had used countless others. Walker was simply a courier. His amateurish attempts to find me, the son of his friend, varnished him with a layer of plausibility as a bungling do-gooder. All of which made him a believable vehicle to carry precisely the information Reese wanted delivered at just the right moment.

Just like my father and the network he had turned over to Isadora in the 1980s. Just like Everett Walker and so many others before and after them. Almost everything they gave the Soviets and, later, the gunpoint capitalists of the new Russia, was authentic, reliable, and valuable. But planted in the rich soil of all that good information were seeds of disinformation. And when those seeds took root, grew, and bore fruit—when a project failed because of faulty data or a promising breakthrough turned out to be a dead end—when those things happened, somebody other than Reese took the fall.

I believe that everything Bassoff and his predecessors received directly from Reese was verifiably true down to the tiniest detail.

Except for Reese's final delivery—the strip of microfilm hidden under the sharkskin grip of my knife. This delivery is fool's gold, I decide, although I'm sure it won't be as easily detected as pyrite. Reese had planned this attack for years, maybe decades, and so he framed his biggest lie against a devastating backdrop of beautiful truth—reams of the scientific information that Bassoff and the GRU most lusted after.

Best of all, Reese plotted to make his last package arrive on Bassoff's doorstep in a way designed to make Bassoff believe he had gotten it through his own brilliant deduction and by manipulating players across two continents.

I sit up, settle back in my seat, and draw a mental scorecard, clicking through the players in my mind.

Rykov: an honest Russian, an honorable career with the GRU. I don't buy the story Santori told me in Albuquerque that Rykov gave information to the CIA.

Isadora, or Katarina as she was known during her days in America: sellout. Probably before, during, and after her turn as the deputy *rezident*, all that mattered to her was the price. My father made many mistakes, but she might have been his worst. "The one he loved," as Mary Montoya put it, there in her rocker at the feet of the painted mountains framed in the window behind her. Isadora was the woman "who was always in his thoughts."

Everett Walker: a Soviet and Russian agent unwittingly turned into a double agent by Reese. He never lost his love for the poetry of the proletariat. Walker's heart may have been in the right place, but he was duped by Reese as surely as dozens of others must have been.

And the final verdict on Stepan: failed patriot. Loyal to Russia to the bitter end, but used badly by Reese and Isadora.

Maybe I'll never know for sure. But after two weeks with nothing to do but think about it, I decide that Reese is using me in the same way he used all the others. I am the patriotic Russian, the good soldier, the messenger above reproach, unsuspecting and beyond suspicion.

I don't know what Reese's final report contains. But I know this much. It is designed to do the most harm possible to Russia.

Bassoff will swallow every word of it.

chapter 78

The passengers in my section are asleep or watching the movie. The nearest flight attendants are aft, behind a bulkhead.

I slide out of my seat and limp to the lavatory. No line. It smells both feculent and antiseptic. I detach my knife from its slot in my prosthesis. Unscrew the cap on the butt and remove two wooden matches, then force back the metal lip to release the end of the sharkskin grip and unwind it in a long, springy helix. The coil of film appears on the metal handle as the final loops spool out. I remove the film the same way I did the grip, then hold parts of the film up to the light like an X-ray, but all I can see are white blemishes against a dark background. Somewhere on this translucent strip Reese's biggest lies nestle in a fertile bed of truth.

I disable the smoke alarm. Slice the tape into long ribbons. Twist the ribbons into a rough braid, set it on the counter, and chop it like parsley, rolling the blade with my free hand on top of the spine, tossing and retossing the pieces until only a pile of particles remains. I sweep the pile into my cupped hand and pour it into the dry bottom of the toilet. Strike a match with my thumb and burn the bits into oily black smoke. Sift through what's left and do it again until only greasy ashes are left. Then I flush the toilet and watch them whoosh away.

I rewrap the handle, slot the knife into my prosthesis, and return to my seat. Minutes later a flight attendant hurries past, following her nose toward the smell of smoke.

I close my eyes, but sleep eludes me.

Somebody on the American side had to have known about Reese. He couldn't have acted alone, not for so long at such a high level. Who was his control? I recall the final smile Matthews gave me, and the way he pulled my knife out of his pocket like an afterthought. Think back even further, connecting dots that might bear little or no relationship to one another—his visit to my office the day I found out where Lachek was hiding; Pavel the machinist spotting him and Bassoff, maybe, as they entered my warehouse; Valya following him to Bassoff's headquarters; his sudden appearance in L.A. and the tumult on the side of the freeway—had that been arranged?—that allowed me to escape to the hotel room.

I had underestimated Matthews once before. Maybe I had done so again. Maybe he was the man behind Reese. I suppose the answer matters to someone like Bassoff, the Russian half of Reese's double-dealing, but not to me. Let Bassoff worry about it.

Still, all those years, and on opposite sides of the world in two radically different regimes, Reese must have been handed down from one control agent to another like a fragile vase from a vanished dynasty. Where did it start, I wonder? How did a man like Reese become a spy?

The captain makes an announcement about federal law prohibiting anybody from disabling the smoke alarm in the lavatory. One of the flight attendants eyes me suspiciously. The woman in the seat next to me scoots out to the aisle to retrieve something from the overhead compartment.

I push up the plastic window shade and gaze outside. We are somewhere over the Arctic. Everything below blazes white. Around and above us are broken gray clouds and snapshots of blue sky. I close my eyes and picture my father, feeling the icy coldness in the cockpit as he pulls back the throttles and starts the enormous Bear on a long descent toward fate.

BRENT GHELFI is the author of *Volk's Game*, nominated by the International Thriller Writers for Best First Novel of 2007 and by *Mystery News* and *Deadly Pleasures* magazines for a Barry Award for Best Thriller, and also critically acclaimed *Volk's Shadow*. His novels have been translated into seven languages and optioned for film. He is currently working on the fourth novel in the Volk series.